CRETE:
ITS PAST, PRESENT AND PEOPLE

CRETE

Its Past, Present and People

by
ADAM HOPKINS

illustrated by Victor Shreeve

FABER AND FABER
London & Boston

First published in 1977
by Faber and Faber Limited
3 Queen Square London WC1
First published in this edition 1979
Printed in Great Britain by
Butler & Tanner Limited
Frome and London
All rights reserved

British Library Cataloguing in Publication Data

Hopkins, Adam
    Crete.
    1. Crete – History
    I. Title
    949.98   DF901.C82

ISBN 0–571–11361–3 Pbk

949.98
H79

Contents

59682

Illustrations

The people of Crete unfortunately make more history
than they can consume locally –

'The Jesting of Arlington Stringham'
SAKI

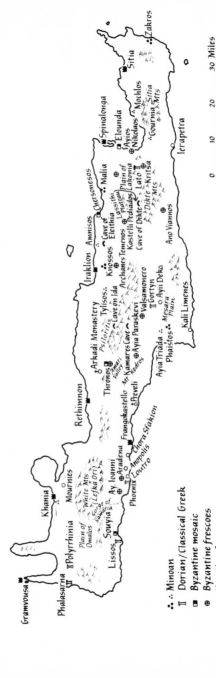

Prehistoric and historic Crete

Gramvousa
Phalasarna
Polyrrhinia
Khania
White Mts (Lefka Ori)
Plain of Omalos
Mournies
Gorge of Samaria
Ay. Ioanni
Souyia
Lissos
Aradena
Phoenix Loutro
Anopolis
Chora Sfakion
Frangokastello
Preveli
 Amari Valley
Thronos
Arkadi Monastery
Rethimnon
Psiloritis
Cave on Ida
Tylisos
Mt Kamares Cave
Ayia Paraskevi
Ayia Kedros
Ayia Triada
Phaistos
Mesara Plain
Ayii Deka
Gortyn
Valsamonero
Archanes
Knossos
Temenos
Iraklion
Amnisos
Cave of Eleithia
Kastelli Pediados
Plain of Lasithi
Lyktos
Cave of Dikte
Dikte Mts
Lato
Krista
Plain of Lakonia
Kali Limenes
Ano Viannos
Ierrapetra
Gournia Mts
Gournia
Ayios Nikolaos
Mochlos
Elounda
Spinalonga
Sitia
Sitia Mts
Zakros
Malia
Chersonesos

∴∴ Minoan
ΙΙ Dorian/Classical Greek
▣ Byzantine mosaic
⊕ Byzantine frescoes
■ Venetian fortress

30 Miles
50 km
0   10   20   30   40
0   10   20   30

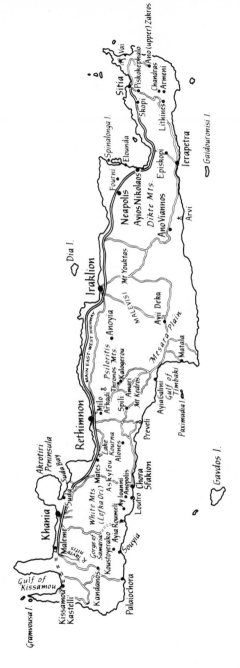

Modern Crete

Gramvousa I.

Gulf of Kissamou

Kissamou I.
Kastelli
Kandanos
Palaiochora
Souyia
Koustoyerako
Ayia Roumeli
Gorge of Samaria
Taurri Mts
White Mts (Lefka Ori)
Askyfou
Anopolis
Ay Ioanni
Loutro Chora
Sfakion
Preveli
Alones
Lake Kourna
Mates
Maleme
Suda
Suda Bay
Akrotiri Peninsula
Khania
Rethimnon
Milo
Spili
Amari
Mt Kedros
Arkadi
Psiloritis
Thronos Mts
Kalogerou
Anoyia
Anoyia
Mt Youktas
MALEVISI
Ayii Deka
Mesara Plain
Ayia Galini
Gulf of Timbaki
Matala
Paximadia I.
Iraklion
Dia I.
MAIN EAST-WEST HIGHWAY
Fourni
Neapolis
Ayios Nikolaos
Dikte Mts.
AnoViannos
Episkopi
Arvi
Elounda
Spinalonga I.
Sitia
Vai
Piskokephalo
Ano (upper) Zakros
Chandras
Armeni
Skopi
Lithines
Ierapetra

Gaidouronisi I.

Gavdos I.

0   10   20   30 Miles
0   10 20 30 40   50 Km.

Introduction

Few people will arrive in Crete without some image of the island ready formed – a compound, most probably, of Minotaur and Minoans and of Cretan heroism in World War II. I certainly knew little more than this when I first visited Crete fifteen years ago. It was springtime – the wild flowers were out, snow lay on the mountains and I rejoiced in a land made up of myth and the vivid legacy of the Minoans. But at the same time I recoiled from what I read as a harsh obduracy in the faces of the people, stern old men sitting in long lines along village streets at evening and women all in black flustered at the presence of strangers. Once or twice, for no reason I could easily explain, I experienced a sense of emptiness and dread. I think now this was partly stranger's nerves. I was living at the time in a more comfortable part of Greece and simply failed, confronted by these arresting people, to find within myself the warmth that would have been a passport to the extraordinary warmth and vitality of the Cretans. Some visitors are lucky enough, and open enough, to encounter it right away. For me, the knowledge came later and transformed my first tentative and limited view of Crete. As I became involved with Cretan people I also began to realise how the island's many layers of medieval and modern history had combined to make the Cretans so proud and singular a race.

Clearly, in writing about an island so ancient and so complex in human terms there are many different courses one could follow. I hope that this book, though it is not intended as a guide, will serve as a companion to the Minoan civilisation and that it will also have something to say about most other aspects of the island, both for travellers and for those interested simply in reading about Crete's past and present. It is an attempt to provide for others the kind of knowledge and understanding I lacked when I first went to Crete.

I did not realise, for example, how much religion counted nor how many survivals there were from a thousand years of (interrupted) Byzantine rule. After the Byzantines came the Venetians. Their magnificent honey-coloured castles were plain to see; but I hardly understood that Byzantine wall-painting continued to flourish at the same time in country churches, so that, as well as the treasure-house of the Minoan period, there is a second and little-known store of outstanding, though considerably ruined, works of art in Crete. I have done what I can to make this painting accessible to the reader. After the defeat of the Venetians in 1669, there followed two hundred and fifty years of harsh Turkish rule. This ended in 1898 and in 1913 Crete became part of modern Greece. But the two and a half centuries of repression had reinforced a revolutionary tradition which was to surface again during World War II. I have written about the Turkish period and tried to give a fair account of the war itself. And I have also tried to give an impression of Cretan places, of Cretan people and their activities and of the condition of modern Crete.

During the writing of this book I have travelled in almost every part of the island, discovering as I did so that I feel more alive in Crete than in other places – challenged, exhilarated, appalled, entertained and touched by turns. The island has a way of taking people by the throat and refusing to let go.

I find also that I have come to value personal contacts and friendships above everything else in Crete, and I should like to thank all those people, whether Cretans or Greeks from elsewhere, who have given more help, kindness and hospitality than I can ever hope to repay. In particular, my thanks and the dues of friendship go to George and Katina Nikolorakis and to George Mathioudakis, each of whom has patiently answered hundreds upon hundreds of questions; to Dr. Costis Davaras, Ephor of Antiquities for Eastern Crete and Director of the Archaeological Museum at Ayios Nikolaos (he has explained much and suffered through early drafts of my manuscript); to Eleni Nakou for great help and encouragement; to the architects Anastasios and Voula Zervas who took me with them on several journeys during a survey of Cretan village architecture; and to Ilias and Sozonga Lecos, doctors of medicine, who helped to fire my imagination and to make me see Crete with greater sympathy and understanding. Of people in Britain who have helped me I would like to give special thanks to Jean Robertson, travel editor of the *Sunday Times*.

It is impossible to render Greek names in the Roman alphabet to everybody's satisfaction. In matters of archaeology I have mostly followed the current habits of archaeologists. As a gesture of respect to the origins of the gods and mythical figures mentioned in the text, I have given their names in an equivalent of Greek spelling rather than in the Latinised version – Daidalos in place of Daedalus, Ikaros for Icarus, Hephaistos for Hephaestus. I have also used the spelling 'Achaian' rather than the more familiar 'Achaean'. Over the names of modern places and people I have followed what I take to be the most common contemporary usage. In doubtful cases I have pleased myself.

1. Landscape and legend

Almost anything anybody says or thinks in Crete is said or thought against a background of mountains. They dominate the landscape everywhere and nothing in Crete makes sense without them. You see them from the towns, you see them when you travel, you see them when you roll over on your back and drift a little way into the summer sea. Because they rise so sharply from the coast they achieve a magnificence far greater than one might expect from their eight thousand feet or so of altitude and, because they are limestone, many of the higher peaks have a bare and craggy aspect which can only be matched, one feels, by rugged, arduous and lofty thoughts. In winter these mountains are intimidating, but in spring, when you look up at their snows from soft green valleys, they seem delectable. Summer gathers a bluish haze about them, a kind of wistfulness. Then, when it is hot and heavy in the plains and when the sun beats down all day along the beaches, then above all is the time to put on your boots and seek the upper breezes along the ankle-twisting limestone tracks. I think it is fair to say that those who have walked the mountains of Crete carry the memory with them everywhere, a source of delight, even of inner strength. And the mountains are bound to be an important part of the perception even of those who never leave the coast and merely look up at them from a distance.

There are four main ranges. They rise east to west in massive bumps like the vertebrae of a dinosaur, in many places effectively barring north from south, despite the short distance in measured miles. In the east are the Sitia mountains, craggy enough but slight by Cretan standards. Next, moving east to west, comes the fine Dikte massif, snow-covered for months at a time and with several flat and sunken plains hidden among its heights, a characteristic feature of the Cretan uplands. The best known of these plains is the Lassithi plateau, the home of thousands of little windmills which flutter like butterflies in early summer. Moving on towards the west, the next mountain outcrop is Cretan Ida, known today as Psiloritis. Its vast and peaceful contours preside over central Crete and over the low-lying, olive-heavy plain of the Mesara. This is to the south of Psiloritis, a rich and drowsy place with huge-boled olive trees, marvellously twisted. To the south again a line of lesser mountains stands between the Mesara and the sea.

All these ranges are fine enough; but the finest by far rises in the west of the island. Here the White Mountains (in Greek, the Lefka Ori) make a different kind of country, wild, intractable, intoxicating, a place where eagles hang on the wind and the human voice dies across the screes, a place of gorges and chasms, the centre virtually uninhabited and for centuries a stronghold of revolution and brigandage. Here, when in some boulder-ridden solitude you meet a shepherd still wearing the little black turban fringed with blackest beads, the proud knee-boots and the wide breeches of Crete, you feel more strongly than elsewhere a sense of surprise that he no longer has a pistol and a pair of silver-handled daggers in his belt. This is the most stirring of all Cretan landscapes, particularly along stretches of the south-west coast where the sheer rock of the mountains climbs up and up straight from the Libyan Sea.

Long ago the mountains of Crete were thickly forested, except on the high peaks, but little by little, and above all in the time of the Venetians, the cypress forests were cut back until today there are only a few stringy remnants, mostly on the upper slopes of the west. These forests attracted the rain and held moisture so that, in all probability, small brooks ran all year and springs gushed where no springs gush today. The forests also held the soil, which is now eroded, as it has been for the last few hundred years, by every storm. The process is completed, and regeneration prevented, by the seedling-hungry domestic goat which is everywhere in Crete.

Eight centuries before Christ, Homer described Crete as 'fair and fertile', or 'rich and lovely', depending on your translator; and as recently as 1609, when Crete was known as Candy or Candia, the traveller William Lithgow wrote of the area round modern Khania in the west: 'For beauty, pleasure and profit, it may easily be surnamed the garden of the whole Universe, being the goodliest plot, the Diamond sparke, and the Honney-spot of all Candy.'

Today the first impression Crete makes is one of obdurate rockiness, but much survives of the gentler beauties praised by Homer and by William Lithgow. The area behind Khania is luxuriously fertile with many succulent fruits, often sheltered by tall brakes of waving cane. The olive and the vine grow almost everywhere in the lower-lying parts of the island and there is a strip of notably fertile plain along the north coast, rich in grapes, vegetables and corn. Most of the island's hotels are scattered along this coast. Down in the south-east, farmers specialise in Europe's earliest tomatoes, cucumbers and melons, and in the valleys that run among the mountains you will find a rich variety of produce. Here, perhaps, the land will be shaded by chestnut trees and in winter and spring there will be the sound of running water.

The towns of Crete – bustling, noisy Iraklion, sleepy Rethimnon, alert and vigorous Khania – stand on the northern plain between the mountains and the encircling sea. And the sea itself, glimpsed far below from a turning on a mountain road, or through the leaves of olives, is as much a part of the Cretan landscape as the mountains. Sometimes it roars and threshes quite surprisingly. On other days, particularly in the south, it takes on a luminous stillness, a dreamlike intensity that will always be remembered by those who have experienced it. It is a stillness not interrupted by the hammering of cicadas, the bleating of goats or the voices of fishermen calling across the water. Parts of Crete have been spoiled by tourism, but much remains inviolate.

As with sea and mountain, one is almost always conscious of the weather. The winters are rough among the mountains, but clean and pleasant at sea-level with sunshine swiftly following rain and racing cloud. Spring begins early, a season so fresh and full of promise it is almost unbearable; for months the island is brilliant with wild flowers. Summers are very hot, but often marred, in August, by a north wind that comes blustering out of the Aegean. Autumn, by contrast, is a tranquil and deeply satisfying season.

The presence of legend is everywhere almost palpable. Few landscapes in Europe, even in the world, are more instinct with myth than Crete. Only the smallest act of the imagination is needed for one to feel a shiver down the spine.

For the ancient Greeks, perhaps the most powerful of all these legends was the story of the birth of Zeus in a Cretan cavern – either on Mt. Dikte or on Psiloritis (scholars still argue which). Rhea, Zeus's mother, was terrified that the father, Kronos, would devour this baby as he had his other children, so she gave birth to him deep within the earth and round her, to drown the cries of the infant god, her helpers the Kuretes danced with wild shouting, beating on their shields. When Kronos learned that a baby had been born and demanded she should bring it, Rhea gave him a stone wrapped in swaddling clothes which he obligingly swallowed.

Zeus later came back to Crete in the shape of a white bull. It was here that he brought Europa and he delighted in her on the banks of the river where the ancient town of Gortyn later stood. The Cretans also had a story which said that Zeus was dead and lay entombed in Mt. Youktas (just behind modern Iraklion). Seen from the north, this mountain certainly has the profile of a recumbent warrior in a helmet; but the idea that Zeus was mortal was heresy enough to provoke the saying that all Cretans are liars, a tag that has endured for thousands of years.

Zeus does not touch modern man so closely as he did the ancients. But it is a different matter with Minos, Minotaur and labyrinth.

According to the myths current among the ancient Greeks, Crete had long ago been a great and wealthy island, ruled over by a king named Minos and by his brother Rhadamanthys. Both were mighty lawgivers and Minos every nine years talked face to face with Zeus. His wife was named Pasiphae – 'lewd and luxurious Pasiphae', William Lithgow called her, for she fell in love with a bull. From this union there sprang a fearful beast, half-man, half-bull and called the Minotaur. It was confined underneath the palace of King Minos at Knossos, in an endless labyrinth which had been built by Daidalos, engineer to Minos, and every nine years a tribute of young men and women was brought here from Athens. They entered the labyrinth and there they were devoured by the bellowing monster.

In the time when King Aegeus ruled in Athens, his son Theseus resolved to end the tyranny of the Minotaur. Despite the entreaties of his father, Theseus took his place among the Athenian youths and girls sent to Crete in tribute. Here he was lucky, for Minos' daughter, Ariadne, fell in love with him. Ariadne had a passion for dancing; Daidalos the engineer had built a dancing floor for her at Knossos. Being in love with Theseus and wanting to help him outwit the Minotaur, she again sought the help of Daidalos. He provided her with a ball of thread which she gave in turn to Theseus so that when it was time to go down into the labyrinth, he would be able to unwind it as he went and thus, if he could kill the monster, retrace his steps by following the thread back to the entrance. The plan worked perfectly. Theseus slew the Minotaur, escaped by following the thread, and he and Ariadne quickly made off, together with the young men and women from Athens. But now things began to go wrong.

Theseus abandoned Ariadne as she lay sleeping on a beach. Then, as he returned to Athens, he forgot to change the black sails of his ship for white, a prearranged signal of success. Seeing the black, King Aegeus plunged from a clifftop into the sea which now bears his name. As for Daidalos, he later fled from Crete with Ikaros, his son. To do so, he made two sets of wings with feathers embedded in wax. But Ikaros flew too near the sun; the wax melted; he fell into the sea and drowned.

Daidalos now took refuge in Sicily with Kokalos, king of the island. But Minos was enraged and followed him there, locating him by setting a puzzle so ingenious that when it was solved it was clear that only Daidalos could have provided the solution. But Daidalos lived on and Minos died. For Minos, according to Apollodorus, was 'undone' after his bath by the daughters of Kokalos. He went down to the Underworld and there, with his brother Rhadamanthys, became the lawgiver of the dead.

·It is an extraordinary and extraordinarily disturbing tale. Crete was also thought by the ancient Greeks to have been associated with many other deities, nymphs and generally numinous figures. Athena herself was sometimes said to have come from the island. The Cretan Diana, Britomartis, was born, some say, in the great gorge of Samaria in the west. Coming from an island so worthy of veneration, Cretan priests were considered peculiarly effective in restoring purity to places which had gone astray.

Homer, though he does not record the Minotaur legend, adds an important element to the tales surrounding Crete. In a series of references scattered through *The Iliad* and *The Odyssey*, he tells how Minos's grandson, King Idomeneus, set out from the island for the Trojan War with a powerful fleet and he conveys a strong impression of a rich and populous land. In doing so, he mentions many place-names.

All of the Minos story, in the form recorded here and in most of the Homeric references, seemed purest fantasy until about a hundred years ago. At that time archaeologists began to uncover evidence of a previously unknown civilisation at Troy in Turkey, and on the Greek mainland. Then in Crete, starting in 1900, excavations at Knossos revealed a vast and labyrinthine palace, far older even than the palatial sites excavated on the Greek mainland. A second Cretan palace was found and excavated at the same time at Phaistos, on one of the most lovely sites in all Greece. It stands on the inland edge of a little ridge running back from the sea into

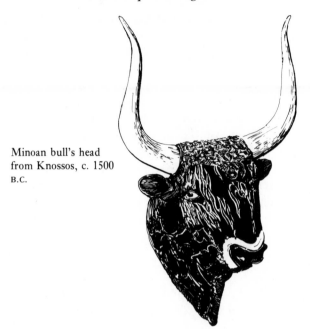

Minoan bull's head
from Knossos, c. 1500
B.C.

the Mesara. From it one can look across the olives of the Mesara
and up to the heights of Psiloritis and the Dikte massif. A third
palace site was cleared at Malia on the north coast, again under a
splendid backdrop of mountains.

From these three principal sites and from many lesser settlements
and shrines, the archaeologists recovered everyday objects which
told much about the life of those who had lived there, and also a
wide range of works of art of an entirely individual kind. Their exuberance and beauty, their grace and naturalism were astonishing.
There were huge quantities of a vivid and beautiful pottery scarcely
matched in later times; there was exquisite jewellery, enchanting
miniature sculpture, extraordinarily accomplished seal-stone
engraving; there was fresco-painting, faience work, work in bronze
and gold. The best of this is now collected in the Archaeological
Museum at Iraklion with some lesser but representative works in

local Cretan museums, notably at Ayios Nikolaos and Khania. The Iraklion collection is without doubt one of the greatest museum displays anywhere and has been greatly enriched by the discovery and excavation during the 1960s of a fourth, and unplundered, palace at Zakros in the extreme east. All the works of art and other prehistoric objects described in the following chapter are on display in this museum, unless otherwise stated (see p. 63). Here, it would seem, in this long-lost but highly developed civilisation (now referred to as Minoan) lies the origin of many Cretan myths. The discovery of the Minoan civilisation seems also to make some sense of the only factual-sounding tradition of Minos. This was recorded by Thucydides in the fifth century B.C. and it portrays the Cretan as a powerful sea-king:

> Minos is the first ruler we know of who possessed a fleet and controlled most of what are now Greek waters. He ruled the Cyclades and was the first coloniser of most of them, installing his own sons as governors. In all probability, he cleared the sea of pirates, so far as he could, to secure his own revenues.

It is, then, with the Minoan civilisation that an account of Crete should start.

2. The Minoan period

Most of the Minoan sites which the visitor sees today – Malia, Zakros, Phaistos, the little summer palace at Ayia Triada and the delightfully situated township of Gournia on the Gulf of Mirabello in the east – were burned down in mysterious circumstances in about 1450 B.C. Knossos probably survived for another eighty years or so before destruction overtook it too. But the Minoan civilisation was old when it came to an end. After a slow emergence from the neolithic age, it grew and flourished and changed for a millennium and a half before the final catastrophe. During this long period there were many outstanding achievements, but the peak came just before the end, in about 1500 B.C. or soon after (see note on dating, p. 74). Much is known about how the Minoans lived, worshipped and enjoyed themselves at this time; but the best way to approach this epoch is to start at the beginning and little by little build up a picture of the civilisation. This cannot be done without some account of the process of archaeological discovery.

The story began in Turkey in the 1870s when Heinrich Schliemann, an inspired and enormously wealthy amateur archaeologist, uncovered the site of ancient Troy. In doing so, he showed that some historical substance, however, vague, lay behind *The Iliad* and *The Odyssey*. He next proved his point further by excavations at Mycenae in the Peloponnese. Here, in one of the most astonishing digs ever undertaken, he revealed, just where Homer had suggested to him that it might be, the remains of an advanced warrior civilisation. The implications were stunning. These were early days for archaeology and Schliemann himself was more intuitive than scientific. But what he had discovered were the relics of some five hundred or more years of civilisation in Mycenae, ending in about 1150 B.C. It seemed clear that Homer's epics of the Achaians and their princely halls, composed some three hundred years later, were built around surviving memories of these people. Moreover, since the epics were proving so revealing over place-names, it seemed that traces of the Achaians (or Mycenaeans, as they are often called) might be found in many of the centres named by Homer as having sent Achaian contingents to the Trojan War. Knossos was one of these.

This was not the only pointer. In 1878 a Cretan enthusiast with the eminently suitable name of Minos Kalokairinos uncovered remains of impressive storerooms with big pottery jars on a mound near Iraklion called Kefala. It seemed likely that this was the site of ancient Knossos. A new museum had been established at Iraklion; local Greek interest was running high and chance finds from round the island were being funnelled into it. Schliemann decided that the time was ripe to dig at Knossos. But the island was still under the obscurantist rule of the Turks and Schliemann was unable to buy the site from the owner on what he considered fair terms. In the end he abandoned the enterprise. This was probably all to the good, for the next person of note to become interested in Knossos was a man with the same strong streak of intuitive romanticism and the same huge energy, but with wider knowledge and a more tidy mind.

Arthur (later Sir Arthur) Evans was born in 1851, the son of a wealthy antiquary. He grew up in a learned atmosphere and studied history at Oxford. As a young man he then spent some years adventuring in the Balkans, supporting the liberal, anti-Turkish cause in partisan dispatches to the then *Manchester Guardian*. He was flamboyantly on the side of all Slavs against all their masters, at one point so incensing the Austrian authorities of Ragusa that they flung him – briefly – into gaol. This was a prelude to his expulsion and to a return to Oxford, where, at the age of thirty-three, he became Keeper of the Ashmolean Museum. Evans was a keen amateur archaeologist and became an effective museum director. But it was not until the start of his third career, some fifteen years later, that he found a role commensurate with his energy and intellectual range.

This began in Athens in 1893 with a study of Schliemann's Mycenaean seals. But it might perhaps never have started without a physical peculiarity of Evans's, recorded by his half-sister, Dr. Joan Evans, in her book *Time and Chance* and singled out by Leonard Cottrell in *The Bull of Minos*, a breathless but highly readable account of early archaeological discoveries. Her brother, wrote Dr. Evans, 'was extremely short-sighted, and a reluctant wearer of glasses. Without them he could see small things held a few inches from his face in extraordinary detail, while everything else was a vague blur. Consequently the details he saw with microscopic exactitude, undistracted by the outside world, had a greater significance for him than for other men.'

Having looked at the tiny surfaces of Schliemann's Mycenaean seals, Evans found similar seals with what appeared to be hieroglyphic writing in an Athens antique shop. The dealer said they came from Crete, and, in order to investigate this pre-Greek writing, Evans set out for the island. It was an interesting journey and he collected a great number of the seals – they were called milk-stones and used by Cretan mothers as charms to help with breast-feeding. He also noted, though he did not make much of it at the time, some pottery finds which antedated the Mycenaean period.

When Turkish rule ended in Crete in 1898, things became easier for archaeologists. Evans returned to Crete, bought the site of Knossos and obtained permission to dig. The excavation began in 1900 and immediately revealed a great hoard of tablets inscribed in an unreadable pre-Greek script. 'It is extremely satisfactory,' wrote Evans to his family, 'as it is what I came to Crete seven years ago to find, and it is the coping stone to what I have already put together.' But this was barely the beginning. Discoveries came at a huge rate. The number of workmen on the site was increased from thirty to a hundred and it became clear that a huge palace had been discovered. Almost at once Evans realised that he was dealing with a civilisation older than the Mycenaean.

Meanwhile at Phaistos another romantic figure, the Italian Federico Halbherr, was also involved in a spectacular dig. Halbherr had been interested in the island for a number of years, dashing about on a black Arab mare and occupying himself with the more recent remains of the ancient Greeks. At Phaistos, though, he was tackling something of a different order and he pressed ahead with speed and thoroughness, emerging with results similar to those at Knossos. Thus the two men found a lost civilisation and accomplished a second revolution in archaeology, extending Aegean prehistory far back beyond the Achaians, themselves so recently rediscovered.

The task now was to find out everything about these remains to which Evans, never at a loss for a telling word, had given the name Minoan. He showed indefatigable energy, excavating year by year and promulgating theories as he went. Evans had his share of faults. To his fellow countrymen he was high-handed and to Greeks he behaved with that assumption of superiority characteristic of an arrogant age. This has done nothing to make his memory loved in Crete, no matter how deeply it may be respected. But the first systematic evaluation of the Minoans was the product of his great physical and intellectual drive.

Other archaeologists, Greek and foreign, quickly joined the fray and before very many years it was possible to build up a reasonably convincing picture of the evolution and the set-backs of the Minoan civilisation. Later excavators – particularly the Greek professors Platon and Marinatos – have refined and modified this outline and many of our accepted ideas may yet be confounded by fresh discoveries. But even if the picture must be framed in ifs and buts it is a fascinating one.

The first arrivals in Crete were neolithic people who came by boat between 6000 and 4000 B.C. Their main settlement was at Knossos in the centre of the island on a low knoll overlooked by undistinguished hills. Elsewhere they lived in caves or easily defensible positions in the east and centre of the island. Though this suggests that fear played an important part in their lives, they were also surprisingly advanced. They no longer buried their adult dead underneath the earth floors of their houses and child burials in houses soon came to a halt. Their pottery, in the words of one modern archaeologist, looks as if it is 'the heir to a long tradition'. If exact parallels for it can be found, this pottery may one day show whence the first settlers came; for the moment the best answer is simply that they came from points eastward.

The neolithic people brought the cult of the fertility goddess, making figurines which represent her as so monstrously buttocked and heavily thighed that the term 'steatopygous' has been borrowed for them from a deformity found in some parts of Africa. By the late neolithic period their architecture had also become rather singular. Ruins of houses found at Knossos, says the archaeologist R. W. Hutchinson, author of the useful if somewhat dry Penguin volume *Prehistoric Crete*, show 'the basic principle, or lack of principle that is so characteristic of the Minoan architecture of the Bronze Age'. The early Cretans seem simply to have added extra rooms of all shapes and sizes as the need arose. 'The resulting plan', Hutchinson concludes, 'was rather haphazard in outline, giving the impression of an organic cellular growth rather than of architectural design.'

Over a very long period the life of the neolithic peoples of Crete slowly became easier. There were at first no sudden revolutions in style or extravagant new departures. But round about 2600 B.C. remarkable things began to happen. The most striking is that settlements now began to be chosen for their harbours or their proximity to the sea, a radical reversal of habit which must have indicated confidence and perhaps a fresh wave of immigration from the east – for the new townships were established in eastern Crete. The island had begun to make the most of its relationship to the sea. Cultural dominance had at the same time passed eastwards from Knossos, not to return for several centuries. There had also been great progress in pottery-making in the east and south. Looking at all these developments together it is possible to see in them the start of what is regarded as the Minoan era. One of its main characteristics is the comparatively fast pace of change.

Within a couple of hundred years, starting from about 2400 B.C., there appears to have been a common civilisation in the inhabited parts of the island. The population had grown considerably in the Mesara, possibly because of another wave of immigration, this time from Libya.

But though the south made great progress, the east retained its cultural leadership, producing from about 2600 to 2300 B.C. a new and rather entertaining kind of pottery known as Vasiliki ware. The basic shapes of the vessels are more elegant, but the spouts are often quite absurdly long. The other oddity is the colour, a strange mottling, dark on a light background, produced by deliberately uneven firing. This style, one of several in vogue in early Minoan times, became quite widespread in Crete.

. But by far the most exciting known artefacts of this period were stone jars – and one or two pieces of associated stone carving – which remain ravishing to the eye. The Minoans must have borrowed the idea from Egypt, and they refined it without revolutionising it, turning out the kind of fluid and graceful shapes that were to be so characteristically Minoan. Making stone jars was a slow and difficult business. The shapes were probably blocked out in the rough, then hollowed to their final finish with a reed drill, using sand as an abrasive. The skill lay in achieving a beautiful shape which harmonised with the natural colouring of the stone. All kinds of veined rock were used and the results must be seen in three dimensions to be fully appreciated. Even behind the glass of the Museum they convey an astonishing sense of purity. A great number of these stone vessels were uncovered in eastern Crete in burials at Mochlos – now an island but then probably a port on a spit accessible from either side. R. B. Seager, the excavator, also unearthed a mass of frail but attractive gold jewellery. (Something of the tone of early Cretan archaeology resides in the epitaph pronounced on Seager by Evans, presumably as an honour, after his early death in Iraklion. He was, said Evans, 'the most English American I have ever known'.)

One unusual object of this period deserves a special place of honour. This is a carving of a tired dog lying across the lid of a stone jar. This Minoan mongrel with its cropped ears and curly tail is the essence of all lowly canine creatures. J. D. Pendlebury, whose *Archaeology of Crete*, published in 1939, remains one of the most sensitive accounts of Minoan art, calls it a 'half-starved village hunting dog . . . of the kind which today accompanies you on your walks, stealing and poaching without shame'; and it is remarkable to see a Minoan artist catching in stone at such an early date something so everyday yet so utterly a part of life as the undignified sprawl of this leggy animal. The dog is anatomically inexact, with length of leg exaggerated for effect; it is this impressionistic treatment, as in many later representations of people and animals, which helps to make it look so very much alive. It is an early example of the joyful and frequently playful naturalism that was to be perhaps the major mode of Cretan art, distinguishing it from the stiff and dignified productions of contemporary civilisations in Egypt and the Middle East.

The next two hundred years or so, down to about 2000 B.C. or a little later, are marked by an advance in pottery towards the kind of designs that seem most typically Minoan. The potters are still working basically in dark colours on light and they have begun, with apparent relish, to specialise in curvilinear and spiral designs. Many of these run into one another, the designs spinning towards the top of the vessel so as to take advantage of the flow of the shape both roundwards and upwards. This is often referred to as the principle of 'torsion'; it is peculiarly Minoan and entirely delightful. Decorations inside circles – later to turn into the ubiquitous Minoan rosette – make a first appearance and animals sometimes crop up in rather a sketchy way.

In the Mesara the carving of seal-stones now became a speciality.

Just as, some three hundred years before, the stone-vase makers of Mochlos had made an Egyptian art their own, so now the engravers and carvers of the Mesara took a second Egyptian art, adapted it to their own naturalistic approach, and wielded it with mesmerising skill.

Seals were used to make an impression on clay. They were both a mark of origin or ownership – a monomark – and a guarantee that a packet, a door or a jar had not been opened. Minoan seal-stones from very early on bore miniature representations of a great number of human and animal subjects. There were rosettes, meanders, processions of lions, ships, dolphins. The design itself may in some cases have been intended to deter and there are seals showing scorpions and what may be the rogalida, a poisonous spider which lives in Crete. (Cretan workmen digging on archaeological sites today are more horrified by these than they are by scorpions. In historical times the cure for those bitten by either scorpion or rogalida was prolonged and frantic dancing.) The handles of the seals were themselves sometimes carved in the form of animals, and these carvings too were of the highest standard.

The next major development, round about 2000 B.C., was even more remarkable than the establishment of coastal settlements six hundred years before. This was the construction of a series of huge palaces – known to archaeologists as the Old Palaces, since others were later built on the same sites. Crete must have been enormously prosperous for anybody to have conceived the idea of such vast projects; but we have so little information about the social order at this time that it is scarcely worth hazarding a guess as to how a royal or aristocratic palace society developed from the simpler type of neolithic order.

Knossos had, it seems, once again become the dominant force in the island. Here the top of the accumulated mound of neolithic debris was levelled off into a platform to make space and foundations for a single massive building. Very little is known about this early palace. It was probably a centre of religious life, but it is also noteworthy that at about this time the mountain peaks began to be used for religious purposes. Presumably they were regarded as sacred and many votive offerings were left among the highest pinnacles. Human figurines, in attitudes of worship, were left behind to stand in for those who had put them there. Bronze had by now arrived – a critically important development – and many of the little figures were made of this durable material. Male worshippers stand in a distinctive pose, one hand on forehead, chest and pelvis thrust right forward. Women in worship seem to have placed both hands beneath their breasts. Models of bulls and other animals were also contributed to the shrines. Of these figurines, those in clay are often crude, but many of the bronzes are extremely powerful, with details suggested rather than actually rendered, much in the manner of Rodin. The same predilection for worship in high places has been expressed by Christians in the peak-top chapels which abound in Crete.

The Minoans also worshipped in caves. At first these had been used mainly for burials, but now they too began to accumulate votive offerings. The most important caves were the Diktean, just above the Lassithi plateau, and the Psychro and Kamares caves on Psiloritis (Mt. Ida).

The art of the Old Palaces was in general as fine as the miniature sculpture of the shrines. One of the best objects surviving from the period is a ceremonial sword from Malia, made of bronze with gold-plated ivory hilt and pommel of crystal. Glyptic art – that is, the engraving in miniature of seal-stones and gems – continued to excel.

Another fine achievement was the jewellery of Malia. Many readers will perhaps be familiar with the much-illustrated pair of bees or hornets with pendants hanging from their wings and tails, above their joined heads a gold ball in a kind of bird-cage and between them what looks like a honeycomb held by the most delicate of legs. Experts write with enthusiasm of the way the techniques of embossing, filigree and granulation have been handled in this piece, and even if one cannot delight in the technicalities, it is apparent to all who see it that this is a masterpiece. It was retrieved by Malia's French excavators from Khrysolakkos, the so-called

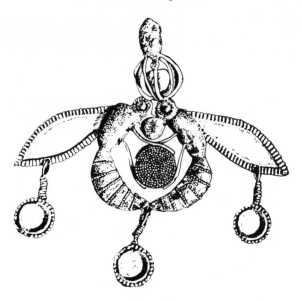

Art of the Old Palaces. Hornet pendant from Malia, c. 1700 B.C.

Gold Hole between the palace of Malia and the sea. In the mid-nineteenth century the British Captain (later Admiral) J. A. B. Spratt, surveying Crete for the Royal Navy, found villagers digging for gold all round the ruins of Malia, and Khrysolakkos is said to have enriched many tomb robbers. Similarities of style suggest that it may even have been the source of the British Museum's exquisite 'Aegina Treasure'.

The art of pottery also developed during the time of the Old Palaces. Potters had been using a wide variety of colours, achieving handsome polychrome effects. From about 1900 B.C. the handling of these new colour schemes began to improve dramatically, as did the technique of turning. The most successful vessels of the succeeding century have a leaf-like lightness, while the shapes are the kind you wish to cradle in your hands – a particular favourite being a big cup with a ribbon handle and the rim widening delicately out-

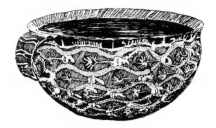

Kamares 'eggshell' cup from
Phaistos, c. 1800 B.C.

wards. This shape has never, I think, been improved on. Most of
the vessels in this pottery – known as eggshell ware – are imitations
of vessels in precious metals which have long since vanished. Fluting
and embossing are common and the glaze is sometimes given a
metallic sheen. But the most beautiful colour schemes are polychrome patterns in light colours on very dark backgrounds; these
are often floral, with daisies a frequent theme.

At the same time, much more massive vessels were being turned
out – using similar but even bolder colour schemes, great sweeps

Large polychrome vase from Phaistos,
2000–1800 B.C.

and swatches of light-on-dark, spiralling and curvetting across the broader surfaces. This magnificent pottery was often encrusted with clay flowers and other ornaments. At about the same time, there was also a period of naturalism in pottery, still light-on-dark, of rather spiky palm trees and great fish enmeshed in nets. Sometimes flowers grew from an undulating band which stood for rocky country. Pendlebury described this inclusion of the setting as 'a naturalistic impulse which no other ancient people attempted to follow until after the downfall of Crete'.

Refinements of technique were made possible largely by the introduction of the fast potter's wheel. (Characteristic concentric circles can now be seen on the base of many vases where the pot was cut with a string from the still-revolving wheel.) 'Technical advances of this kind sometimes stifle artistic inspiration,' writes Sinclair Hood in *The Home of the Heroes*. 'Not so in Crete. There is a fantastic elaboration in the pottery of this period and the best of it, made for the palaces of Knossos and Phaistos, is infinite in variety and often of great beauty; though restraint and taste are sometimes recklessly abandoned in that exuberance of fancy which appears to be characteristic of Minoan art.'

Both the eggshell pottery and the more massive polychrome vessels of the period are known as Kamares ware after the cave, for it was here that the first examples were found. Kamares ware represents the first great period of Minoan pottery.

Everything flourished at the time of the Old Palaces. The seals show a tremendous variety of scenes and activities; a numeral system had arrived; an early form of hieroglyphic writing, still undecipherable, had begun to take on a more developed form. But in about 1700 B.C., when all this activity was at its height, each and every one of the existing palaces was destroyed by earthquake.

The confusion, however great, was not long-lasting and the economic life of the island seems scarcely to have been affected. Towns and villages began to spring up round Knossos, and fresh palaces were erected. These great buildings – damaged in their turn by earthquake around 1570 B.C. but restored again – were the last of the Minoan palaces; it is their ruins, as retrieved and sometimes restored by the archaeologists, which we see today. They are known as the New Palaces.

Knossos was pre-eminent. From outside it was unattractive, a louring mass of stone and mud-brick, probably without external windows, with big houses up against its southern walls and many lesser homes nestling around.

Inside, the palace was an extraordinarily ingenious assemblage of courtyards and ritual chambers, of workshops, storerooms and living quarters, so big as to be almost a city in itself. Its labyrinthine quality is very striking; parts of the palace recall most menacingly the tale of Theseus and the Minotaur, but others are full of charm and ease. The architects, whoever they may have been, had faced up to a great many problems, foremost among them lighting, drainage and movement from floor to floor, solving them brilliantly. What appear to have been the residential and secular areas of the palace were also extensively ornamented with frescoes. The originals are now in the Iraklion Museum, but reproductions have been installed at appropriate points among the ruins.

One of the main points of entry to the palace of Knossos was, and still is, a narrow passageway in the northern wall (see ground-plan, p. 38). Here, in the portico, was a magnificent relief of a charging bull, a creature whose fiery presence as doorkeeper indicates that the Minoans themselves associated Knossos with the bull.

Entering the palace at this point where myth and Minoan reality meet, one soon comes into a broad central courtyard. Much timber was used in the construction, providing a pleasant contrast in materials rather as in Tudor England. Conjectural sketches by the architect who worked on the site with Sir Arthur Evans show huge two-horned emblems all around this courtyard. These are known as horns of consecration and almost certainly evolved, as the archaeologists' term suggests, from the depiction of real horns. The other great symbol of the palace, and one which remained closer to its actual origin, was the double axe. Sometimes these axes had huge bronze blades and were set upright on shafts $1\frac{1}{2}$ to $2\frac{1}{2}$ metres

Knossos

1. Northern entry with bull bas-relief
2. Central courtyard
3. Throne room and lustral chamber
4. Pillar crypt
5. Grand staircase
6. Hall of the Double Axes
7. 'Queen's sitting room'
8. Corridor of the Procession
9. Storerooms
10. Archway
11. Theatral area

high (the shafts have long since rotted but there is plentiful pictorial evidence); or they were made as miniatures (of gold, bronze or, rarely, silver). Sometimes they were painted on pottery or scribbled on walls and sacred pillars in the palace. The ancient name for the double axe was *labrys* and Evans believed, though it has been strongly disputed, that the word labyrinth began with the double axe, was applied after that to the palace of Knossos and finally came to refer to mazes in general.

The palace, with its many emblems, seems to have served as an important religious centre. The holiest places were along the right of the courtyard as one entered past the charging bull and they appear strange and frightening to a modern eye, mainly because they are half-underground and very dark. The first room in the series was equipped with throne and benches. Next to it was a room with a deeply sunken floor into which steps descended. This – and it has important parallels among other Minoan remains – is referred to by archaeologists as a lustral basin and presumed to have been the scene of rituals of purification in which a king with priestly functions was the central figure. The association here of throne and ritual chambers strongly suggests that the state ruled from Knossos was theocratic in nature.

A little further along the right-hand side of the courtyard came a second series of sacred chambers, the so-called temple repositories and pillar crypt. Here a series of not very impressive pillars was the focus of attention. Libations were poured on them, running down to the bases over double axes scrawled into the rock. It is probable that the pillars were held to be a manifestation of the divine – they also held the roof up.

The opposite side of the court is generally believed to have been the centre of day-to-day royal life – despite recent assertions in *The Secret of Crete* by H. G. Wunderlich, a professor of geology in Stuttgart, that the New Palaces were not residential buildings at all but 'cult structures built for the veneration of the dead'. Professor Wunderlich argues, unconvincingly, that the gypsum used in the interiors would have resisted neither feet nor contact with water.

The various storeys of this part of the palace were reached by a stairway which was one of the most impressive architectural achievements of prehistory. Sir Arthur Evans called it the Grand Staircase. It rose perhaps two floors above the level of the court, giving access to rooms of which one can conjecture little. Below the court, where it can still be seen, it descended round a rectangular light well down the side of the hill into which this part of the palace was cut. Leading off the stairway there was a fine series of rooms opening on to a terrace overlooking gardens. There was also a large 'reception room', which could be extended by swinging open a series of double doors. This is known today as the Hall of the Double Axes. Another series of apartments includes what may have been a sitting room, where dolphins painted in fresco gambolled on the walls. Maze-like corridors led from one room to another in this suite, but despite its somewhat cavernous look today, most archaeologists agree that it was once modest, gay and comfortable. It has usually been presented as the queen's living quarters and the rooms immediately above associated with the king. One of the most remarkable aspects of the queen's suite was the underfloor drainage system which carried away not only washing water but also, according to the conventional archaeological view, sewage from a flushing lavatory. Throughout the palace one finds evidence of close attention to water-supply and drainage – well-made interlocking pipes and drainage conduits built in parabolic curves to restrain the water of flash rainstorms. There is nothing comparable until Roman times. Another interesting feature is the use of light wells.

Of even greater interest is the elaborate ceremonial or 'theatral' area just outside the north-western corner of the palace. Two finely built flights of shallow steps rise at the end of a paved road, dividing to make room for a stone platform. Quite possibly this was used for ceremonies or entertainments involving the priest kings and queens.

Most of what I have described can still be seen at Knossos. The theatral area remains intact, so does a large part of the portico (with reproduction bull – the original is in the museum). The central courtyard survives, with ritual chambers to the right, and to the left the Grand Staircase leading down to the royal apartments. Above the courtyard no original structures stand more than one storey high, so the courtyard feels open and exposed rather than the centre of one great complex. Outside this core of courtyard, ritual and residential areas – to which the fine southern entrance should be added – many other discoveries remain *in situ*. Visitors will find Stylianos Alexiou's *Guide to the Minoan Palaces* helpful. (It is worth trying to avoid the crowds which nowadays attend almost incessantly at Knossos. Being inland and very hot in summer, the site is often emptiest at midday. If you can bear the heat, this might be the best time for a visit.)

All this having been said, the aspect of Knossos likely to make the most immediate impression on the visitor is the ubiquity and insistence of the restoration work. As Evans dug deeper and deeper into the accumulated layers at Knossos, the problem of how to preserve the ruins he was uncovering grew more urgent. On one occasion a leaning wall was hoisted straight by sixty men with ropes while it was cemented into position. Then there was the Throne Room which needed roofing to preserve the floor and the throne itself. The worst problem was the Grand Staircase.

Evans's bold solution was to rebuild whole areas as he concluded they must have been. The site was his own, the money he was spending in such profusion was his own, and he considered his rebuilding a process of 'legitimate reconstruction'. Those who come after are bound to feel that he overdid it wildly, imposing his personality to an unwarrantable extent. Parts of his work are acceptable – the lower courses of the Grand Staircase, for example – but in other places, for instance the set of rooms above the Throne Room, the reconstruction appears to be almost totally conjectural. The choice of materials was also crude. Where Evans thought there had been wooden beams, he placed beams of brown-shaded concrete. (He hoped these would withstand earthquakes.) They were accompanied by great numbers of odd-shaped pillars, widening upwards from a narrow base. These were introduced mainly on the basis of frescoes, but it is hard to believe that they were quite so numerous or quite so ugly as Evans has made them. The general effect of Knossos today is of genuine ruins inextricably interlaced with artificial ruins, and the latter are both massive and unattractive.

And yet one must not be too ready to condemn. The Cretan climate is hard on ruins. Evans's roofs have saved many of the original features from the winter rains and because his reconstructions preserved the levels of the eastern part of the palace, in particular of the Grand Staircase, they allow one to catch a powerful impression of the intimacy and occasional grandeur of the original.

It is all a far cry from Phaistos (see ground-plan) where reconstruction was kept to a minimum. The position of Phaistos is extremely lovely in its own right and the uncluttered ruins take on a kind of purity. Another distinction is that the massive foundations of the old palace are still to be seen, running at a slightly different angle to ruins of the newer façade built on the platform they created. It is fair to say, however, that a visitor to Phaistos will understand it a great deal better after he has seen Evans's reconstructions at Knossos. The same is true of Malia (ground-plan, p. 45) and of Zakros.

As at Knossos, the main rooms of Phaistos were grouped around a central courtyard. The upper storeys, apparently including a dining room, looked down on it while at the level of the courtyard there were ritual rooms, the main residential quarters and storerooms lined with broad jars taller than a man. These are called *pitharia* by modern Cretans – they are still used – and *pithoi* by classical scholars (*pithos* in the singular). They were full, most probably, of olive oil, among the most valuable crops of the Bronze Age Mediterranean. All these groups of rooms might seem, like Early Minoan houses, to have been assembled in a random way, but recent calculations have shown that Phaistos appears to have been built to a predetermined plan, and to have been constructed on a standard measure of 30.36 centimetres, fractionally less than the imperial foot.

Phaistos was different from Knossos in one important respect. Where the interior of Knossos was much decorated, the finishing

Phaistos

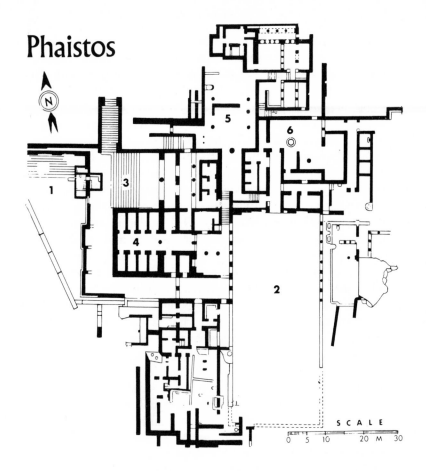

1. Theatral area with steps
2. Central courtyard
3. Staircase
4. Storerooms
5. Small court with columns
6. Small court

materials at Phaistos – gypsum, marble and alabaster – were beautiful in their own right and seem to have been left, like those of
modern architecture, to make their own impression. The fine
quality of the external stonework is also very striking at Phaistos. An
important point of resemblance is that here, as at Knossos, there is a
paved theatral area to the west, in this case rising in shallow, ceremonial steps (raised slightly in the centre) to meet a high blank wall.

Only three-quarters of an hour's walk from Phaistos, back along
the ridge towards the sea, there was another, smaller set of palatial
buildings, erected perhaps after the earthquake of 1570 B.C. This
was the 'summer palace', now named Ayia Triada, or Holy Trinity,
after a Christian church on the site. In Minoan times the sea came
right up to the hill on whose flank it stood. It must have been a
peculiarly lovely spot, for even without the sea, now some distance
away, it remains delightful.

The palace complex here consisted of a handsome set of linked
buildings. To one end was a village and a row of what look like
shops – if they are, these are the only Minoan shops on record. Some
of the rooms of the main buildings were decorated with marvellously
naturalistic frescoes. One showed a cat stalking its prey, all stealth
and cruelty. It was painted without symbolism or any conventions
awkward enough to distract a modern eye. What the painter had been
after, and what he caught to a degree unparalleled at that time unless in China, was the pure essence of what he was depicting – in
this case, cat. This fresco can be seen in the Iraklion Museum today.
It is a little hard to make out, but entirely ravishing once you have
spotted the cat crouched cunningly amid the herbage.

Malia (see ground-plan) is also worth a visit, though it is a
less expressive site than either Phaistos or Ayia Triada. Again, it
follows the architectural pattern of the main palaces with central
courtyard surrounded by the principal centres of palace activity.
What I like best about it is its position on the coastal plain in front
of the ramparts of Dikte. On a stormy day, with thunderclouds
blowing about the crags, the place is majestic. So it is also in moonlight when one may perhaps see in the mind's eye the hand that

Malia

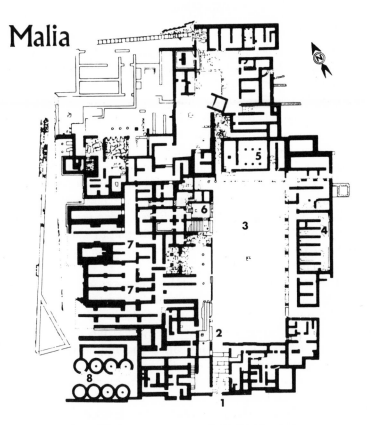

1. Southern entrance
2. Altar
3. Central court
4. Storerooms
5. Hall with columns
6. Lodge
7. Storerooms
8. Granary

held the great bronze sword and the flesh behind the gown to which the Khrysolakkos hornets were once pinned.

Zakros, in the extreme east, has rather less to show than Malia – though it has one significant advantage for the visitor. Since it was newly created during the final Minoan period its ruins are on one archaeological level only. This makes it the easiest of all the Minoan palaces to understand. Like Knossos, it has a central court-yard surrounded by treasure chambers, storerooms, state chambers and shrine. The situation is also very fine: the ruins lie behind the sea on a little up-and-down plain behind which mauve-tinted mountains rise in a semi-circular sweep. Except for Knossos, all the main Minoan sites and most of the lesser ones are in superb positions, a fact which seems to indicate that the Minoans shared with us – may even have helped pass on to us – a notion of beauty in landscape.

All the five New Palaces yielded great works of art, now drawn together in Iraklion. In discussing them, the frescoes make a good starting point, since it is from these that many modern visitors derive their keenest pleasure. They were true frescoes, painted straight on to wet plaster, and they show Minoan naturalism at its most perceptive. A number of scenes, like the cat fresco from Ayia Triada, depict animals going about their own affairs in their wild state, and people, when they are represented, are shown chatting gaily in crowds or performing acrobatics. It is highly significant that none of the subjects is military. In Cretan art at this period there is a total absence of the pomp and savagery found so commonly in other civilisations of the same era. This absence, together with the choice of undefended coastal sites for cities, is perhaps the most telling indication we possess of the whole tenor of Minoan society.

The pity of the frescoes is that most of them were in an appalling condition when rediscovered, mere crumpled heaps of plaster. They have been reconstructed jigsaw fashion and the many missing parts have been supplied on the basis of information deduced from the rest of the picture or from other paintings. The restorations sometimes strain credulity. One famous example is the 'saffron gatherer', a set of fragments first put together to show a boy picking flowers from ornamental pots. After some years and vigorous counter-interpretations, Nicolas Platon and the Cretan painter Thomas Phanourakis reassembled it to show not a boy but a blue monkey with a long wavy tail! In the past, therefore, it was necessary to rely a good deal on the eye of faith to make the best of the frescoes. This has been made unnecessary by excavations carried on from 1967 in the island of Santorini (also known as Thera), one hundred kilometres north of Knossos. Here great quantities of frescoes were found in good condition and they are as lovely as even the most optimistic could have hoped. (They can be seen in the Archaeological Museum in Athens.) All that had previously been said in praise of Minoan grace, naturalism and colour seems, by inference from Santorini, to have been surprisingly exact.

In Crete at this period some of the finest frescoes came, as we have seen, from Ayia Triada. Phaistos yielded little, but a considerable quantity came from the district of Knossos as well as from the palace. A house at Amnisos on the coast had lilies and other flowers on the walls, the so-called caravanserai just outside the palace was decorated with hoopoes and partridges in a rocky landscape (it was an oddity of Cretan art that rocks were often shown both underfoot and above the heads of the people or animals represented). At the palace itself there were a great number of frescoes and, in these, women were painted white and men in red. Several show animated crowds, possibly watching some spectacle: some details are barely suggested, others sketched in with exactitude. One fragment in particular stands out. This shows the face of a woman, often referred to as La Parisienne: she has a huge and knowing eye, red lips and a big bump in the middle of her nose – an alert and entertaining face providing an early glimpse of the individual artist at work on portraiture of the individual.

Round about 1500, the palace artists got to work on much larger scenes – among them the famous Cupbearer and Procession frescoes. They also produced running friezes and big bas-reliefs, most notably one of a prince strolling among lilies. These have become

Art of the New Palaces. 'La Parisienne' – fragment from Knossos fresco, c. 1500 B.C.

the picture-postcard trademarks of the Minoan era: they were spectacular, but rather formal and did not suit Minoan talents quite so well. For the Minoans were, above all, successful miniaturists and at their best when most naturalistic. These talents are magnificently exemplified in Minoan miniature sculpture. As intensely as in painting, and to my mind even more delightfully, Minoan artists reached out, as one modern critic has observed, to catch for as long as their artefacts endured, the essence of the passing moment. They were deeply interested in the human form, particularly the human form in movement, and one of the best examples of this is an ivory statue of an acrobat, only thirty centimetres high. John Pendlebury

Ivory athlete from Knossos, c. 1500 B.C.

describes it as reaching 'the highest and most exquisite level of miniature sculpture attained in the ancient world, even including Egypt'. The acrobat is poised on his hands in the early stages of a somersault, probably from the horns of a bull now missing. 'The play of the muscles and the very veins', writes Pendlebury, 'are shown in such a way as not to give the effect of laborious detail but merely to heighten the impression of nervous energy.' Length of limb is emphasised rather than muscularity and the comparative smallness of the head reinforces the impression of a lithe and graceful body in full movement.

Men and women were also frequently portrayed in bronze miniatures, as we have seen in the context of the peak shrines. But perhaps the best known of all Cretan miniature sculptures are two little faience figures of about 1600 B.C. which were buried under the floor of the Knossos temple repositories. One is a goddess on whose head sits what seems to be a bird. She holds up a snake in either hand and her breasts are full and bare. The arms and body of the other figure, presumably her assistant, are positively alive with snakes. Two charming and delicate little faience plaques were associated with them, one showing a deer (or goat) with kid, the other a cow with calf.

Faience goddess with snakes, Knossos,
c. 1600 B.C.

Seal-stone carving was also superb at the start of the New Palace
period. Nicolas Platon observes that the Minoan talent for
miniature work found a perfect expression in seal engraving. 'On
minute round or elliptical surfaces', he writes, 'they contrived to
depict a world of action and movement, taking their subjects from
nature and religion.' 'World' is the operative word. The seals show
all kinds of animals, both wild and domestic. Almost all of these,
however tiny, are instinct with life, like the Mochlos dog. It is won-
derful that such grace can be achieved in so small a compass. There
are olive sprays, ships of various kinds, carpenters' tools, ploughs,
jugs and musical instruments. Human figures are quite common,

the men sometimes wearing baggy trousers like those still worn by a handful of the very oldest inhabitants of Crete. The stones are nearly as various as the designs. Carnelian, steatite, chalcedony, haematite, greenstone, agate and onyx were all favourites. But before the end, the engravers began to produce excessively distorted images, with animals sometimes bent almost double to fit the surface of the stones and, among the subjects, too many demons for comfort.

Apart from the seals, the best stone carving of the period – it is possible to find critics who consider it the most animated and naturalistic small-scale carving of antiquity – occurs on the shoulders of a black steatite (a kind of soapstone) vase from Ayia Triada, all that survives of the vessel. This is customarily referred to as the Harvester Vase, though it may represent a spring scene

The Harvester Vase, Ayia Triada, c. 1500 B.C.

with sowers. It shows two groups of peasants, sowers or reapers, marching along gloriously happy. One man has fallen down (too much to drink?) and others are singing lustily. One group is led by a man in a skull cap rattling an Egyptian instrument called a sistrum, the other by an old man in a quilted coat. The vase is a truly cheering piece of work, perhaps the most humane of all surviving Bronze Age scenes. The use of perspective to show groups four abreast in low relief has been managed most skilfully. Two other fine steatite vases were also found at Ayia Triada, one showing what seems to be the gift of oxhides to a prince, the other, savage scenes of boxing, in sharp contrast to the peaceful jollity of the Harvester Vase. From Zakros there comes a particularly elaborate and lovely chlorite vessel about thirty centimetres high, showing, among other things, a peak shrine and a bounding ibex.

All four of these vases were conical and used as ritual vessels for libations (this type of vase is usually known as a rhyton). Magnificent plain stone vases of this shape were also being made and a delectable rock-crystal rhyton with green bead handle was found at Zakros – shattered into many pieces but now satisfactorily reassembled. These vessels could not stand without support and were probably lowered into circular stands when not in use. At about this time potters, too, were making the same conical shape, though it is very difficult in clay.

The potters were skilled enough, however, to work almost any marvels, for this was one of the great ages of Minoan pottery – the first having occurred three hundred or more years before with Kamares ware. Now, in the period of the New Palaces, the shapes were so various, the decorations so many and so accomplished, the colours so bold and subtle, that it is hard to achieve much by description. The best pieces are illustrated in art books, but it is the mass of excellence which is so impressive: here it is only possible to pick out one or two major themes.

From about 1500 B.C. one style was shading into another. The first was a naturalistic style, in which abstract motifs, used for a long time, had been extended to representations of leaves, flowers,

Leaf-pattern jug from Phaistos, c. 1500 B.C.

branches and so forth. These forms, based in nature, flow and blossom over the surface of the pottery, often associated with the rosettes and cursive spirals the Minoans loved. 'Torsion' remains a major principle, helping to give the pottery an extraordinary liveliness. The designs were mostly picked out in shades darker than their background (which allowed gradation of tone). The commonest colour scheme was a lustrous red-black paint on a yellow background.

In due course this type of pottery gave way to the riotous and splendid marine style. Now vessels were decorated, often in blue, with writhing octopi, argonauts with waving tentacles, conch shells, dolphins, seaweed – any and every form of marine life. Plant designs still persisted and so did abstract patterns. There were many double

Marine-style amphora from
Knossos, c. 1500 B.C.

Large jar with double-headed axes,
c. 1400 B.C.

axes. But it is the energy and grace of the sea creatures which delight the eye and dwell in the memory. They possess an epic quality – Byron, so to speak, instead of Keats.

An astonishingly high proportion of Minoan art objects possess a deep and lasting loveliness based on a naturalistic representation of the world still relevant today. But Minoan artists put a higher premium than is currently fashionable on physical beauty and the ravishing of the senses. Their works reveal a constant inventiveness, an understanding of form and movement and a sense of spontaneity and fun.

As well as offering great satisfaction to the visitor, Minoan art provides much information about religion and daily life. In religion, the central figure in the cosmogony appears to have been a great goddess, capable of taking many forms – a goddess of the earth in the Knossos pillar crypt; on seals and many exquisite golden signet rings of the period, divine huntress and mistress of the animals; and, most significant of all, as the wild and lovely goddess of nature who is often seen in a grove dancing with ecstatic attendants or, with a priestess, engaged in severing a bough from a tree on an outdoor altar. This 'golden bough' presumably implies the death of the year and its regeneration, as also does the occasional presence of a young man – most probably son and lover of the goddess. Nature itself appears to be charged with religious significance. But it is always the female principle which dominates. Interestingly, we know from a variety of sources that women played an important part in religious ritual. One of these sources, though of a rather later period, is a fascinating painted sarcophagus from Ayia Triada which shows women performing the main priestly functions in ceremonies dedicated to the dead.

The scanty evidence we possess suggests that the Minoans viewed death in a tolerably cheerful light. During the period of the New Palaces many tombs were cut deep into the soft Cretan rock; the dead were buried there in handsome clay chests – some of which had previously done duty as baths – and were accompanied by a few objects which they were clearly expected to need in an after-life.

It is significant that this grave furniture, though decent and often extremely beautiful, was not usually of a munificence to beggar the living. On the whole, and even though they may have worshipped their ancestors, the Minoans were too intent on the joys of the day to indulge in the gloomy over-attendance on the dead so fashionable in Egypt. Some commentators have suggested that the Minoans may have contributed the notion of Elysium, as opposed to the harsher northern Hades, to ancient Greek civilisation.

Whether or not the Minoans felt obliged to propitiate dark and destructive forces is an interesting question. Much religious art appears to express joy and ecstasy. On the other hand some of the most sacred ceremonies seem, as at Knossos, to have been conducted in dark and secret places. Snakes were involved (witness the little faience snake goddess from Knossos and a number of strange clay vessels in which sacred snakes were probably kept). But we should not read too much into this for the snake is regarded as a benevolent force in Indian and occult tradition and survives in the emblem of medical associations and in the sceptre of Greek Orthodox bishops. The omnipresence of the bull motif opens up wider questions.

We have noted the great bull by the north entrance to Knossos, the horns of consecration and the bronze and clay bulls of the peak shrines. Two of the most splendid libation vessels of the New Palace period – one from Knossos (p. 23), one from Zakros – are in the form of bulls' heads, the horns gilded, eyes of rock crystal with a jasper centre. They are so striking it is hard not to believe they were of particular significance. But the most intriguing representations of all show athletes somersaulting with uncanny grace along the backs of charging bulls. A fine bull-leaping fresco was found at Knossos and the theme occurs frequently enough to make it virtually certain that something of the sort actually happened – though there are difficulties in understanding how. Bulls hook sideways with their horns, yet the bull-leapers appear to grip both horns at once to pivot themselves up and over and into the arms of a waiting helper.

The evident element of risk in connection with bulls leads one to speculate on a connection with the Minotaur story. Could it just possibly have been that girls and youths were brought unwillingly from Athens to participate in the dangerous Cretan ritual of bull-leaping? This is purest speculation, but it is worth noting that there is no evidence whatsoever in Crete of human sacrifice. Bulls, on the other hand, were certainly sacrificed.

In more general terms, Nicolas Platon has speculated that, just as the omnipresent goddess embodies the female principle, so, in the general absence of a male god, the bull may have represented 'male creative force' and have been associated with sun and moon, the sea and the nether-world. Sir Arthur Evans also thought the bull of profound religious importance to the Minoans. At one spot in Knossos he found evidence of earthquake damage which had never been repaired; among the fallen blocks two great pairs of bulls' horns were associated with the remains of altars. Homer, Evans pointed out, had said that 'the Earthshaker delighteth in bulls'; and he interpreted the horns as evidence of sacrifice to the god of earthquakes who, in Greek times at least, was known as Poseidon and was often associated with bulls. Bulls and earthquakes seem to have been closely involved with one another at Knossos and earthquakes were critical in the history of the Minoans.

Fashion is one of the subjects on which Minoan art provides most information. Unfortunately the damp winter climate of Crete, so different from that of Egypt, has destroyed all fabrics and leather, not to mention the wooden furniture which was almost certainly in daily use. But we know leather was used, among other things for boxing gloves, as on the Ayia Triada boxing rhyton, and for shields, as can be seen on a huge Knossos frieze showing figure-of-eight shields made of oxhide. For fabrics, frescoes provide some evidence, though disappointingly there appears to have been an in-hibition against representing the human form on pottery. In the Cupbearer and Procession frescoes from Knossos the men wear kilts of rich colour and design, suggesting that weaving was well advanced.

Quite frequently prehistoric religious art shows modes of dress which were once traditional but which may have fallen out of use by the time they were last represented. Even bearing this in mind, it seems likely that men at an early period wore very few clothes and that these consisted mainly of a tight belt, often with a dagger stuck in it, and a codpiece larger than one might have presumed strictly necessary. The awareness of the body indicated by the modelling combines with this provocative fashion in clothes to emphasise sexuality. Moreover, men are almost always portrayed in paintings as broad-shouldered and wasp-waisted, extraordinarily graceful. Most interesting of all, women's fashions were as provocative as the men's. Long flounced or flowing skirts covered the lower parts of ladies whose breasts were often bare. Hair styles were various and elaborate, as were hats.

It is usually the case around the Mediterranean and in the near East that when women occupy a low position in society they are obliged to cover their bodies and even to veil their faces. Their sexuality must not be revealed in public and is usually repressed in private too. Because the sexuality of Minoan women is recognised, it seems rational to suppose that they occupied a high position in society. They are shown in frescoes as participants in the same events as men and it is indisputable that they exercised an important function as priestesses. Another factor is the Minoan reverence for the female principle as exemplified in the presence of the goddess. It is quite possible that inheritance was through women.

As to the entertainments that may have been enjoyed, presumably by both men and women – the kind of people shown in the Knossos miniature frescoes – bull-leaping seems to have been highly significant, if one may judge by the dramatic quality of the illustrations which depict it. Music was important, with lyre and pipe the main instruments. Dancing must surely also have been popular. The ancient Greeks believed that dancing was invented on the island and Daidalos, according to myth, built Ariadne a dancing-floor at Knossos (some people connect this with the theatral area). One charming pottery group from Palaikastro shows a ring dance in progress and there is a famous passage in *The Iliad* which links this kind of circular dance with Knossos. The god Hephaistos has just made a shield for Achilles and now he is decorating it:

> Next the god depicted a dancing-floor like the one that Daedalus designed in the spacious town of Cnossus for Ariadne of the lovely locks. Youths and marriageable maidens were dancing on it with their hands on one another's wrists, the girls in fine linen with lovely garlands on their heads, and the men in closely woven tunics showing the faint gleam of oil, and with daggers of gold hanging from their silver belts. Here they ran tightly round, circling smoothly on their accomplished feet as the wheel of a potter when he sits and works it with his hands to see if it will spin; and there they ran in lines to meet each other. A large crowd stood round enjoying the delightful dance, with a minstrel among them singing divinely to the lyre, while a couple of acrobats, keeping time with his music, threw cart wheels in and out among the people. [Book XVIII, trans. E. V. Rieu.]

This kind of dance is still performed in eastern Crete and it may be that it has descended virtually unchanged from Minoan times.

Art has little to tell us of what the Minoans ate and drank, but archaeologists provide a fairly thorough picture from other sources.

The Minoans possessed the Mediterranean triad of corn, vine and olives. There is a misleading Greek tradition that the olive was first cultivated on Crete, but if we may judge by the vast storage jars of the palaces, great quantities of oil were collected either as secular tax or in religious dues. At the same time, the Minoans had many other crops. They had figs, apples, pears and the quince (a native of western Crete). There was barley, there were broad beans, peas and lentils, the multitudinous herbs which still grow more profusely on the island than anywhere else and the many delicious wild vegetables (*horta* in modern Greek) which are still much prized – the more so, in fact, as the modern exodus from the land continues, leaving fewer unoccupied hands to pick them.

For meat, Cretans of 1500 B.C. had a few cows (the terrain is mostly unsuitable for them), goats (not yet a symbol of poverty), a good number of sheep and quite a plentiful supply of pigs. They hunted the wild ibex, that splendid mountain goat known in Greek as the *agrimi* and today almost extinct, the red deer, and hares and rabbits. There were no chickens, but they may have had the small domestic goose from Egypt – a series of deductions based mainly on the work of Joseph Hazzidakis, one of the earliest Cretan archaeologists, at the ruins of a series of Minoan manor houses at Tylisos, a few miles west of Knossos. (There also came from Tylisos a series of gigantic bronze cauldrons, remarkably similar to those used today in the mountains by makers of cheese and curdled milk.) The early Cretans had plenty of fish and shell fish. For sweetening they used honey. They probably knew pepper and certainly used salt – the archaeologist Costis Davaras recalls finding a pot of salt near Zakros. 'Some of it went to the museum, the rest into our salad, and it tasted fine,' he says. Apart from tomatoes, potatoes, bananas, citrus fruit and sugar, the Minoans ate very much what Cretans eat today – a conclusion announced with suitable awe by economists undertaking a survey for the Rockefeller Foundation just after World War II.

But to turn from food to more problematical matters. One of the many things that are unknown – and this is a major gap – is whether the Crete of the New Palaces was one or several states. There seems to have been a unity of culture with Knossos pre-eminent, but one cannot go much further. Even more important, we do not know what language or languages were spoken, though it is probable that Greek had not yet arrived. Philologists believe, however, that certain words in currency among the Minoans were later absorbed into Greek. One common Minoan word-ending may have been -*sos* (as in the place names Knossos, Tylisos, Amnisos). *Kiparissos*, the modern Greek word for a cypress tree, may be Minoan. Pendlebury suggests as Minoan *thalassa*, the sea. Sinclair Hood thinks the Greek words for thyme, sage, marjoram and mint may be Cretan, as also *sandalou* for sandal. R. W. Hutchinson, an enthusiastic player of the game, adds calamint, sesame, silphium and wormwood. He even suggests that the Greek words for pepper and mustard, very similar to their English descendants, came from Crete. It is a pleasing thought that Minoan words may be tripping off our tongues at lunch and dinner.

By 1500 B.C. the early hieroglyphic system had developed into a linear script. This, too, remains undeciphered but seems to have been used mainly for administrative purposes connected with the palaces (and in Phaistos far earlier than in Knossos). This script is called Linear A, to distinguish it from a later form of writing, the famous Linear B, which is discussed later.

A good deal can be deduced about foreign relations, trade and manufacture at the time of the New Palaces. The Minoans, like the neolithic people before them, not only made beautiful things, they made them for other people as well, an important step in social evolution. There was also at least one small town devoted to a considerable extent to manufacture: Gournia, on the Gulf of Mirabello. It occupied a pleasant site on a knoll running down towards the sea and its remains are interesting since it is one of very few ancient Cretan sites to have been excavated in its entirety. Finds included carpenters' kits, potters' wheels and many other indications of industry. Visitors to Gournia are often puzzled by what seems to have been the tiny size of the rooms. It took me a long time to realise that the ruined walls are those of basements which would have been reached from above. Access to the houses themselves was by steps up from the street, and the arrangement of their rooms may have been quite unlike that of the basements below. Another point of interest – there was a public shrine in Gournia, a fact which suggests a highly developed communal life.

In essentials Crete was self-supporting. Its main exports were probably timber and corn, wine and olive oil; but the materials for many of its luxury goods had to be imported – tin, some copper perhaps; obsidian, mainly from Melos; emery from Naxos; veined white alabaster from Egypt; lapis lazuli from Afghanistan.

Seal-stones tell much about the ships that carried the Minoan trade. These appear to have been high at the prow, low at the stern and in some cases big enough for thirty rowers, fifteen on either side. The sail, presumably the main method of propulsion except in calm or crisis, was square and supported by a central mast. This meant that ships could not sail close to the wind and greatly restricted the range of harbours that were safe and easy to approach. Once in harbour these ships would have been dragged up on the beach. This created a preference for harbours on sandy coasts, particularly spits of sandy land towards which it was possible to sail from either side according to the wind. There was also a tendency (the reason for which remains obscure) to use as harbours inshore islands like Pseira in the east.

By 1500 B.C. the Minoans were trading extensively with Egypt, the eastern Mediterranean, the Aegean islands and, most significant for the future, with the mainland to the north of Crete. This was now inhabited by the Achaians (or Mycenaeans). Their much younger and more warlike culture was greatly influenced by the Minoan and at this time the two societies probably eyed one another neutrally, exchanging ideas and art-forms while year by year the power of the Achaians grew.

Crete quite possibly ruled the Cycladic islands, one of which is Santorini of the frescoes. Others are Melos, Naxos, Paros, Andros, Mykonos and Delos. Minoan remains have been found in many of them. This would tally with Thucydides's description, written a thousand years later, of how Minos established his sons as governors in the Cyclades and cleared the sea of pirates. It would certainly have been in the Minoan interest to suppress piracy and it is also unlikely that the Minoans would have been able to live in undefended cities without confidence that their ships could maintain the integrity of the seas around. Their influence may have followed trade. In any event, the Minoans do not seem to have imposed themselves by fire and the sword, for, as Pendlebury observes, there is no sign of general catastrophe in the Aegean during the period of their supremacy. This seems as fine a recommendation of their civilisation as one could wish for.

The sites of the New Palaces convey, in their state of ruin or restoration, a strictly limited impression of this great civilisation. The finest distillation available is in the Archaeological Museum of Iraklion. The visitor to the Museum will find exhibits arranged in chronological order. The first room (Gallery I) contains finds from neolithic and Pre-Palatial periods, including the Mochlos stone jars and the dog on the stone lid. This is now shown with an almost identical dog from Zakros. Galleries II and III deal with the Old or Proto-Palatial period; then comes a magnificent series of rooms devoted to the New Palaces. In these the visitor will find the pottery, sculpture and other works of art described here, not to mention surprises such as the Phaistos disc – a curious and handsome clay tablet stamped with a unique and, up to now, impenetrable script. The pottery collection in these rooms has few rivals in the world. After this comes another group (Galleries X to XII) which follow the story from the end of the palaces right down to 600 B.C. Gallery XIII returns to the Minoans with a fine collection of sarcophagi – some of them surprisingly comical in their decorations – while the frescoes are upstairs in Galleries XIV to XVI. The best way to see the Museum is to make a preliminary trip, taking not more than an hour or two and perhaps using the clear and helpful guide of Stylianos Alexiou, the current Director. This will allow the visitor to come back later for a closer look at what he most enjoys. The consequences of trying to take it all in at once are cultural shock, visual indigestion and exhaustion. (One should also remember that the Museum can get exceedingly crowded by mid-morning.)

Standing either among the pottery or the frescoes of the New Palace period the visitor perceives a society perhaps excessively aristocratic, dominated by priest and palace, but one which in many other ways shines by comparison with our own. Art, industry and agriculture flourished astonishingly in a mountain island at peace with itself and its neighbours.

All this came to an end at about 1450 B.C., when all the palaces except Knossos were burned. Nor was it only the palaces. Towns and country houses alike were devastated. Little built by man appears to have escaped. Knossos endured, producing some fine works of art, but the glories of Minoan Crete, considered as an entity, were over.

What was the reason for this terrible catastrophe? Enemy action, local revolution, earthquake and tidal wave are all hypotheses which at one time or another have looked attractive, and experts have supported each of them.

Even at the time of Evans's death in 1941 it was clear that the question of how and when Knossos was destroyed had not been satisfactorily settled. (Much interesting material about Evans and about the curators he appointed to Knossos – among them John Pendlebury and R. W. Hutchinson – has been assembled in *The Villa Ariadne*, by Dilys Powell. It takes its title from the name of the house that Evans built for himself near Knossos.)

Evans had been involved for many years in a vigorous scholarly dispute with Professor J. B. Wace who was working at Mycenae. The main point at issue was the extent of Cretan influence on Mycenae and vice versa. Wace thought that Knossos in its final days had fallen under the cultural domination, at least, of the mainland city, Evans assumed a continuity of civilisation at Knossos right up to the time of its destruction, which he attributed to earthquake. Pendlebury followed the continuity theory in a memorably romantic passage, though ascribing the final burning of Knossos to an attack from Mycenae, which he pictured as a Cretan colony rebellious at subjugation. 'On a fine spring day,' he wrote, 'when a strong south wind was blowing which carried the flames of the burning beams almost horizontally, Knossos fell.

'The final scene takes place in the most dramatic room ever excavated – the Throne Room. It was found in a state of complete confusion. A great oil jar lay overturned in one corner, ritual vessels were in the act of being used when the disaster came. It looks as if the king had been hurried here to undergo too late some last ceremony in the hope of saving the people.'

This theory of attack from the mainland seemed quite plausible – except for an absence of human bones – until, in 1953, a young

English architect, Michael Ventris, announced that he had succeeded in reading documents written in Linear B.

Linear B was a well-developed script current at Knossos during its final period. Great quantities of clay tablets bearing this script had been preserved, presumably by accidental baking during the last fire. Evans assumed that they were written in the dominant language of the Minoans, whatever that may have been. Ventris's decipherment came as a major event to the scholarly world because

Linear B.

his readings were obtained on the assumption that Linear B was written in Greek. If this were so, then it meant that Crete was almost certainly in the hands of Greek-speaking Mycenaeans *before* the destruction of Knossos, with Knossos Greek-speaking in its final days. Not surprisingly some scholars were ready to say, with much asperity, that Ventris had got it wrong.

Ventris had been determined to solve the mystery of Linear B since hearing Sir Arthur Evans lecture during his childhood. He worked at first on the assumption that the language of the tablets was of Oriental origin, Hittite or something of the sort. There had not been much material to go on, for Evans published few of the Knossos tablets. But in 1939 a fresh batch of tablets was discovered on the Greek mainland at Pylos and these were published in 1952. At the same time, Linear B tablets were turning up at Mycenae and the results were passed by Professor Wace to Ventris and his collaborator John Chadwick. Most of the remaining Knossos tablets were finally published in the same year. Working like wartime cryptographers, and bearing in mind the mainland source of much of their new material, Ventris and Chadwick soon began to explore the possibility that the language was Greek. Very quickly Linear B began to make some sense. They were careful to make only modest claims at first, but four years later they published a substantial volume – *Documents in Mycenaean Greek*. According to this, the tablets were mostly lists – as Evans had conjectured. They contained appropriate place-names, the names of individuals involved in transactions and, most interestingly, the names of deities to whom various offerings had been made. These were the same as names of gods who later figured in the Homeric cosmogony.

The trouble with the Ventris decipherment was that to make it come out as Greek, it had to be assumed that some of the signs had different values on different occasions. These variations were expressed in an elaborate set of rules – for instance, that L, M, N, R and S are omitted at the end of words or before other consonants. This meant that some words could be read in a number of different ways and it was the main reason for criticism of the decipherment. The arguments on both sides are many and complex and generally impenetrable to outsiders. In the end, I think, a mere enthusiast must simply choose an expert who is convincing on other matters and follow him. I am greatly swayed by the fact that Professor Platon, after careful review of the evidence, came down in favour of Ventris. Another pointer was the publication, after the decipherment, of the famous 'tripod' tablet. This showed in ideogram (or picture form) a set of tripods with varying numbers of handles. There was writing beside them in Linear B. Deciphered by the Ventris method, the script clearly referred to tripods with the appropriate number of handles. Since it was impossible for Ventris to have seen this tablet before its publication, many scholars take it as proof that he was broadly right, though his decipherment is open to improvement. It does not produce a reading for all the tablets and it contains too many variables. Ventris himself died in a car crash in 1955, leaving the debate to others.

If we accept that the language of Knossos when it was destroyed was Greek, this suggests that Crete had passed on its art-forms and much of its culture to a warrior civilisation which had responded by swallowing its teacher. As for the final destruction of Knossos in 1400 B.C., may it have been the work of native Cretans rebelling against Mycenaean masters? Hutchinson, at least, thought so.

These speculations were in the air when a new champion appeared, maintaining that there was a fundamental error in the dating of the destruction of Knossos. Far from falling in 1400, said Professor L. R. Palmer, a Cambridge philologist, Knossos had survived another two hundred years or more as a brilliant centre of Achaian/Mycenaean civilisation. This would have brought Knossos much nearer to historical times, comfortably producing Achaian heroes from Crete for the Trojan War and explaining, perhaps, how Minos the sea-king was still remembered well enough for Thucydides to write of him. It is in many ways a most engaging theory.

Professor Palmer first began to examine this possibility because he felt that the language of the Knossos Linear B tablets was too modern for 1400 B.C. (It had long bothered scholars that the tablets from Pylos and Mycenae, in an almost identical script, dated from about 1200 B.C.) Various philologists have rejected Palmer's conclusions on this; another difficulty is that he can only be right if Evans misrepresented the evidence from Knossos. Palmer at first refrained from saying this, but the assumption is implicit in *A New Guide to the Palace of Knossos*, a spirited work published in 1969.

The argument is over the nature of the pottery originally found with the Linear B tablets, and from which those tablets were dated. Palmer alleges that Evans, when he came to publish, mangled the information contained in the notebooks of his assistant Duncan Mackenzie, producing an unrealistically early date for the tablets. If this were so, argues Palmer, then major areas in the palace itself would be much later than Evans maintained. Many archaeologists are horrified at the thought that Evans could have erred so greatly, and the passions stirred by the controversy are deep without being attractive. Matters have now reached the point where Evans's views would look more convincing if they were thoroughly supported by fresh evidence.

But while the Palmer dispute was argued this way and that,

another solution to the general destruction of 1450 B.C. began to look more credible. This was the tidal wave theory, first propounded by Professor Spyridon Marinatos. As Director of the Iraklion Museum in the 1930s, Marinatos was already considering this possibility, and his own dig in Santorini from 1967 has reinforced the theory. Briefly, Marinatos suggested that the volcano of Santorini had erupted about 1450 B.C. with devastating results. He argued by analogy with the great Krakatoa eruption of 1883. This triggered off huge tidal waves which were highly destructive in themselves and which in turn started up a great many fires in homes where lamps had been lit against the unnatural darkness of the day. The size of the Santorini crater indicated that the explosion would have been much greater, as also the tidal waves, because of the depth of sea between Santorini and Crete. (The deeper the water the bigger the waves.) The darkness associated with the eruption would likewise have been more intense. And this would account, thought Marinatos, for destruction and burning all round the coast of Crete. But when he first began to dig on Santorini this theory looked a little shaky. The Minoan town which he unearthed at Akrotiri (a site which all Minoan addicts will wish to visit) seemed from its pottery to have been destroyed around 1500 B.C., not in 1450, and expert evidence on the volcano suggested that there had been one eruption only during this period. Soon, however, analysis of discoveries began to suggest that Akrotiri had been destroyed by *earthquake* round about 1500 B.C. and that the eruption followed fifty years later. This made the tidal wave theory look very plausible. It seemed at first to lock in with another piece of evidence produced by Platon during the 1960s in the most exciting dig on Crete itself since Evans and Halbherr first caused others to pick up the spade. Platon undertook his dig at Zakros convinced by a mixture of logic and intuition that there must be substantial remains on this remote little coastal plain. Excavations by the British archaeologist David Hogarth at the turn of the century had revealed a series of large Minoan houses, but Platon thought that eastward trade would have demanded something more. Then there was the intriguing story of Dr. Giamalakis, a notable collector of antiquities in Iraklion.

Shortly before World War II, Dr. Giamalakis was summoned to Upper Zakros to the sick-bed of a village farmer on whom he had operated many years before. Giamalakis had taken no payment at the time, but the message which brought him hastening on the long journey from Iraklion – which he completed, late at night, by mule – spoke of valuable objects for his collection. These turned out to be an exquisite gold diadem, a gold pendant of the head of a young bull and a shallow and elegantly shaped golden bowl. They were, wrote Platon, 'undoubtedly the products of a royal workshop and probably the possessions of a person of high status in Minoan society, perhaps even a member of the royal family'. In return for them the doctor emptied his pockets, the old man accepting a gold watch, a few British sovereigns and a little Greek money. He said that the objects had come from Lower, or Kato, Zakros. (The Giamalakis Collection is shown in Gallery XVII of the Museum.)

This remained the strongest pointer until Platon made a trip by boat along the rugged coast near Zakros. At Kato Zakros itself there were a few big blocks of *poros* stone lying on the ground and now Platon found a place where huge quantities of this favourite Minoan material had been quarried. The transport of this stone from the quarry to Zakros implied more than the construction of houses, however substantial. Patches of land where crops of legumes were particularly rich also caught Platon's eye. These often occur in places which have been inhabited for a long time, because of an accumulation of fatty substances in the soil. The Cretans, Platon observes, describe than as *'Lenika* (Hellenika), Greek lands. Taken together these indications were enough. Backed by American benefactors, Platon began to dig.

In his book on the excavation Platon tells how, within yards of Hogarth's dig so many years before, he immediately struck the ruins of a palace. Its magnificent pottery and libation vessels showed that it was one of the New Palaces and though it had been destroyed round about 1450 it had never been plundered. Season after season, glorious and revealing treasures of Minoan art were recovered.

Some of the most significant results came from the palace shrine. Here the impression of an interrupted ceremony was even stronger than at Knossos, and lumps of pumice were scattered about the floor; to Platon this indicated that in this room a ceremony of propitiation had been interrupted by a pumice-bearing tidal wave. If this were so, then it would follow that all the palaces except inland Knossos were overwhelmed by the same disaster. Platon thinks that Knossos, now or soon afterwards in Mycenaean hands, endured another seventy years before it was destroyed in about 1380 B.C. After this, the Mycenaean chieftains may have moved to other sites. The impression we are left with is of a beautiful but fragile civilisation almost obliterated by natural disaster and with its remnants firmly in the hands of mainland chieftains. But even this theory is beginning to look a little frayed, having been vigorously assaulted by the French scholar Paul Faure. It certainly seems wrong to attach so much importance to pumice. This material has been used since time immemorial for rubbing and cleaning and, since its discovery in Zakros, has turned up as a grave-good in a tomb near Sitia, placed there a thousand years before the catastrophe. Clearly, pumice could travel without benefit of tidal wave. It is a complex matter, but one which may yet be elucidated satisfactorily, by studies of the fall-out of volcanic ash and other evidence concerning seismic activity.

One interesting effect of the tidal wave theory, however, has been to provoke speculation that Plato's lost island civilisation of Atlantis was based on Crete. There are some curious parallels between Minoan Crete and the story which Plato tells in the *Critias*. One of the most intriguing is his description of how 'every fifth and every sixth year alternately' the ten kings of Atlantis gathered to consult in the temple of Poseidon by whose commands they ruled. Now it so happened that 'there were bulls who had the range of the temple of Poseidon; and the ten kings, being left alone in the temple, after they had offered prayers to the god that they might capture the victim which was acceptable to him, hunted the bulls, without weapons, but with a stave and nooses; and the bull which they caught they led up to the pillar and cut its throat over the top of it so that the blood fell upon the sacred inscription.' In the Archaeological Museum in Athens there are two gold cups, found at Vapheio in the Peloponnese but of Cretan manufacture. They show a bull hunt with stave, nets and nooses.

Then there was Plato's account of the wealth and fertility of the island – including the export of timber – and of the order and stability on which its society was founded. Plato cites Egypt as the source of his story – and who better to preserve a memory, however garbled, of the civilisation of Crete and of its inundation?

Many other aspects of Atlantis bear no obvious Minoan mark. The most important argument against the Cretan candidacy is that Plato fixed his island in the Atlantic, giving it a mythic quality which suggests that he invented everything – even the Egyptian source.

If this is disappointing to Atlantis-hungry speculation, it has been suggested that there may be a memory of the Santorini eruption in the Argonaut story as told by Apollonius Rhodius in the third century B.C. It seems that after terrible trouble with Talos, a rock-throwing giant of bronze who guarded Crete, the Argonauts sailed north.

And then straightaway, as they moved swiftly over the great Cretan deep, night terrified them, the night which they call 'the pall of darkness'. No stars nor moonbeams pierced this deadly darkness. It was black darkness coming down from the sky, or some other darkness rising from the inmost recesses of the earth. They did not in the least know whether they were voyaging on the water or in Hades. Helplessly they entrusted their safe return to the sea, to carry them whither it would. [Quoted by J. V. Luce. See Bibliography.]

But however much tales of Atlantis and the Argonauts may stir the imagination, they are not susceptible of examination like the actual artefacts of Minoan Crete, arrayed for all to see in the Archaeological Museum. Here, surrounded by the finest known artefacts of the first European civilisation, the visitor may well ask himself whether the many centuries of oblivion mean that the Minoan achievement was wasted. Surprisingly, the evidence shows that this is not the case.

First, perhaps, we should look at non-essentials, if only to establish that there were survivals. There are several obvious instances. The fact, for example, that some villagers still use the same type of vast clay storage jar and that there has been until recently an unbroken line in the way the flat roofs of their houses are built – first, rafters with branches laid across them, then several inches of earth on top and a layer of hard-stamped clay to make a watertight seal. We have already noted the persistence of the ring dance, not to mention individual words passed on to modern Greek. It is clear that some elements of the Minoan way of life endured.

There is, too, another area where the Cretan inheritance was far greater, affecting, most probably, the Achaian heroes of whom Homer wrote, surviving tenuously through the Greek dark ages and emerging again to flower in the classical Greek civilisation. Through this medium it has had a profound effect on Europe and other parts of the world. This is the religious inheritance of the Minoans.

At the obvious level there is the great quantity of religious myth involving Crete, the birth of Zeus being a case in point. The association with goddesses – goddesses both of household and of what the archaeological writer Jacquetta Hawkes has called 'the wild places and the unconscious mind' – is extremely striking. Athena, whether or not she came from Crete, certainly possessed in classical Athens the sacred symbols of the Minoan household goddess – snake, pillar and dove.

The names of some Greek divinities appear in Mycenaean script but are very likely to have been Minoan in origin and to have been absorbed by the Mycenaeans. Though one cannot say for certain just which details of Greek religion are Minoan, they are undoubtedly many and important.

But what ancient Crete seems beyond all question to have passed on was the sense of a world instinct with divinity – fertile, sometimes ecstatic and in many of its aspects feminine. At its best it brought humanity and nature into a full relationship. Minoan art suggests that gods perhaps and goddesses certainly could find their epiphany in trees and rocks and birds; and the main Minoan contribution to Greece was surely a sense of the miraculous possibilities of nature.

NOTE ON DATING

The first dating scheme for Minoan prehistory was worked out by Sir Arthur Evans on the basis of pottery finds at Knossos.

Evans described three broad periods which he called Early, Middle and Late Minoan. He subdivided each of these into three: Early Minoan I, II and III, Middle and Late Minoan similarly numbered. This produced nine periods, some of which had to be further subdivided – Middle Minoan Ia and b, for example. (The notation for these is MMIa, MMIb, etc.) The total in the end was fourteen periods preceded by three phases of neolithic development.

An absolute chronology was achieved by cross-dating with Egypt. Egyptian dates are accurately known and objects from the two cultures have been found in a datable association on many sites in both Egypt and Crete.

The Evans scheme, however, was extremely cumbersome and there were other snags. The scheme was based on Knossos, but other parts of the island developed at different speeds, so that one style might be in vogue in Knossos, quite another in the east. Moreover the styles on which two of Evans's periods were based turned out to have been confined to Knossos and Phaistos. Thus the Evans scheme presents difficulties for the specialist and can be totally bewildering to the layman.

A more satisfactory scheme, based on actual events, has been provided by Professor Platon. He splits Minoan history into four broad periods – Pre-Palace, Old Palace, New Palace and Post-Palace. Each of these is subdivided into three phases. It is an altogether more elegant system and is quickly superseding that of Evans. The table overleaf compares Platon's chronology with Sir Arthur Evans's scheme.

	Nicolas Platon's chronology	Absolute chronology	Comparison with Sir Arthur Evans's chronology
	Neolithic Age	B.C.	*Neolithic Age*
PROTOMINOAN AGE	Early Neolithic I Early Neolithic II }	6000–4000? }	Early Neolithic Middle Neolithic
	Middle Neolithic	4000–3000?	
	Late Neolithic	3000–2600?	Late Neolithic
	Pre-Palace Period		*Early Minoan*
	Phase I	2600–2400	Early Minoan I
	Phase II	2400–2200	Early Minoan II
			Early Minoan III
	Phase III	2200–2000 {	*Middle Minoan*
			Middle Minoan Ia
	Old Palace Period		
	Phase I	2000–1900	Middle Minoan Ib
	Phase II	1900–1800	Middle Minoan IIa
	Phase III	1800–1700	Middle Minoan IIb
	New Palace Period		
	Phase I	1700–1600	Middle Minoan IIIa, b
MINOAN AGE			*Late Minoan*
	Phase II	1600–1450	Late Minoan Ia, b
	Phase III	1450–1400	Late Minoan II
	Post-Palace Period		
	Phase I	1400–1320	Late Minoan IIIa
	Phase II	1320–1260 }	Late Minoan IIIb
	Phase III	1260–1150	
	Subminoan Age	1150–1000	*Subminoan*

(From *Crete*, by Nicolas Platon. See Bibliography.)

3. From Knossos to Byzantium

The Minoan civilisation, however perplexing some of its elements remain, is in a real sense accessible to all. But Crete possesses another great body of art which up to now has remained by comparison exceedingly obscure. This is the fresco painting in almost a thousand churches and chapels dotted about the valleys and mountainsides from one end of Crete to the other. Most of it was painted under Venetian rule which began in A.D. 1204, but it is entirely Byzantine in character, an art which could hardly be more different from that of the Minoans – symbolic, spiritual, ritualised, concerned as much with heaven as with earth, more with salvation than with daily life. Often the painting is hard to see or in shocking condition, and its appreciation requires patience and an effort of mental projection which we are never called upon to make by the Minoans. Yet once one is equipped with a bare minimum of background information, its exploration becomes a fascinating and often a moving occupation.

Twenty-five centuries, however, elapsed between the fall of Knossos and the most fertile period of Byzantine fresco painting in Crete. During these centuries the island's fortunes were extremely varied and much of interest survives. Crete, was, after all, in the hands of the Achaians, the Dorians, the Romans, the Byzantine emperors, the Saracens and the Byzantines once again.

Archaeology apart, the only real source on Achaian Crete is

Homer, and to me Homer's most interesting phrases occur just after his famous reference to the rich and lovely island of ninety cities. The whole passage runs like this:

> Out in the dark blue sea there lies a land called Crete, a rich and lovely land, washed by the waves on every side, densely peopled and boasting ninety cities. Each of the several races of the isle has its own language. First there are the Achaeans; then the genuine Cretans, proud of their native stock; next the Cydonians; the Dorians with their three clans; and finally the noble Pelasgians. One of the ninety towns is a great city called Cnossus, and there, for nine years, King Minos ruled and enjoyed the friendship of almighty Zeus . . . [*The Odyssey*, Book XX, trs. E. V. Rieu.]

Strabo, the Greek geographer, considered that the Kydonians (Kydonia is the ancient name of Khania) and the 'genuine Cretans' of this passage (called Eteocretans by translators unwilling to beg the question) were the original inhabitants of Crete – none other, it would now seem, than elements of the Minoan population living on still in cities of their own. And one of the most extraordinary facts in the history of Crete is that these Eteocretans managed to hang on in the east until at least the third century B.C. They preserved their own language, leaving behind them in Praisos a number of inscriptions still undeciphered but recognisable as being in a Minoan language.

In general, though, the Achaians seem to have ruled the polyglot populace of Crete. They were a warlike people and their art, while still substantially Minoan, took on an increasingly militaristic tone.

But some time in the twelfth century B.C., disaster overtook the Achaian civilisation, just as had happened to the Minoans before. The mainland cities and citadels were destroyed and the Achaians of Crete seem likewise to have melted away. The survivors took to the mountains, building places of refuge in inaccessible sites, among them Karphi, near the Lassithi plateau. Below, the valleys and plains fell into the hands of the Dorians, a Greek-speaking people from the north. They were fierce and energetic, and in due course came to dominate the island, building themselves substantial cities which were to evolve into the Greek city-states of classical Crete. The earlier Dorian cities were probably founded in the eighth and ninth centuries B.C.

The most exciting of these sites is Lato, reached from the village of Kritsa, an awesome set of ruins on a saddle between high crags. It commands a view down through the foothills to Ayios Nikolaos that makes the unsuspecting visitor gasp as he reaches the crest.

On a smaller scale it is reminiscent of that great sweep of hill going down from Delphi to a distant sea. But the atmosphere is very different. There is something intimidating about Dorian ruins, a threatening quality in the huge grey blocks of stone; nevertheless, Lato is extremely fine, a place worth many visits. I recall on one occasion standing among the great blocks of masonry as the sun sank on one side and on the other a full moon rose over sea and mountain; and once again I felt the original thrill of beauty and repulsion.

The Dorian cities, unlike the Minoan, were built as strongholds. But Lato both incorporates Minoan elements and prefigures the classical Greek city. This makes it the most interesting archaic Greek site in Crete. The agora, the open space in the middle, seems to have been a meeting place for citizens in what was to become the classical manner; but it is commanded by a tier of steps which recalls the theatral areas of Knossos and Phaistos. A characteristically Greek element is the dominance of the temple just above the steps. There is a deep pit in the middle of the agora, which archaeologists believe to have been a public cistern, for, unlike the Minoans, the Dorians had to place safety before a good supply of running water.

There are fine ruins of the same period in western Crete – particularly Polyrrhinia, another citadel on a crag, with lovely views over the Gulf of Kissamou and the two wild promontories that reach forward like the arms of a sleep-walker. Nearby, on the west coast proper, are the ruins of Phalasarna, probably a somewhat later foundation and in its day a famous port. Now it has been left high and dry by the rising of the land, a phenomenon first observed by Captain Spratt during his mid-nineteenth-century survey. He noted, quite correctly, that much of western Crete had risen by a whole eight metres. It was also believed, wrongly, that eastern Crete had sunk to a comparable extent. Recent work by Costis Davaras has shown that the problem was more complex. Some parts of eastern Crete have sunk, others have actually risen.

The remains of Phalasarna are fragmentary (except for what looks like a gigantic throne of solid stone), but the wide bay at whose northern extreme it stood is most inviting on a calm day. Lissos, most easily reached by boat from Souyia in the south-west, is to my taste more fascinating, though it is a later site again – classical Greek shading into Roman. Here there was an Asklepieion or healing centre (only recently discovered), where the sick came to be treated by a strange mixture of medicine and magic, often effective, despite the poor advertisement provided by the great number of tombs in the neighbourhood. I have even heard of a modern visitor who owes much to the Asklepieion – a kidney stone having been shaken loose by the rough-running engine of the boat that took him over!

In Dorian times the leading city of the island was no longer Knossos. Gortys, or Gortyn, just by the site of Phaistos in the Mesara, achieved a primacy it was to hold for at least a thousand years. (Zeus's dalliance here with Europa is commemorated on many coins of the classical period.) It became a substantial city and we know a good deal about its daily life.

The organisation of Gortyn under the Dorians was as deeply conservative as that of Sparta. (One tradition asserts that Spartan institutions came from Crete.) It was a completely aristocratic society with a rigid system of class divisions. There were slaves and serfs, the latter with greater rights than the slaves – surprisingly, they were allowed to marry free women. Then there were free people of a low status and finally the ruling classes. These divisions were perpetuated and emphasised by laws which were progressively more severe the lower the social status of the offender. Thus a rapist who was also a serf came off much worse than an over-passionate aristocrat. But the serfs of Gortyn do not seem to have lived in rebellious resentment like the Helots of Sparta. This class in Crete was made up largely of the descendants of the pre-Dorian population, and they kept up some of their old traditions – living, in a tantalising phrase of Aristotle's, 'according to the laws of Minos'.

The men and boys of the ruling classes took their meals together (a system known as the *syssitia*); and the education of young men was based, as in Sparta, on hard living and militarism. Arms were valued above everything else.

Some of our information about the city can be deduced from one of the most remarkable inscriptions ever found in the Mediterranean basin. This is the code of Gortyn, an incomparably beautiful piece of stone-cutting which cites a great number of early laws dealing with property and family matters. The inscription, on large marble slabs (discovered and pieced together at the turn of the century), is displayed at Gortyn. Every letter is so clearly engraved that the whole looks very easy to read – until you begin to try. Many of the characters differ from classical Greek and in any event the script runs from right to left.

This and other monuments from Dorian Crete show that the island played a great part in the development of the Greek alphabet from its Semitic-Phoenician antecedents.

Plato and Aristotle both admired the ordered society of Crete and their commentaries on the island are another valuable source. In his old age, Plato, never a political progressive, came to idealise the island, describing with approval a supposed rule that forbade young people to question which laws were good and which were bad. Instead they were meant simply to affirm that all were divinely ordained. Whether this was fact or fiction, Plato seems to have been reflecting the spirit of a rigidly conservative society.

The Dorian period coincided with the Iron Age, a time of increased efficiency in agriculture and warfare. Cretan pottery during these centuries did not approach the standards of Attica, having at best a rustic vigour. But one very notable find from early on was

made in the Idaian cave on Mt. Psiloritis. This was a series of ornamental bronze shields with fine relief work, done in a somewhat
Oriental manner (Archaeological Museum, Gallery XIX). The best
shows a bearded god holding a lion above his head.

But the most interesting works of art from Dorian Crete are the
fine statues which were made in the seventh century B.C. These
represented a first step towards the splendid sculpture of the Greek
archaic period and the even better-known sculpture of classical
times. The style is called Dedalic. The statues and statuettes show
sharp-chinned, animated faces surmounting bodies done with
Egyptian formalism (this kind of body was to evolve into that of
the monumental *kouros* figure of archaic sculpture). More austere
and warrior-like than this Dedalic sculpture was the frieze from a
temple at Prinias near Malevisi, one of the best achievements of
early Greek sculpture (Archaeological Museum, Gallery XIX).

But soon the torch passed to the mainland. Work of this calibre
was no longer produced in Crete. By the fifth century B.C. the cities
had fallen into petty wars and the island entered a period of violence.
From now on Crete was famous mainly for its pirates, and armies
all round the Aegean employed its mercenary archers. Alexander
the Great used Cretan units against chariots and elephants. The
historian Polybius describes them as 'invincible' in ambushes, raids,
the capture of prisoners and night patrols – everything, he says,
which involves trickery and small-scale actions.

Inevitably, Crete's warring cities took part in conflicts which
drew in Rome, the great new Mediterranean power. The Romans
intervened on several occasions during the second and first centuries
B.C. In 71 B.C. Mark Antony's father attacked Crete, only to retire
discomfited at the unaccustomed unity of the islanders in their resistance to him. Then in 69 B.C. Metellus (later known as Metellus
Creticus) attacked. For three years there was bitter fighting; but
in the end Crete fell and responsibility for its government passed
overseas.

Gortyn became the capital of a Roman province which included
large tracts of Africa. Crete prospered hugely, achieving a popula-

tion probably greater than that of the island today. It was a time of feverish town-building and the erection of monuments. Roads were laid, aqueducts constructed and large irrigation works were undertaken in the Lassithi plateau.

An amusing story of the time tells how the ground split open at Knossos, revealing a tin box (perhaps one of the lead-lined cists of the Minoan storerooms). This contained tablets with strange writing which were promptly passed to the Emperor. He passed them on to his savants who quickly deciphered them – as a narrative of the Trojan War.

Then there was the visit of St. Paul. Readers familiar with the Acts of the Apostles will remember how the ship taking Paul as a prisoner to Rome put in 'at a place which is called the fair haven' – Kali Limenes, near Phaistos on the south coast. Paul advised that they should stay there. The ship's owner and the centurion in charge of Paul thought otherwise.

And because the haven was not commodious to winter in, the more part advised to depart thence also, if by any means they might attain to Phenice, and there to winter; which is an haven of Crete, and lieth towards the south-west and the north-west.

And when the wind blew softly, supposing that they had obtained their purpose, loosing thence, they sailed close by Crete.

But not long after there arose against it a tempestuous wind called Euroclydon.

And when the ship was caught, and could not bear up into the wind, we let her drive.

And running under a certain island which is called Clauda, we had much work to come by the boat:

Which when they had taken up, they used helps undergirding the ship; and fearing lest they should fall into the quicksands, strake sail, and so were driven.

Clauda is the island of Gavdos, Phenice (or Phoenix) was next door to the site of modern Loutro in Sfakia. The story has meant more to me since the occasion when, half-way up the mountain above Loutro, I watched a late summer storm come out of nowhere. It lifted the whole surface of the sea in a single sheet of white and underneath this spray-cloud short, sharp, vicious little waves got up in seconds. The force of the wind was extreme on the mountain and must have been terrifying on the water. Big trading caïques appeared from beyond the horizon, racing for land; and in the high village of Anopolis the priest declared himself ready to set out for Loutro if I thought, from what I had seen, that anyone was hurt. Captain Spratt, who was caught in a storm of this very nature just off Kali Limenes, believed that this wind was the Euroclydon; and he, with all his experience of seamanship, was as impressed by it as I.

As for St. Paul, his ship was now swept on by the tempest to Malta where it was wrecked. It was in Malta that Paul was bitten by a snake and felt no harm. Local legend claims wrongly that this happened in Crete; there is even a version by which he landed at Loutro only to receive a beating for his irritating ideas.

Paul in due course organised the Church in Crete, dispatching Titus to be bishop there, and sending after him the outrageously self-righteous epistle in which he endorses the view that 'the Cretians are always liars, evil beasts, slow bellies'. This view did not prevent ten of them – the Holy Ten or Ayii Deka – standing up for Christianity at the cost of their lives during the reign of Decius (A.D. 249–251). The village of Ayii Deka near Gortyn is the site of their martyrdom and their memory remains alive among modern Cretans.

Martyrdom ceased to be necessary under Constantine in the fourth century. Marching to battle, he and his army saw a great cross shining in the sky with 'Hoc vinces' written across it. Soon the archaeological endeavours of his mother Helen were rewarded with the discovery of Calvary and the excavation of the True Cross, the sponge, the lance and the crown of thorns. Christianity had triumphed and a long age of piety was beginning.

The new religion demanded a new capital. In A.D. 330 Constantine inaugurated anew the city on the Bosporus which became known as Constantinople, though he called it New Rome. This east-ward shift of empire reflected the impact of Christianity, the strongest of the eastern mystery religions, and it also opened the way to those many other Oriental influences which were to be such an important aspect of Byzantium. Almost at once, for instance, the republican tendencies of Rome were abandoned and the emperor became an awesome potentate in the Oriental manner.

Around the sovereign was ranged a vast hierarchy of courtiers and officials who regarded the empire which they served as the supreme expression of earthly civilisation. It was the direct heir of Greek culture and of Roman reverence for law and efficiency and it was animated by a religion which promised salvation. Con-stantinople was immensely wealthy, the empire appeared coherent and unified. The Byzantines believed their duty was simply to preserve it.

In retrospect, the empire was clearly under pressure from the start – from tribesmen along the Rhine and Danube and above all from the Sassanid Persians in the east. The history of Byzantium was to be that of an eleven-hundred-year-long holding operation against the onrush of the barbarian world. Life on this earth came increasingly to seem so dark and dangerous that the Byzantines, while retaining their notion of the earthly perfection of Byzantium, preferred to live, so far as they were able, in the pure and abstract realms of spiritual devotion.

The western part of the empire had, of course, from early on de-veloped separately, but in 395 Crete was assigned to the east, in whose wealth and order it was able to share for several centuries. Order was perhaps the most striking aspect of the system. In the capital the vast imperial bureaucracy provided for everything – prices, wages, hours of work, jobs for the unemployed. The same suffocating attention to detail extended to the provinces. There was little individual liberty. To maintain the social order (and to make taxation easier) travel was usually forbidden and migration was at first firmly discouraged. In the sixth century the Emperor Justinian even ordained that sons must follow in their fathers' professions.

But this fanatical devotion to stability probably paid off in agricultural terms. It seems likely that Crete was well and thoroughly tended during this period, retaining the agricultural importance it had had under the Romans. Byzantine farming, like Byzantine society, was directed towards stability. In the eighth-century Farmers' Law, for instance, the central concept is that the consequences of disorder ramify outwards almost indefinitely, like ripples in a pond. Thus a man who stole a sheep dog became responsible for the whole flock, the thief of a cow bell for the cow.

The capital at this time was the centre of a great web of commerce reaching from the Baltic to China and specialising in the luxuries of the east – above all in silks and spices. The wealth of Crete was demonstrated by the basilicas of the early Church which were numerous and far more ample than anything achieved in medieval times.

These basilicas retained the feeling of Greek temples. They were roomy, rectangular buildings, triple-naved and divided into colonnades, and with wooden roofs slightly raised in the centre. Nothing of them remains above ground, but many had mosaic floors and these are now being revealed one by one as interest in the Byzantine period grows – at Elounda in the east, for example, at Chersonesos in central Crete and at Souyia in the south-west. Most of these mosaics are a mixture of geometric designs interspersed with frolicsome scenes of birds and animals in the Hellenistic manner. The fish represented Christ, the peacock immortality and the vineyard Holy Communion. The standard of execution is very low compared to many Byzantine mosaics, but to me at least they give a certain melancholy pleasure. Faded under the summer sun, encroached upon by thistles and dust, they look as venerable and as vulnerable as they are.

The mosaic at Souyia, just behind the beach, includes peacocks, the sacred fish and a much-ruined deer among its otherwise largely cursive and geometric designs. But an ugly little modern church, far smaller than the mosaic, stands right in the middle of it, the tessellated floor seeping out under its walls like water.

The story is that, during World War II, a villager sleeping out at night dreamt that the ruins of a church lay beneath him. He awoke certain that he had received a divine message – God would spare the village if a new church were erected on the spot. The people of Souyia did enough digging to check they had found the site and then complied with the heavenly directive. This, at any event, was the account given to Xan Fielding, an Englishman who had worked as a British secret agent on Crete during the war and then returned for a year in 1952. (His excellent book, *The Stronghold*, is about his experiences on his return.)

An even odder story is told about Souyia. Robert Pashley, a Cambridge don who travelled in Crete in 1834, recording all he saw with the greatest intelligence, good humour and learning, heard in Souyia of a marble slab with inscriptions (the Asklepieion of Lissos is just along the coast) which had recently been removed by an unknown caïque. One hundred and ten years later, Fielding was told what may have been a version of the same tale though much improved with time. For a start, it involved the invention of a village (in Pashley's time there were only ruins in Souyia) and the transformation of the caïque into an English man-of-war whose captain and officers disembarked with a barrel of rum and threw a magnificent party on the beach. When the villagers were quite incapable, the officers signalled to the ship and a boatload of sailors came ashore with picks and shovels. Before the village people could recover their wits – an event which occurred next morning – ship and crew had vanished with a treasure.

This story reflects the belief held by Greek village people throughout the eighteenth and nineteenth centuries that all foreign travellers were treasure seekers. Pashley was much irked by this assumption, but even though he was not interested in gold, he nevertheless carried off a fine sarcophagus from Arvi to the Fitzwilliam Museum in Cambridge. From Elgin to Schliemann and Evans, no matter how lofty their ideals, the most dedicated lovers of 'antiquity' have been acquisitive. The insistence of modern states on retaining archaeological finds has helped to right the balance, but even today there is a trade in Minoan objects which nobody has managed to suppress.

But to return to Byzantine mosaics. Thronos, a small village at the head of the Amari Valley, south of Rethimnon, takes its name from its early Byzantine status as an episcopal see. Here too a mosaic has been partly obliterated by a small church built on top of it. The mosaic goes running out into the churchyard, under the churchyard wall and finally into the street where cars may sometimes be found casually parked on it. But here at least the 'new' church – which is medieval – contains a fine if sombre series of wall paintings.

The era of the basilicas came to an end during the rule of the great Emperor Justinian (527–565) and the forms that we now think of as most typically Byzantine began to emerge. In building Santa Sophia in Constantinople, and commissioning buildings from Ravenna to Mt. Sinai, Justinian presided over a decisive modification of the old classical and Hellenistic concepts. The glories of the basilicas had been largely external; now a religious building was conceived of as an interior, giving physical expression to the idea that it was the inner life which counted above all. The interiors were not only grand in themselves but magnificently decked out, with fine stonework, silk hangings, rich ornament and above all with wall mosaics. Some of the finest surviving mosaics are in Ravenna and they show how greatly the old traditions of Hellenism had been changed. Those who visit them must be struck not so much by the individuality of the figures as by the way they combine together, silhouetted in a non-dimensional setting, to create a total impression, almost a processional rhythm. This idea of rhythm – a deeply spiritual concept – was to remain central to Byzantine art, still animating the fresco painters of Crete nearly a thousand years later. The soul is led, as it were, from one figure to another among a set of compositions which are all part of the one whole. Byzantine artists saw the abstract, spiritual world to which their works gave expression as one, entire and perfect.

Another important change was that, after Santa Sophia, domes or little round towers capped with cones of tiles were regularly used to surmount religious buildings, whether these were square, rectangular or cross-shaped. This style became the most obvious external trademark of the Byzantines.

In Crete substantial ruins of a grand and domed cathedral, clearly influenced by Constantinople, still survive at Gortyn. Paul's envoy Titus had become a saint – he is now the patron saint of Crete – and this church was named for him. Gortyn must at this time have been a remarkable sight, with its Greek, Roman and Byzantine monuments. Buondelmonte, an Italian monk who travelled in Crete early in the fifteenth century, described it as being even then 'equal in grandeur to our own Florence'.

As for the empire, matters were good and bad. In 628 the rival Sassanid empire of Persia was destroyed. But from 634 the dangerous force of Islam was on the move. The Muhammadans took Syria and then Egypt, destroying the libraries of Alexandria, last bastion of Hellenism. In 697 they took Carthage and, not long after, Spain. Their outposts were now ranged around the empire and their philosophy was one of continuous attack. Soon all Byzantine subjects were being instructed to store enough provisions to last them for three years if necessary.

The empire itself was desperately riven by theological disputes. Since the world was now considered a mere anteroom to heaven or hell, it is not surprising that these were taken so seriously. The main issue was the proper definition of Christ's nature. Was it one and entire, or could a distinction be made between his human and his divine nature? Particular nations became identified with particular theological systems – or at least made them a war-cry – so there was a danger of the empire breaking up along nationalistic lines.

Another controversy revolved around representational art. Statues had been banned for centuries, but now pictures came under attack from the Iconoclasts (today we use the word 'icon' to describe the movable pictures of the Orthodox faith; in Greek the word refers to pictures of all kinds). In 717 Leo the Isaurian became Emperor and made Iconoclasm the official – though bitterly resented – policy of the empire. The churches were redecorated with abstract designs.

In Crete there is one survival from this curious period. This is a delightful little church of the ninth century, made of warm brown stone and surmounted by a small round tower capped with heavy tiles. It stands on a promontory a few hundred yards north of Ayios Nikolaos, threatened on one side by a large hotel, under construction as I write, and approached from the waters of the inlet by a long and ugly flight of concrete steps. When this church was cleaned, fragments of iconoclastic frescoes were revealed in places where a later layer of painted plaster was missing. For the work of an age apparently so severe, they seem extraordinarily pretty and varied, once again echoing the charm of Hellenistic art. There are interlocking diamonds of red and blue, each going through three gradations of colour. There are interlacing hoops of pastel shading, a serpent-sinuous figure-of-eight and a kaleidoscope suggesting petals and flowers with leaves spread out like butterflies' wings.

More churches of the period might have survived if the strategists of Constantinople had not neglected the navy. Crete had been attacked by Muslim raiders in 673 and 715. In 827 it fell to a band of Arabs. Thrown out of Cordoba, they had spent thirteen years raiding from Alexandria. Now, under their leader, Abu-Hafs-Omar, they swept into Suda Bay with forty vessels. In due course they set up a fortified camp surrounded by a huge ditch, on the site of modern Iraklion. This ditch – El Khandak – gave its name to the town. The name Candia – applied both to town and island during the Middle Ages – was derived from it. (Under the Turks the town was called Megalo Kastro – the big fort. It was finally given the name of Iraklion – which commemorates the Cretan Herakles – at the time when Evans was excavating and the frenzy for antiquity was at its height.)

The Arabs held Crete for one hundred and thirty-four years. There is no evidence of building during this period, and a large part of the population was probably sold into slavery.

The island's new masters used Crete as a base for attacking the

Peloponnese and raiding northwards into the Aegean. In 901 they sacked Salonika, a blow almost as grave for the empire as the loss of Crete itself.

Early attempts to recover the island ended badly, but in 961 the Byzantine general (and later, Emperor) Nicephoras Phocas laid siege to El Khandak, incidentally catapulting the heads of captured Muslims into the fortifications. After ten months he recaptured the island and built a massive inland castle at Temenos to control the route to the Mesara. He in his turn enslaved the Arabs, Greek colonists from Constantinople receiving twenty-five apiece.

Meanwhile the empire had turned its back on Iconoclasm. The Ecumenical Council of 787 finally ruled that, since Christ had taken human form for divine purposes, painters representing him were carrying on the good work. It was a simple but ingenious solution. Accordingly the churches were again redecorated; but by now the manner in which this should be done had been codified. Holy scenes had to be arranged in a predetermined order and painted in the approved manner.

In Crete, according to the chronicler Michael Ataliates, Nicephoras Phocas had established a church replete with 'the shining faces of the saints'.

Other churches were built and decorated in Crete during these centuries, though what survives is scanty and of interest mainly to the specialist. The strongpoints were refortified and order returned to the island. From now on Crete was ruled largely through the Archontopouli or 'Sons of Nobles', an aristocracy of grand families imported from Constantinople.

There is little precise information about Crete at this time, but the attitudes and perceptions which informed the great flowering of Cretan fresco painting from the thirteenth century onwards must have been developing in the island. This whole complex of attitudes centred on Orthodox Christianity; and long after Constantinople was swept away, Orthodoxy and all it implied lived on as the essential constituent of Greek nationalism. Modern Greek culture derives to a surprising degree from the old empire and it is tempting to see some traits of Greek character – such as excessive subtlety and love of disputation – as having survived undiluted from that time. In order to understand both modern Crete and medieval frescoes it is worth looking a little more closely at Byzantium.

For the fresco painters, one important aspect of the empire was the physical appearance of the emperor and courtiers. The smooth cheeks of Rome had long ago given way to beards. Togas had vanished in favour of long, stiff robes of bejewelled brocade. Women wore fantastic head-dresses. Everyday objects were elaborately ornamented and devotional objects – particularly crucifixes and gospels – were fantastically adorned with precious stones and metals. The Byzantines dressed like this and surrounded themselves with these objects not out of vanity or sensuality but because, from the Emperor downwards, they considered themselves to be the courtiers of God. The finery was for His sake and painters seeking to glorify God would do so by portraying His saints in a splendour not unlike that achieved by the great ones of the empire.

The two imperial palaces of Constantinople were extraordinary places, made up of endless, rambling chambers which housed an untold wealth of art and holy objects. The bewildering elaboration of these palaces and of the city itself were echoed in the domes and towers and cupolas, the dream buildings that so often form the background to Byzantine painting.

Surprisingly the empire was efficient. It was administered by men of high intellectual calibre whose loyalty was to the institution rather than to the man who held the throne. Some of the most distinguished of these were eunuchs. Debarred from holding the throne and unable to found new dynasties, they were regarded as safe and trustworthy. Nor was any stigma attached to their condition – indeed, to have a child castrated might well give him a good start in life!

Given the empire's embattled position, diplomacy was inevitably one of the main preoccupations of the court. It was conducted with all the subtlety the Byzantines put into their theology. One of the aims was to induce awe among lesser peoples, and visiting ambassadors were as tightly controlled as western diplomats in Moscow today. Their interviews with the Emperor were apt to be terrifying. At one period the imperial throne was surrounded by golden lions which roared and the throne itself would suddenly and disconcertingly rise to the ceiling. Another object of diplomacy was to protect the empire by setting its enemies at one another's throats. This involved great duplicity.

When protective diplomacy failed, the emperors resorted to war. In the chivalrous west, feats of arms were all the rage; but Byzantium's standing army was for defensive purposes. So was the navy, even though it possessed the devastating weapon of Greek fire, an early type of incendiary bomb which exploded into flame on impact. The army was meticulously maintained and included a large corps of non-combatant engineers and ambulance men. The navy, however, showed a tendency to disorganisation and had to be thoroughly reformed after the capture of Crete by the Arabs. As for tactics, the watchword was caution. The best source for this is Leo VI's *Tactica*, written while Crete was in Arab hands. It shows forethought and subtlety of a kind quite alien to the western nations at this time. The strengths and weaknesses of individual enemies were carefully analysed so that the former could be avoided and the latter turned to good advantage. Trickery was highly commended. On the other hand, Leo says that a pledged word must be kept, that women must be unharmed and the lives of prisoners spared.

These last two points are extremely important. It is often said that the Byzantines were cruel, and so they were at times. But they were perhaps somewhat more tender-minded than their contemporaries. Mutilation, which so horrifies us today, was considered, reasonably perhaps, a humane alternative to the death penalty. And it is only by assuming a sensitivity to pain and mental suffering that one can explain the great tenderness of much Byzantine painting, particularly in its later phases and above all, perhaps, in Crete.

There were other elements of Byzantine culture which had an even more direct bearing on painting. One was the love of learning and literature, and particularly of stories. Courtiers sometimes knew all Homer virtually by heart; and the Bible stories seem to have been well known to every citizen, no matter how ignorant otherwise. These, of course, were the main subject of religious painting; at first they were rather limited in number, but as time went by the range of stories accepted into the painters' canon gradually increased.

As for religion, life itself was seen as a liturgy, the church merely as a place where worship was more intensive. Pleasure came after piety. During Crete's second Byzantine period religious art in the empire had developed again, achieving, particularly under the Comnene dynasty from 1081, a new power and spirituality, a marvellously hieratic tone–without much individuality, admittedly, but full of rhythm, force and dignity. The magnificent mosaics at Daphni, outside Athens, are an excellent example, and there was much fine work in Sicily and in Venice–a city swayed by Byzantine art from a very early date.

Alongside the main themes of Christianity there existed a great range of secondary superstitions. The reverence for holy relics, bones and corpses was one facet of this, the ready acceptance of dubious miracles another. The Byzantines, like medieval Europeans, also believed in demons, omens, dreams, signs and symbols. Fortune-tellers had a great following. The world of fantasy was weird and horrifying, and this element is strongly expressed in the wall-paintings of Crete.

Crete remained relatively peaceful during the second Byzantine period, but it was no longer prosperous. Churches, for example, had now become small and simple. Meanwhile the empire was in progressively greater danger. In 1071 disaster at the Battle of Manzikert gave all Asia Minor to the Turks, a destructive people newly arrived on the scene. A fresh menace materialised with the Crusaders, who often turned out to be freebooters masquerading under false pretences. Imperial finances were also in a very poor way. The provinces of the empire groaned under taxes imposed too late to save the day but severe enough to make foreign domination sometimes look preferable to Byzantine rule. Agricultural enterprise dwindled. Trade fell into a decline and its remnants were almost entirely in the hands of the Genoese and the Venetians, both of whom, though hated, enjoyed special concessions in Constantinople.

The inevitable catastrophe occurred in 1204 when the Fourth Crusade turned on Constantinople and sacked it, in the greatest act of vandalism of the Middle Ages. What they did not burn the Crusaders looted and, for the time being, the glory of Byzantium was eclipsed.

For Crete, this meant the end of Greek rule for seven hundred years. The island was assigned to Prince Boniface of Montferrat, leader of the Crusade; he ceded it to Venice for a nominal sum and concentrated on establishing a mainland enclave. But before the Venetians had established themselves, the Genoese seized the island, energetically fortifying the strongpoints. It was not till 1212, after a bloody war, that Crete genuinely became Venetian territory. Even then the Genoese did not give up. They enjoyed the support of the Cretans and in 1263 they once again took Khania, maintaining a foothold in the island for another twenty years.

The Cretans themselves frequently rebelled. Though many Venetian families had been settled in the island to form a new aristocracy, the Byzantine Archontopouli remained strong. Their names – particularly that of the Kallergis family – occur again and again in accounts of the revolutions. The Venetian colonists themselves also rebelled from time to time – in 1268 and again, more seriously, in 1363. They trampled St. Mark's banner in Candia and proclaimed their conversion to Orthodoxy. But in the end the will of Venice prevailed and the island settled down to a period of peace.

Strangely, in view of its implicit nationalism, the Venetians left the Greek Church untouched. They built (Catholic) churches and cathedrals for their own purposes, of course, many of them large and handsome edifices in the Gothic and later the Renaissance manner. The Greek Cretans had nothing like the same wealth to dispose of and their churches were like those of the second Byzantine period – modest structures, generally with just one nave and only rarely surmounted by a tower. One or two are exquisite, but most are merely chapels, which from outside might be mistaken for the places of worship of a population that was spiritually as well as materially subject. Inside, however, the fresco painters of Venetian Crete have concentrated an astonishing wealth of paintings from the Byzantine repertoire. Indeed, part of the singularity of this art is its unstinting profusion, since the painters were following a scheme of decoration evolved for buildings many times larger.

One of the main ideas governing the painters was that the Church itself stood as a symbol of the universe, divided into heaven and earth and supervised from above by Christ the Pantocrator, ruler of all. In grander Byzantine churches he stares down from the dome. Given the absence of a dome in Cretan churches, the most domi-nant position that can be found for him is the top segment of the little rounded apse beyond the altar. From this position, not so very far above head height, he customarily surveys his symbolic universe, sometimes stern and awesome, sometimes impassive, sometimes tender. He is in heaven, while below him in the apse (on earth) the Holy Fathers and Evangelists are clustered. Mary often occupies an intermediate position, symbolising her intercession between heaven and earth.

The main body of the church depicts the divine essence of the universe through the stories of Christ and his saints. Scenes from Christ's life generally cover the little barrel-vaulted ceilings, starting on the Pantocrator's left hand with the Nativity and criss-crossing the ceiling to end diagonally across from where they started. Origin-ally these scenes represented the main festivals of the Church, arranged not in historical sequence but according to their place in the calendar. By the time of the Venetian conquest the repertoire included not only such necessary subjects as the Nativity, Baptism, Crucifixion and Resurrection but also themes like Herod's feast, Salome's dancing and various miracles. Interspersed among these tableaux there were often scenes from the life of the saint to whom the church was dedicated. At first the Crucifixion usually occupied the west wall, at the far end of the church from the Pantocrator, but later this position was taken by the Second Coming and scenes such as the punishment of the damned and the sea giving up its dead.

All these scenes are in the upper part of the church. Below there is usually a frieze of full-length saints, male and female and including such military men as St. George and St. Demetrius. They are often joined by the founder of the church, his wife and children. Sometimes, between the saints and the narrative tableaux, there is a row of medallions each containing the head of another saint.

For nearly a hundred years after 1204 the Cretans continued to paint in a provincial version of the old Comnene school – idealised, rather inexpressive figures with large eyes, arranged in formal compositions. There are a few examples in the Pediados area to the north-west of the Lassithi plateau. But the real moment was yet to come.

Events in Byzantium proved decisive. Though the old empire had been shattered by the Fourth Crusade, fragments survived in several places. One of these was at Nicaea, not so far from Constantinople. In 1260 its ruler, Michael Palaeologus, took over the old capital and succeeded in putting together a fair-sized empire. Under him and his descendants there now occurred a revival of Byzantine art. It found in Venetian Crete an expression which was extraordinarily rich, while neither grand nor monumental. In sharp contrast to other admired periods of Byzantine art, its essence and appeal lie largely in its intimate, rustic character.

The Cretan painters accepted the conventional subjects of Byzantine iconography but tried to express the *human* drama of the scenes they painted. This was a revolutionary change. Though the basic compositions remained the same, individual character and emotion now came bursting through the old hieratic forms, creating a conflict and intensity which is both visually exciting and extremely moving. The old sense of rhythm was retained, even if in a more crowded manner (each scene, incidentally, was now framed in a deep red band). The whole church, as before, remained symbolic of the spiritual order; but the tendency to abstraction was replaced by

Detail of Byzantine fresco.

vivid colours and gestures, by a wealth of incidental detail and pro-
fuse decoration. Sometimes the painting is crude, even grotesque,
at other times it is elegant and accomplished, though without being
cosmopolitan.

One must not expect, however, to find all the elements together
in one place. From the Turkish conquest until a decade ago these
paintings were systematically neglected. Sometimes the plaster has
come away from the walls, leaving only fragments of fresco behind;
sometimes leaking roofs and walls have allowed damp to smear the
pictures; often they have been blurred and streaked by a precipita-
tion of salts from the plaster behind. In many cases the Turks put
out the eyes of the figures and frequently local people have simply
covered them over with whitewash.

Renewed enthusiasm for the Byzantine heritage led in 1964 to
the start of a programme of cleaning and restoration, during which
many previously unknown paintings have been discovered. But it
is a long, expensive and difficult job and one comes across a cleaned
church only occasionally. The visitor learns to travel pessimistically,
which leads in turn to a disproportionate sense of pleasure in striking
lucky.

The golden rule is to take time over each church. On a blazing day it will be a minute or so before one sees anything at all. Then perhaps, as one's eyes adjust, a few panels will stand out, bold and delightful. With patience there is almost always more to see; often a chapel which you might think had surrendered itself at once will continue to yield secrets for half an hour or so. It is worth carrying a torch to pick out details.

One learns quite quickly to recognise many of the main scenes. Find an ox or an ass and you will soon locate a cradle with a baby, and next, perhaps, the reclining Virgin. The ox and ass may look quite comical, but the Virgin's face and posture are usually deeply and movingly serene. The Baptism is easy, too – Christ stands in Jordan (often surrounded by fish) with huge crags on either side of him. John the Baptist is almost always rendered with great power. So is the Crucifixion. Far from the calm spirituality of earlier Byzantine treatments, Christ's body is now atrociously contorted in the spasm of death. In one beautiful and appalling version (at Archanes Temenos) the Virgin falls fainting and angels weep in the sky, hiding their eyes against Christ's agony. There is no problem, either, in recognising the Last Supper. But other, and extremely beautiful, compositions are less familiar.

The raising of Lazarus is puzzling until one realises that the coffin is shown as standing on its end with Lazarus apparently upright, though bound in grave-clothes. In the descent into Limbo, Christ is shown standing on fallen gates which look like snow-shoes, crossed at the front. He reaches out over the river of death to Adam, who likewise stretches out his hand. One of the finest scenes is often the Dormition of the Virgin. She lies, composed and gentle in death, on a bier surrounded by holy figures. Behind her stands Christ, cradling her soul (represented as a baby) in the crook of his elbow. Often this is one of the biggest scenes and it is almost always an effective blend of the old formalism and new humanity.

The file of haloed saints on the lower level is another important element of each church. They are shown facing straight outwards in the Oriental manner and, being far too holy to have need of *terra firma*, float against their background with toes pointing downwards like those of ballet dancers. While the figures in the Bible stories are almost always simply dressed, the saints, being the courtiers of God, are splendidly robed and carry richly bejewelled objects. In older Byzantine painting the folds of the robes were often arranged geometrically, but now, in Crete, they follow the contours of the body. The women saints are often most eloquently painted and there is an impressive muscularity about the military saints and their huge-buttocked mounts.

It is hard to know which part of Crete to begin with in pursuit of frescoes. There are a great many in the western province of

Church of St. Fanourios, Valsamonero.

Selinou (here a higher proportion are signed – some by Ioannis Pagomenos, John the Frozen). The Amari Valley is rich in them; so is the area round Kastelli Pediados. One of the most famous churches is that of the monastery of Valsamonero (only the church survives) in fine country south of Psiloritis. It is a place of oddity as well as charm and it has a great variety of scenes. But many of them are unfamiliar and so rather hard to identify; they will give most pleasure to the practised eye.

There is not much doubt that the original effect can be imagined most accurately in the church of the Panayia Kera (Our Lady the

Virgin), at Kritsa, in the hills above Ayios Nikolaos. This lovely building, heavily whitewashed and set about with cypresses (it stands some three hundred and fifty metres before the village, hidden away up a little lane on the right-hand side of the road), has three naves and a little round tower capped with a cone of heavy tiles. Inside it is at first too dark to see much, but quite quickly, as you become used to the gloom, you will see that almost the whole range of paintings has been preserved.

The south aisle, nearest the road, is most brightly painted and best lit; but one does best, perhaps, to start in the central aisle under the eye of the Pantocrator since the paintings here are oldest (probably dating from the end of the thirteenth or beginning of the fourteenth century). They are an extraordinary mixture of the primitive and the sophisticated. On the left, as you stand with your back to the altar, Herod's Massacre of the Innocents is powerful and primitive, a panel full of short-torsoed soldiers with tough, heavy faces, misshapen and expressive and quite lacking in the elegance of the painting of the Last Supper which is higher up and on the right. This is a delicate and graceful composition with much fine detail, including black-handled knives and some elaborate Venetian glassware. Crude paintings on the west wall, placed so as to give pause to those leaving the church, show the nasty and degrading punishments envisaged for sinners. But the distinctions in style do not impair the total effect, which is one of immense narrative variety, full of human emotion and religious force, contained within a thoroughly Byzantine framework.

The north aisle has many beautiful scenes. The haloes of the saints in the Second Coming recede into the distance in pastel colours, like a vast cluster of hot-air balloons. There are numerous other scenes from the Second Coming – including some splendidly medieval beasts. Delicate portrayals of Paradise are full of floral sprays with birds at rest on them. On the rear wall, by contrast, are some boldly sketched heads and torsoes, caricatures of a kind found hardly at all in earlier Byzantine art. Then, just by them, there is the founder of the church (unfortunately rather ruined).

His wife wears a charming wide-bottomed gown with an elaborate shawl over her shoulders – an everyday figure, agreeable to encounter among the throng of the blessed and the damned.

There is far more to see in both these aisles than I have mentioned here. But it is in the south aisle that Cretan painting can be experienced at its most tender and humane.

This aisle is presided over by the figure of the Virgin in the apse. She seems to sorrow as she blesses with hand stretched wide. Cracks in the plaster running over her left cheek add to the sense of calamity. The barrel-vault is taken up with smaller, red-bordered panels telling the story of Anne, Mary's mother, and of Mary and her marriage, stressing the theme of virginity. Here tenderness and personal observation are more evident than gravity. Anne prays in her garden among trees in blossom while a bird with its wings closed, in typical Byzantine disregard of gravity, floats in mid-air to feed its nestlings. Anne's long, thin hands open upwards as if to let butterflies fly out of them. When Mary's chastity is put to the test (by making her drink a glass of water which will poison her if she is lying) she squints down the glass as if it were a telescope. The best panel of all shows Joseph grieving over Mary's pregnancy. She sorrows in sympathy while an angel reaches down to offer him comfort.

In the Panayia Kera at Kritsa the fused spirituality and humanism of the unknown painters carry the visitor into a world where the religious experience is central. The scale is intimate, but here as much as in soaring cathedrals one can understand the meaning of medieval piety.

My last visit to Kritsa was on a day in late January. I came out again to a sky grey and soft as doves' feathers. The almonds were already in blossom and oranges hung incandescent on the trees. I could hear ravens in the crags above Kritsa; and an old woman, dressed all in black, came clopping past on her donkey, the stones sounding hollow beneath its hooves. Fishing deep in a bag she carried, she pulled out two oranges and placed them on the wall beside me, then rode on without waiting for thanks.

But if Kritsa is the most complete of the churches, I nevertheless carry round with me the memory of many others where individual scenes or details have moved me quite as much. In the plain of Lakonia, a few miles from Kritsa and just under Lato, in the apparently insignificant little church of the Archangel (which has a large veranda of reinforced concrete), there is a set of six figures on a gold-ochre background, as vivid as anything in Crete. They stand in pairs, a favourite Byzantine arrangement – Helen and Constantine holding the True Cross; the founder of the church and his wife (he holds in his hand a church far grander than the one he actually financed); and two local men in parti-coloured clothes. One has a quiver so full of arrows that they burst through the red band confining the panel.

Another, nastier memory comes from the church of Ayia Pelaya in Ano Viannos, the other side of the Dikte massif. Here a dozen or so naked women, drawn extremely crudely, are being tormented by snakes which bite their breasts and assault them sexually. The women are labelled in a strange Byzantine hand, one as a prostitute, another as a woman who will give no milk. Two of the women hang upside down. Another is swarming up a snake as if up a rope, her legs drawn up suggestively around its body. These scenes occur just near one of the tenderest of all Cretan nativities. There are many other unpleasing scenes among the Cretan frescoes – renderings of torture, monsters and demons. The Sea giving up its Dead is often peculiarly eerie, with human heads protruding from the mouths of fish and octopuses.

Another important aspect of the churches is their part in the landscape. The church-builders tried to ensure that God was nowhere neglected. You will find chapels in the oddest places, half-buried by a grassy bank, perhaps, or hidden away behind the fold of a hill. Some of the sense of how it may have been can be recovered by visiting as many churches as possible in a particular area – a pastime which demands stout walking shoes and a little Greek for locating the painted churches.

Early one spring, with a group of Greek friends, I spent several days pottering among the churches of the Amari Valley. Psiloritis rose in a great mound of snow on one side, Kedros white and lumpy on the other. Wild flowers shone brilliant among the freshly washed pastures. The villages are dotted along the valley floor and up the lower mountainsides: the churches are everywhere. We did not succeed in finding them all, but from this journey we brought back an incomparably rich jumble of medieval images – here a fine Last Supper, there a painfully treacherous Kiss of Judas, a sombre and magnificent Dormition, a bitter Lamentation over the dead Christ.

The same year, on a burning August day in Sfakia, I climbed alone from the coast to the mountain village of Ay Ioanni, perhaps the most remote year-round settlement in Crete. A shepherd boy accompanied me the last few hundred yards and insisted on showing me the village's two churches. It was hot and I was tired after the long climb. But there, in the cool gloom of these ancient buildings, fragmentary and crumbling, the saints of Byzantium lived on.

4. Venetian days

The Venetians changed the look of Crete. Iraklion, Khania and Rethimnon became Venetian cities, all with a strong family resemblance. Each was fortified and refortified and by the end of the Venetian period made a considerable impression on those who saw them. In 1589 General Giambattista del Monte called the castle at Iraklion 'la piu bella fortezza d'Europa'. And William Lithgow included Khania in a roll-call of honour: 'Truely this city may equall in strength, either Zara in Dalmatia, or Luka, or Ligorne, both in Tuscana, or matchlesse Palmo in Friuly: for these five cities are so strong that in all my travels I never saw them matched.' Rethimnon was the largest single Venetian fortress ever built.

Sitia was fortified on a smaller scale, and a network of military installations sprang up – inland to hold down the populace, and on the coast to keep marauders and pirates at a distance. Several offshore islands were also fortified, though not until the sixteenth century.

A number of the Venetian castles stand in such remote spots that they have never been pillaged even for building stone. The great carved lion of St. Mark, worn thin by time and elements, presides still over a host of abandoned gateways, casting only the tiniest of shadows in the sunlight.

The finest of the Venetian forts – for me, at least – is just a few miles east of Chora Sfakion. Here the great mountains, split by gorges, come sweeping down to sea-level, at a point where the land at their base spills out into a creviced plain. On the seaward edge of the plain, above a sandy beach, stands the apricot-coloured fortress of Frangokastello, dominant over the littoral, puny under the mountains. The colour of the stone, the situation, and the view of the castle from a distance are its most impressive aspects; from close up the outside walls are largely blank – except for a particularly faded lion – and the inner courtyard, despite restoration work, is somehow spiritless and saddening. But it is certainly worth a detour.

The Venetians knew the Cretans hated them. A chronicle of 1252 puts it plainly: 'The Greeks of the Isle of Candia have always held ill feelings towards the dominion of Venice, not accepting their subordination to it.' The number of early revolutions bear this out; and Lithgow, writing about the Venetians in the seventeenth century, can still speak of 'that conceived fear they have of Treason'. This was partly why they walled the cities.

The hatred was not surprising, for though the Venetians left the Orthodox Church alone, they exacted immense feudal dues. The forts were built and the galleys manned by Cretans reluctantly obliged to serve. Peasants had to labour on the land for Venetian masters and give up a large and unvarying quantity of corn and oil whether the harvest was good or bad. Perhaps one reason why Byzantine painting flourished under these conditions was that the very unpleasantness of daily life helped give intensity to the spiritual.

Punishments were brutal, dissidents being executed or condemned to the galleys in chains. In 1263, following a revolt, the Venetians drove all its inhabitants out of the Lassithi plateau, uprooting the fruit trees and threatening death or dismemberment to anyone who cultivated the land. Lassithi lay abandoned for two hundred years. Most daunting of all is the story of the Kandanoleon revolt. The bulk of the information here comes from a Venetian monk named Trivan, writing in the late seventeenth century. Briefly, his story concerns a revolt led by George Gadhanole, a Greek noble of Sfakia who appears to have borne the nickname Kandanoleon. He was elected 'rector' of western Crete by the local population some time in the sixteenth century and succeeded in running a rebel administration parallel to that of the Venetians. But an attempt to marry his son to the daughter of a Venetian aristocrat, Francesco Molini, led to his downfall. Molini pretended to go along with this, and the wedding actually took place amid tremendous celebrations. But these were altogether too tremendous for the Cretans. While they slept drunkenly about Molini's country house, they were bound hand and foot by a large force of Venetian soldiers, summoned from nearby Khania by rocket, as prearranged.

In the morning the Venetians hanged Gadhanole, his son the bridegroom and another, younger son. Eight more people were hanged on the spot and three shot dead. Another eight were dispatched to the galleys in chains. Of the remaining prisoners one group was taken to Khania and hanged at the gate there. Another group was hanged at the castle of Apokoronas. Two final groups were hanged in villages associated with Gadhanole. These were also razed. 'Thus,' says Trivan, 'they were annihilated, and all men who were faithful to God and their Prince were solaced and consoled.'

But this was not enough for the Venetian senate, who dispatched to Crete a special emissary named Cavalli. His first sally was by night to Fotiniaco (near Mournies), a village outside Khania. He turned the people out of their homes, then burnt the houses and in the morning hanged twelve of the leading villagers. Then the bellies of four pregnant women were slit open with cutlasses and the unborn babies wrenched out – 'an act which truly inspired great terror throughout the whole district'. Most of the remaining villagers were put to death in Khania, while the others were banished.

Cavalli next summoned Greeks from all the western villages to make their submission in Khania. Few dared to do so. Cavalli thereupon promised pardon to anyone who came to Khania bringing with him the head of his father, brother, cousin or nephew. The first to appear was a priest with his two sons and two of his brothers. Each laid a head before Cavalli, explaining 'con amarissime lacrime' to whom the heads belonged. In this way, says Trivan, the lives of many former rebels were redeemed.

There are a number of difficulties about this story. According to several modern scholars, the only date to which it can be assigned is 1527. The revolution of that year was put down by Gierolemo Cornaro and not by Cavalli, who was in Crete later. There is doubt over the name Gadhanole and the account of the marriage makes the Cretans sound implausibly naïve. But the fact that Trivan was able to write this story into the record, apparently with confidence that his account would be accepted, means that the brutality must be regarded as within the realm of possibility. Trivan's story adds a dimension to a reference made by the Captain of Candia in 1594. In 1527, he said, it had been necessary 'to execute more than three hundred persons, and send many to exile, to burn and raze their villages, confiscate their property, and exact other severe penalties'.

The object of Venetian rule was to manage Crete for the aggrandisement of the mother city. The need for elaborate defences and a large garrison made this an expensive exercise, but the Cretan countryside was run during the more efficient periods so as to extract the greatest revenue from agriculture. Though the Cretans received no benefit, the cultivated parts of Crete were fruitful and well tended. The traveller Pierre Belon told in 1553 how he had seen 'moult beaux jardinages et vergers d'excellente beauté et de grand quantité qui leur sont de grant revenu, dont les uns sont en pays si plaisant qu'un homme ne s'ennuirait a les contempler'. Jean Struys, in 1668, speaks of 'forêts entières cultivées d'abricotiers, d'oranges, de citronniers, de figuiers, d'amandiers, d'oliviers et même de pommes et de poires.... Ou il n'y a blé ni vignes ce n'est que thym, que marjolaine, que serpolet, que romarin et autres herbes de bonne odeur:... et celles qui ne sentent rien ailleurs sont en Candie toutes parfumées...'

The main Venetian exports were oil and wine – both extremely valuable. Cretan wines had been famous since antiquity. Now, in the Middle Ages, they were called Malmsey and sold from Poland to the Indies. Prince Henry of Portugal stocked Madeira with Cretan vines when it was colonised in 1441. The trade was so important to England that in 1552 Henry VIII appointed a man named Baltha-zari as 'the Master, Governor, Protector and Consul of all and singu-lar the merchants and other his lieges subjects within the port, island and county of Crete or Candia'. This was the first English consul anywhere. Milton mentions Cretan wine in *Paradise Regained* and so does Ben Jonson in *Volpone*.

But though the Venetians fostered agriculture and the vine, they performed an act of ignorance which has had immense con-sequences for Crete. Not knowing that deforestation causes erosion and a reduced rainfall, they cut back the forests mercilessly for the galleys of their great Mediterranean fleet. Standing today among the bare and weather-gouged uplands of Crete it is almost impossible to see how this poverty-stricken terrain could ever have been famous for its timber.

Constantinople fell to the Turks on 28 May 1453, almost exactly half-way through the period of Venetian rule in Crete. The dis-astrous news apparently reached Iraklion on a Cretan ship laden with refugees who had swum out to sea to escape the carnage in the city.

In a contemporary song, the dying Emperor calls to the Cretans to cut off his head and save it from defilement. The symbolism is obvious enough; and after the fall of Constantinople the Greeks of Crete did their best to assume the shot-ridden mantle of Byzantium.

One of the first results was that many of the Byzantine scholars who had been so busy with the recovery and dissemination of ancient Greek literature now moved their operations to Crete. Irak-lion became a centre for manuscript copying and so played an im-portant part in promoting the Italian Renaissance. Venice had, of course, long been involved with Byzantium and for hundreds of years had reflected many of her artistic values; but the recovery of ancient Greek culture was a new and critical departure. Soon Cretan-born scholars began to gather in the new centres of learning in Italy and some of them became extremely influential.

Cretan doorways in Venetian style. Because the climate makes stonework appear prematurely ancient, it is often extremely difficult to ascribe a date to Cretan buildings. Architectural styles, once introduced, tended to remain in continuous use. The difficulty of distinguishing Turkish from Venetian is further compounded by the practice among Cretan villagers of referring to all ruins indiscriminately as Turkish.

Markos Mousouros, to take one illustrious example, edited Plato, Sophocles, Euripides and Aristophanes, all for the Aldine press.

Developments in painting were equally interesting. Towards the end of the fourteenth century, the rural vigour of Crete's frescoes began to be modified by a more aristocratic manner diffused from

Constantinople. The grave and lovely Dormition of the Virgin in the nave of the Virgin at Valsamonero is a good example: the ground-plan of the church is complex and unusual; the painting in question is on the far side of the second nave, opposite you as you enter by the main door. The diffusion of the aristocratic manner was followed early in the fifteenth century by the arrival of a wave of painters emigrating from the Great City. Though the rural population was treated shamefully by the Venetians, Crete was at least at peace and a stronghold of Byzantine culture. The *émigré* painters, some of whose names are known, brought a new elegance, a renewed sense of balance and harmony. There is an excellent example of work from this period too at Valsamonero – a fine and dignified Divine Liturgy (painted by Constantine Ricos in 1431) attended by a procession of harmonious angels described with long flowing lines and curves. There are other striking frescoes in the church of Apano Simi near Viannos, painted by Manuel Phocas in 1453. Throughout the next fifty years the new manner was explored and refined. Of this later period, perhaps the most beautiful church is Ayia Paraskevi at the southern end of the Amari Valley. It has a sophisticated and delightful set of frescoes, revealing a Hellenistic grasp of character, a Byzantine indifference to perspective (the saints still float in air), a marvellously sensual use of colour and a deeply spiritual gravity and rhythm.

This was one of the last churches painted. At this time, probably for economic reasons, the fresco painters abandoned Crete, moving on to work at Athos and at Meteora. The later painters – among them the great Theophanes – are known as the Cretan school, though they did no significant work in Crete. Their paintings on the mainland are the last great frescoes of Byzantium.

In Crete itself, only icons were now being painted. The old rural tradition flourished, with many strange and striking results. Some of these icons are still in the churches, but the best are in Iraklion, either in the Historical Museum or in the battered but beautiful Sinaiite church of St. Catherine just by the modern cathedral.

My own favourite themes are the Root of Jesse (descendants

perch among the branches of a tree like song-birds, holding the emblems appropriate to them) and an extraordinary and often-repeated scene called the 'Zoodokhos Pigi', or Life-giving Well. Pashley was astonished when he first saw one of these: and so, one hundred and thirty years later, was I. The Virgin and the Holy Child are shown seated in a large tub from which there gush copious streams of the life-giving water. In some versions diminutive figures drink from the trough into which it flows. Confronted by this odd scene it is hard to restrain an upsurge of irreverent mirth.

Another tradition of icon painting was a great deal more sophisticated, its practitioners consciously producing a high art. They studied at St. Catherine, then a college, and many of them passed on, like so many scholars, to Italy. Here the neoclassical perspective of the Renaissance was all the fashion, and, naturally, the painters absorbed it.

This was in the sixteenth century; the most interesting of these painters was Michael Damaskinos. He worked for many years in Venice and his pictures are now scattered over what was then the Greek sphere of cultural influence. Returning finally to Iraklion, he produced a number of quite large-scale paintings. Six of these are hung in St. Catherine's as the centre-piece of the icon collection, and they form a remarkable series. The earliest, being the most Italianate, are the least satisfying to those looking for a last flourish of the Byzantine. The Last Supper, for example, and the Adoration of the Magi show a three-dimensional treatment of space which contrasts awkwardly with the beautifully rendered and very Byzantine-seeming faces. The glory of Damaskinos's career came at the end of it when he reverted almost completely to the Byzantine style. The Divine Liturgy, with its mass of angels' wings, is a marvellous composition. Even better is his picture of the first Ecumenical Council, painted in 1591. Here the brightly haloed early fathers sit in semicircular tiers, painted with the same flatness of dimension and in the same relationship to the eye as a deck of cards fanned out in the hand. Their robes are gorgeous; the faces grave and reverend.

The greatest Cretan painter of all – Domenico Theotokopoulos, El Greco – was born in 1541 (the village of Fodhele claims the honour despite evidence which tends to suggest Iraklion). He seems to have lived in the island till he was twenty-five, quite possibly studying at St. Catherine. He carried away with him, first to Italy and then to Spain, the visual richness and spiritual fervour of Byzantium, ready to be transmuted into a new and intensely moving form.

Excellence in scholarship and painting was accompanied by development in Cretan writing. The first stirrings were uncertain, but slowly Cretan writers began to acquire a mature and sometimes a profound voice. Throughout the fifteenth and sixteenth centuries more and more was being written – didactic and courtly poems, satires and histories. From the early seventeenth century there was an extremely rich period during which pastoral idylls, comedies and tragedies were appearing at a positively Elizabethan pace. The tragedies were usually set in imaginary royal courts and were thoroughly bloody, as in the Elizabethan manner. In one, *Rhodolinos*, all the principal characters commit suicide. In *Erophile*, the most popular, a royal bride receives as a present from the king her father the severed head, the heart and hands of her intended bridegroom (to whom she was already secretly married). The comedies were set mostly in Crete and revolved around such themes as confusion over identity and recognition by unusual physical features – a kind of denouement common in Greek drama from the earliest times.

As to the pastoral idylls, one of these, *The Fair Shepherdess*, has been translated into English by John Mavrogordato; and despite the determined archaism of the language it is an altogether charming, and moving, poem. It is unusual and pleasing in that, before its unhappy ending, the shepherd and shepherdess spend some days and nights explicitly dedicated to the joys of the flesh.

Another work full of humanity and humane perception is the remarkable short play *Sacrifice of Abraham*, also translated into the same stiff English by Mavrogordato. It was written, most probably, by one Vicenzos Kornaros of Sitia. The monstrous tale is presented, overtly, as a story of Abraham's moral courage and devotion to God. But the play explores, with terrible anguish, the human reality of the situation. Sarah cannot stop weeping in front of the child as he sets out in his best clothes believing he is going for a day's holiday. On the way Abraham meets his two servants and when he explains to them what God has commanded, one of them tries to persuade him that it must have been an evil dream. But Abraham is inflexible. The most terrible moments come as Isaac awaits death on the altar, a little boy struggling to be brave.

The most significant achievement of the Cretan renaissance is a massive poem only a little shorter than *Paradise Lost* and certainly by Vicenzos Kornaros. This is the *Erotokritos*. It is written in a rich Cretan vernacular, marvellous to roll around the tongue but hard even for Greeks to understand. It was partly this vigour of language which kept the *Erotokritos* alive, despite its later rejection on precisely these grounds by neoclassicists. The poem found its way into the affections of ordinary village people, many of whom knew much of it by heart. Cretans sing it still, to a peculiarly Oriental-sounding plain-song rhythm (there is also a modern musical setting). And passages are often performed by professional entertainers, winning much applause from Athenian as well as Cretan audiences. George Seferis, the Nobel prize-winning poet, recalls how in his childhood the *Erotokritos* was sold in Asia Minor by street vendors, and the profound impression it made on him. It seems that this poem, along with the Orthodox religion, somehow became part of the Greek sense of national identity and thus held enormous importance for Greeks.

The story is a courtly one. It deals with the love between a princess and her more lowly suitor, its many impediments and final triumph. His name is Erotokritos, hers is Arethousa. The poet tells the story, unfolding it wisely and slowly (sometimes slowly to the point of tedium); but Erotokritos and Arethousa also have speaking parts and the human tone often breaks through the courtly, producing the same kind of pressure as in some of the frescoes. Part of the charm of the poem, specially for the Greeks with their love of a tale, is its sheer length as it flows on and on in leisurely balladic couplets. There is no translation into English, but a brief volume of commentary on the poem by John Mavrogordato includes an extended prose summary which conveys a good deal of the atmosphere.

The *Erotokritos* was probably written in 1646. It was published in Venice in 1715, by which time Crete had been in Turkish hands for nearly half a century.

The danger had been plain for a long time. In 1538 the pirate admiral Khaireddin Barbarossa scourged the coast of Crete. Rethimnon, defended by seven thousand men, was sacked and burned. The pirates came back again in 1560 and 1562. In 1571 the whole island, including the Venetian nobles (by now completely hellenised), rose against Venice. It was a bloody affair and three years later Giacomo Foscarini was sent from the mother city to put matters right. He found total disorganisation. The villagers, he wrote, were in a dire situation: 'The cavalieri had reduced the peasants to a worse condition than that of slaves, so that they never dared even to complain of injustice.'

Foscarini briskly set about social and military reforms, incidentally persecuting the Greek clergy and also the Jews whom he blamed for the poor morals of Iraklion. Iraklion had long been castigated in literature for its love of luxury and whoring. But Foscarini does not seem to have had much success in changing things. Nearly a hundred years later, just after the Turkish conquest, the Flemish writer and doctor O. Dapper complained: 'La plupart des Candiots ou habitants Grecs de cette île sont de grans mangeurs, de grandes ivrognes, adonnez au vin, a la debauche, a la gourmandize et a la luxure, et surtout au plaisirs sales et impurs de la chair.'

Foscarini was not much more successful with his other reforms. His successor was soon reporting in terms as gloomy as any he had used. Turkish pressure continued to increase and it became clear that much of the population of Crete might actually prefer the unknown asperities of Muslim rule to the tyranny of Venice. Some Venetians thought the answer was more repression and in 1615 one

Fra Paolo Serpi was urging that 'the Greek faith is never to be trusted'. He went on: 'These, therefore, must be watched with more attention, lest, like wild beasts, as they are, they should find an occasion to use their teeth and claws. The surest way is to keep good garrissons to awe them . . . wine and bastinadoes ought to be their share, and keep good nature for a better occasion.'

The opposite course prevailed. Conditions improved a little, to the great advantage of scholarship and literature. It was a great time for the foundation of monasteries. Meanwhile the Venetians refortified, achieving a semblance of military splendour. But it was too late and the Turks already far too powerful.

The end began in 1645 when the Knights of St. John, those not-so-holy buccaneers (then based in Malta), attacked a Turkish convoy. They made off with a good deal of gold and also, in one account, with a number of ladies bound for the seraglio and the Sultan. The Knights put into a Cretan harbour, furnishing the Turks with the pretext for a general attack.

Khania fell after a two-month siege during which the Turks incurred enormous losses. Rethimnon capitulated within twenty-four hours of the first assault. But Iraklion held up the Turks for twenty years. In a desperate attempt to save the capital and the island, the Venetians created diversion after diversion, initiating a general war in the Levant. But in May 1667 the Turks settled down in earnest to besiege Iraklion.

Europe held its breath as month after month the Venetian garrison held out. The castle could still be supplied by sea and in due course Louis XIV of France dispatched seven thousand men under the Dukes of Beaufort and Navailles. Beaufort lost his life in a sally; Navailles behaved petulantly and departed again with his troops after a short and ineffectual stay. The Venetians fought on under their commander, Morosini, a gallant leader who dressed in red from top to toe. Huge quantities of grenades, gunpowder and cannon-balls were used. There were sorties and counter-attacks, there was devastation on every side. At last, on 5 September, 1669, after a great number of deaths on both sides, Morosini surrendered on

honourable terms. Declining the offer of a robe and sequins from
the Turkish general, he and what was left of his army departed unmolested to their ships. It was the end of the last great battle for
an outpost of Christendom.

Detail of carving from Venetian loggia, Iraklion. Now
in Historical Museum.

5. Struggle against the Turks

'The face of Crete is stern and weathered,' wrote the Cretan novelist Kazantzakis. 'Truly Crete has about her something primeval and holy, bitter and proud, to have given birth to all those mothers, so often stricken by Charos, and all those *palikares*.'

In Crete, Charos is Death, not merely the ferryman of the under-world. He is a constant presence in folk-song, and under Turkish rule, in songs and in reality, he was a frequent and untimely visitor. A *palikare*, by contrast, is a human hero ready at all times to defy Death in the struggle for Cretan liberty. He is bold, bristling with weapons and positively a wild beast in battle. In the two and a half centuries which followed the fall of Iraklion this concept of a harsh, unthinking heroism took deep root and remains quite central to Crete's perception of itself today.

Under the Venetians Crete was famous for its independence of spirit: but those early rebellions seem to have been the intermittent reaction of a population goaded beyond measure. Under the Turks revolution became something of a sacred duty, a profession for *pali-kares*. The movement took a hundred years to build up, but when the revolutions began they came fast and astonishingly furious. Christian Crete rose against Muslim rule time after time during the nineteenth century, often with appalling loss of life. The Turkish contribution to the island is to be seen not in works of art or monu-mental buildings – there were few of the former and fewer of the latter – but in the bearded, hook-nosed faces of their enemies the *palikares*, which now stare proudly down from plain black frames in Cretan schoolrooms and monastery museums. The painters and poets departed to exile – many of them to the Ionian islands – leaving behind an island where only courage counted.

To symbolise their conquest and to minimise the fatigue of building, the Turks took over the Latin churches as mosques, merely adding minarets. They let the towns fall into disrepair. J. P. de Tournefort, a botanist sent by the French king at the end of the seventeenth century to report on plants and men in the Levant, found Iraklion 'the carcass of a large city ... little better than a desert'. 'The Turks', he wrote (in the translation of his contemporary, John Ozell), 'intirely neglect the repairing of ports and walls of towns. They take a little more care of the fountains, because they are great water drinkers, and their religion obliges 'em very frequently to wash every part of their body.' The rundown extended to the countryside and de Tournefort speaks most feelingly of the sorry fruit and neglected orchards of Khania. In Rethimnon he encountered such a shortage of Malmsey wine that he was unable to find a single drop to taste. But these were the more superficial symptoms. The underlying situation was worse.

The Cretans were unlucky that they were the last important Turkish conquest; for the Ottoman empire had been devised as the war machine of Islam. The empire worked so long as it was expanding. When growth stopped, its administrative inadequacies had the most severe consequences for Christian subjects. For example, the Turks felt themselves above trade, but the empire needed cash and heavy taxes were imposed on Christian traders. This naturally had a destructive effect on trade, in Crete as elsewhere. Then there were property taxes. Most hated of all was the *kharatch*, a capitation tax whose payment entitled subject Christians merely to stay alive. The poverty of all Christians was at least as gross as that of the peasants under the Venetians. Even worse was the capriciousness of the new masters. The centre of the empire was often quite unable to control the Pashas in the provinces and the Pashas in turn were unable to

control their own troops. Turks at every level exploited Crete for
their personal enrichment, taking what they wanted on demand.
Life was miserable and uncertain.

De Tournefort describes the rapacity of the Pashas (Ozell calls
them Bashaws) and the punishment of the few early dissidents.
Under the treaty of 1669 the Venetians retained the island fortresses
of Suda, Gramvousa and Spinalonga. (They kept them for some
fifty years.) Cretans caught making common cause with these Venetian remnants were either impaled, the stake being driven through
the body 'leisurely with a mallet' till it emerged at the shoulder,
or else exposed to a machine called the gaunche. This was a wooden
platform festooned with meat hooks and surmounted by two high
poles. Victims were hoisted to the top of the poles, then dropped
on to the hooks where they hung until they died.

Though the Christian religion was officially tolerated, Christianity was, in practice, an immense handicap. Almost immediately
apostasies began.

This had happened elsewhere but never on so massive a scale
as in Crete. More than half the population of the island turned
Muslim and was thus at liberty to prey on these who held firm
(Christians were known as *rayahs* – cattle). The new converts were
perhaps even more unruly than the native Turks. They were also
self-righteous. According to de Tournefort: 'A good Turk says
nothing when he sees the Christians eat swine's flesh or drink wine:
a renegado shall scold or insult them for it, tho' in private he will
eat and drink his fill of both.' On the subject of wine, Robert Pashley
reported in the nineteenth century that Cretan Muslims drank it
copiously, valuing the juice of the grape more highly than a reputation for orthodoxy.

The system was bad to begin with and became worse. In 1770,
for the first time that we know of, Christian Crete rebelled. The
movement was led by one Daskaloyiannis, a wealthy merchant and
shipowner in a district which had been less subject to depredation
than any other. This was the wild and mountainous region of Sfakia
which may, at first, have enjoyed a limited degree of autonomy

under the Turks. Sfakia included most of the White Mountains. Its heart was the upland plains of Askyfou and Anopolis and it had a substantial capital at Chora Sfakion on the south coast. It lived partly off sheep-rearing, but also had a merchant fleet of about forty vessels.

Some of these ships belonged to Daskaloyiannis (the name means John the Teacher – a title of respect accorded him, perhaps, because of his wide knowledge of languages and his habit of wearing European dress). On a journey to the Black Sea, he met the Orlov brothers, Russian agents, engaged on behalf of Catherine the Great in stirring up trouble in the Ottoman empire. Daskaloyiannis became their ally and returned to Anopolis to preach revolution. At first nobody was much impressed. But his repeated promises to 'bring the Muscovite', followed by the appearance of a Russian fleet off the Peloponnese, finally secured his election to lead a revolution. The Sfakiots swept down into the plains of Khania, driving the Turks into the cities.

But the Russians let them down. The Orlovs were interested only in the Peloponnese and it seems that they tricked Daskaloyiannis into creating a diversion which they had no intention of sustaining. The result was disastrous for Sfakia. When the Turks counter-attacked they quickly pushed the revolutionaries back into the mountains; the Pasha called on Daskaloyiannis to surrender. He was persuaded to fight on, and the result was great attrition in Sfakia. Daskaloyiannis was more ready to listen when a second missive arrived from the Pasha. This was accompanied by a letter from his captured brother Nicholas begging him to comply with the Pasha's entreaty to give himself up. His life would be spared and the slaughter in Sfakia ended. But the letter was signed with three capital *M*s, a secret code from his brother to let him know that the Pasha's offer was a trick. Nevertheless, Daskaloyiannis went down to Frangoskastello and there, with seventy followers, gave himself up.

His followers were maltreated. He himself was sent to Iraklion where the Pasha courteously welcomed him, ordering food, wine, coffee and a pipe. Why, asked the Pasha, had Daskaloyiannis rebelled? Did not Sfakia have its freedom? Daskaloyiannis replied that, whatever the situation of Sfakia, the Cretans were treated as animals. He had raised the flag 'first for my country, second for my faith and third for the rest of the Christians in Crete, for even though I a Sfakian be, I am a child of Crete and for me to behold the woes of Crete is pain enough.' For this defiance Daskaloyiannis was taken out and flayed until he died. And so the first revolt against the Turks came to an end.

The source for this account is a long poem, *The Song of Daskaloyiannis*, recited sixteen years after the event by an illiterate cheesemaker in the mountains of Sfakia and copied down by a shepherd bearing the old Byzantine surname of Skordylis. As Barba Pantzelio, the cheese-maker, dictated the story, so the shepherd tells us, tears streamed from his eyes. Sometimes he fell silent at the sadness of his tale. Skordylis the shepherd felt called upon to apologise for the crudeness of the verses; he also asserted that Barba Pantzelio had a perfect memory.

Perhaps; but it is certain that the details have been arranged for dramatic effect, with events exaggerated and time telescoped. (Daskaloyiannis seems in fact to have spent a year in prison before his execution.) But the revolt was real and the consequences dire. A contemporary Turkish document lists the conditions to which Daskaloyiannis was asked to subscribe by the Pasha. These, as well as imposing all the main forms of taxation on Sfakia, abounded in petty humiliations. They forbade the repair of damaged churches, the building of new ones and the building of houses over one storey high. Sfakiots must wear normal *rayah* clothing. The power and independence of Sfakia were ended. Its people, towns and merchant fleet were damaged beyond repair.

Pantzelio's poem ends with a lament for all that was lost – 'girls like cool waters and cool winds, who danced on holiday like lambs, and leaving their handiwork and tasks, went to church like mountain lilies'; brave young men and sailors afraid neither of storms nor monsters. Nor were there any longer 'white-haired old men to sit by the table, to eat and drink, to sing with strong voices, and tell of heroic deeds and the woes of war, and the tables to echo from one side to another'. One by one, Pantzelio calls out the names of the Sfakiot aristocracy. 'Where are you now?' he asks.

The next serious revolt came in 1821 as part of the Greek War of Independence. For some years before it conditions had been even worse. The janissaries, that military body formerly made up of soldiers taken as children from Christian families, were quite out of control and Crete is described as having been the worst-governed province in the Ottoman empire. Demands for money would be sent, wrapped round a bullet, to Christians, to indicate the alternative to payment. The Muslims enjoyed complete sexual licence, taking Christian women as and when they wanted. According to the reports of the French consul at Khania, janissaries on the city walls laid bets with one another on which way Christian passers-by would fall as they shot them dead in sport.

When the War of Independence broke out on the mainland, the Cretan Turks, panic-stricken, embarked on massacres in the hope of preserving their dominance. Armed bands roamed the streets. Christians were strangled, drowned and burned. The Bishop of Kissamou was dragged by his beard half-naked through the streets, then hanged. The Metropolitan (or Bishop) of Iraklion was slaughtered with seventy followers in his cathedral. In the countryside violence was equally great.

Five months after the Greek flag was first raised in the Peloponnese, Crete was in arms from end to end. The mountaineers, inflamed by the massacres, once again drove the Muslim population into the towns and kept them penned there. (The besieged Turks of Khania suffered from thirst, just as the defenders of ancient Kydonia had once done on the same spot.) But by the following year the Ottoman empire was fighting back vigorously. Troops from Egypt arrived in Crete and quickly subdued the eastern end of the island. Villages were burned and trees cut down in many parts. The Christians held out only in the most mountainous parts and many village people took refuge in caves.

In 1834, his interest sparked by reports of an inscription which linked a cave at Melidoni with the myth of Talos, Robert Pashley became the first person to enter that cave since the war. Three hundred people had taken refuge there from a passing Muslim army. According to locals, the leader of the troops had sent a messenger to tell the Christians to come out; they shot the messenger. Next, the Muslims sent a Greek woman with the same message. The Christians shot her too and threw her body out. So the Turks threw stones down into a dell at the mouth of the cave, eventually blocking it. That night the Christians made a small hole to breathe through. After several days of this, the Muslims replaced the stones with combustible material and lit it. Many of the Christians died at once in the main chamber, as Pashley discovered. Some escaped into a second chamber. Others crawled into narrow fissures. 'Alas!' wrote Pashley, 'the passages through which they rushed suffered the destroying vapour to follow them . . .' In the next chamber 'the bones and skulls of the poor Christians are so thickly scattered it is almost impossible to avoid crushing them as we pick our way along'.

Refugees were suffocated in this way in several caves. Christian prisoners were also impaled in the old manner. (The word for the stake used to transfix the body is *souvli* – more familiar today as the skewer on which *souvlaki* is cooked.) The Christians themselves took no male prisoners and on occasion killed women. This was to avoid the contamination of the *palikares* by heathen flesh – apparently the only other possible outcome. It was thus an act of savage piety. Many Christians (according to Pashley) at the same time declared themselves soldiers of the Cross and 'shrunk from the caresses of their wives, as from a pollution, which would most probably be punished by their falling in the next engagement'.

The Church played an extremely active part in the war and in Sfakia conducted special ceremonies in which *palikares* entered into religious brotherhood with one another. This had odd long-term consequences, for after the ceremony the rules of consanguinity applied, making marriage to the close female relatives of a brother in Christ incestuous.

Religious fervour, however, did not prevent the development of fratricidal jealousies between the Christian chieftains. The Sfakiots as usual wished to give the orders. Their leader eventually succeeded in murdering the patriot in charge in the region of Psiloritis. Against this background of dissension, the rising petered out in 1824 (after which the island was for a time governed from Egypt). During these three years of war the population of Crete fell by nearly half.

Pashley reports many villages with only a handful of surviving men and one where the only adult inhabitants were widows. Then there was the Kurmulidhes family in the Mesara. Of sixty-four men, two survived.

The destruction of this family brought to an end a curious episode. The Kurmulidhes, despite Muslim first names and acts of public devotion to Allah, had remained crypto-Christians for generations. They were christened and married in secret by Orthodox priests, and did much to alleviate the sufferings of local Christians. This system, which died with them during the War of Independence, had nearly come to an end once before. On that occasion members of the family, conscience-stricken at their failure to proclaim their faith openly, took their difficulties to the Bishop of Jerusalem. He told them that their pusillanimity would keep the gates of heaven closed. Thirty Kurmulidhes then decided to confess to the Pasha in the expectation of a redeeming martyrdom. But the Metropolitan of Iraklion dissuaded them, arguing that it would lead also to the destruction of all the priests involved. So the clan survived until the rising of 1821.

On the mainland, the War of Independence carried on until Ottoman naval power was broken at the Battle of Navarino in 1828. The Great Powers (Britain, France, Italy and Russia) had for some time been moving towards the establishment of an independent Greece, but in such a way that the balance of strength should remain so far as possible unchanged. Britain wanted the Turkish empire to remain coherent enough to hold the Russians, and it became clear that Free Greece would be a small country unlikely to include Crete. The mainland leader, Hadzi Michali Daliani, accordingly decided to stir things up once more in the island. Landing with a small force he installed himself in Frangokastello and there, in March 1828, decided to stand and fight against a large Muslim army which came swarming at him out of the gorges. His refusal to take to the mountains was one of those gestures of hopeless bravado in which the War of Independence abounded; and his death was so clearly written, says the song about his exploits (a great many *palikares* are celebrated in song), that as he vaulted into the saddle his war-horse wept. Hadzi Michali and his followers were duly slaughtered.

When one visits Frangokastello it all seems very recent. Local

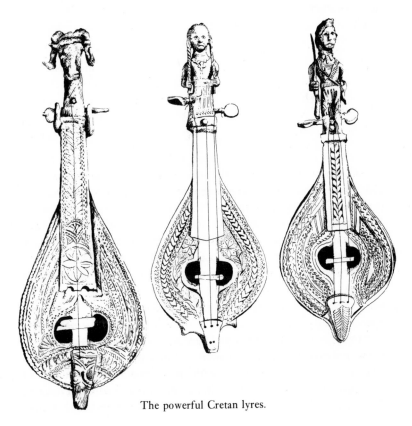

The powerful Cretan lyres.

people declare that in the dawn mists of March they still see Hadzi Michali and his men. They call them the Dhrosoulites, 'Dew Shadows'.

This all took place in Sfakia, and so much of the War of Independence was fought there that one must ask what it was that made this part of Crete the constant centre of resistance. The answer lies partly in the inaccessible terrain, but also in the extraordinary character of its people.

From very early on the Sfakiots aroused the interest of foreigners who encountered them. One of the best descriptions comes from the monumental study of the Greek islands published late in the seventeenth century by the Flemish doctor, Dapper:

> Les habitants de *Spachia* ... surpassent tous les autres en courage & en adresse à manier des armes. Car ils sont des hommes rudes, mal polis & presque sauvages, qui sont acoûtumez à vivre de pirateries & de brigandages. Ils sont les meilleurs et les plus adroits archers de toute l'île; & lors qu'ils sont en presence de l'enemi, ils ne manquent pas de resolution, & combatent ordinairement avec beaucoup de fermeté.

He went on to say that while their women went bare-shouldered and bare-headed, the Sfakiot men wore boots up to waist-level ('Ils vont tous botez jusques au nombril'). They had an inordinate love of dancing, and would pound the earth at height of summer's day without for one moment setting aside their weapons. To be armed at all times was a point of pride with them. This trait has persisted without intermission to the present day. You do not see the weapons carried so obviously, but I have often encountered Sfakiots who turned out to have pistols in their pockets, and no Sfakiot baptism or family party is complete without a ragged rattle of gunfire.

As well as the Sfakiots' love of arms, the essential points for the future were their ferocity, and their habits of piracy and brigandage. The attitude behind these characteristics is endorsed by the Sfakiot version of the Creation, as recorded by Raymond Matton. The story opens with an account of all the gifts God had given to other parts of Crete – olives to Ierapetra, Ayios Vasilios and Selinou; wine to Malevisi and Kissamou; cherries to Mylopotamos and Amari. But when God got to Sfakia only rocks were left. So the Sfakiots appeared before Him armed to the teeth. 'And us, Lord, how are we going to live on these rocks?' and the Almighty, looking at them with sympathy, replied in their own dialect (naturally): 'Haven't you got a scrap of brains in your heads? Don't you see that the low-landers are cultivating all these riches for *you*?'

Their attitude to law (and to their neighbours) was one of disdain. Sheep-stealing was part of the way of life. When they led their raids against the Turks, it was in disregard of the consequences for the less well-protected lowlanders. They were also fierce towards one another, making a fetish of the vendetta. Failure to exact vengeance was a failure in manhood and a quarrel might be pursued for genera-tions, sometimes leading to the extermination of whole families. The Venetian proveditor, Foscarini, reported in the sixteenth century that a Sfakiot, discovering a death which demanded vengeance, would put on a black shirt and never change it till the debt was paid. Pashley was told of the murder of a man because he had killed two Sfakiot dogs, and in Anopolis he was assured that few locals died a natural death. This violence died down on union with Greece, but armed strife between families, mainly because of sheep-stealing, broke out again in World War II. I have come across astonishing enmities in Sfakiot villages. The village of Aradena has been virtually depopulated over the past fifteen years by people seeking to escape vendettas, and in 1972, after a murder in Sfakia, even though the murderer was detained by the police, his whole family left Crete, abandoning land and a general store in hope of personal safety.

The Sfakiots also made a special production of bride-stealing, though this was fairly general in the island. You still meet women who were abducted in their youth (the cheerful wife of the telephone operator in Nefs Amari comes to mind, and a comfortable widow in the Sfakiot village of Loutro); but in the old days, despite the animosities it created, it was reckoned quite the thing. Even where a bride was not abducted she was carried off ceremonially to her husband's village, the groom and his friends singing all the way.

Cretan marriage, incidentally, has been a rich seam for folklore experts. Not surprisingly in an island where Byzantine culture lived on for two hundred years longer than in most of the rest of Greece, it is, or was, loaded with symbolism. A mid-nineteenth-century discussion of the subject mentions that three crowns were placed on the bride's pillow: one of thorns to signify long life and endurance

Carved wooden bread mould. Even today, extraordinarily elaborate loaves are produced for wedding feasts.

under its cares; one of myrtle and orange leaves to signify sweetness and everlasting love; and a third of bread, to stand for peace and plenty. On entering her house, the bride dipped her finger in honey and made four crosses on the door, showing her love to be 'as holy, sweet and strong as the symbol of her faith'. And she would throw down a pomegranate on the floor, scattering its richly coloured seeds as a symbol of the many possessions she hoped the house would one day have.

But to return to the Sfakiots. They were superstitious as well as fierce and believed, to their own discomfort, in vampires. Bodies not properly buried, or the bodies of the excommunicated, roamed the Sfakiot countryside at night, feeding on human liver. They could be destroyed only by the burning of the corpses. The belief seems to have been on the wane in Pashley's day, for he was told of few modern instances. But he collected a great many tales of former vampires. These had some of the annoying habits of polter-geists, and were not above such tricks as pretending they were the husbands of faithful wives and so enjoying their embraces in the dark of night.

Another peculiarity of the Sfakiots was that, despite their ferocity when roused, they often behaved from day to day with a majestic courtesy. There is no better example of this than Captain Manias, a Sfakiot of the early nineteenth century, of whom we are lucky enough to know a good deal. For Manias was engaged as a guide first by Pashley and then, twenty years later, by Captain Spratt. Both were profoundly impressed by the contrast between his record as pirate and warrior and the manly charm of his behaviour.

Pashley established that in the 1821 war Manias had performed acts of signal ferocity and that, after 1824, operating as a pirate in his own caïque, he had captured for ransom sixty-four Muslims from the region of Sitia. For these deeds he had been awarded the title of Kapetan, or Captain, the ultimate accolade to which *pali-kares* aspire. Pashley wrote of him: 'The life of war, rapine and bloodshed which he had led, proved of the highest utility to me, for it had made him so well acquainted with every hill and dale, path and river in the island, that there were few parts of it where he would not have proved an unerring guide even at midnight.' He knew the songs of the *palikares* and sung them; he himself was widely known and welcomed everywhere he went; and he possessed great delicacy of manners. He would not pass the soap by hand to Pashley, believing that this would wash away the friendship between them. (This superstition still exists in Sfakia.) In talking to a Muslim he would never mention the word 'pig', referring instead to 'those animals which have bristles on their backs'.

Pashley, a warm sympathiser with the Cretan struggle for inde-pendence, was evidently fond of him and full of secret admiration. Spratt reflected British foreign policy in approving of the Turks and condemning Cretan revolutionary spirit. His opinion of the Sfa-kiots was low. 'The name of the Sfakiot', he wrote, 'is...a byword

amongst the lowland Cretans, for talents perverted, and for un-
scrupulous intrigue, theft and cruelty. Athletic and active, he stalks
about the island from one extreme to the other, either as an itinerant
merchant or pedlar, or political disturber, and is feared, but not
respected.' Spratt refused on principle to write of Manias's piratical
past, while conceding his unrivalled knowledge of safe harbours and
marine hazards. But he was melted by the man. Manias was 'patient
and gentle and his heart was kindly, though stout; a lion or a lamb,
he had no intermediate quality'. He died of fever in Ierapetra during
Spratt's survey and his English companions buried him as he had
lived – in his boots.

Spratt adds a good deal to our ability to visualise Turkish Crete.
He records the growth on the foreshore near Khania of an Arab
settlement two or three thousand strong, complete with Bedouin
tents. He notes that the Mesara was still full of ruins from 1821.
And he records, with sympathetic horror, that lepers were forced
to beg outside the city gates or to live totally cut off, as in a village
above Ierapetra. One old man among the lepers outside Iraklion
was blind and his horribly swollen limbs, hands and feet were
hidden 'in filthy bags of old rags'. He was attended by his daughter,
a girl of great beauty, seemingly in perfect health. But it turned
out that ten days before, because two of her fingers were slightly
bent and stiff (apparently an early sign of leprosy), she had been
driven out of her village to join her father. She appeared to register
no emotion.

Beneath the island's exotic surface there ran an undercurrent of
horror. But Spratt provides a corrective by describing how, in time
of peace, the Muslims and the lowland Christians were able to live
together with some mutual tolerance.

The mountaineers, however, were intent on their vision of themselves as *palikares* and captains. There was trouble in 1841 and 1856.
The Church, and particularly the rich monasteries founded in the
last century of Venetian rule, became more and more deeply involved. In 1866 Christian Crete was up in arms again, this time
because of Ottoman failure to carry out promised reforms. As the

Pasha summoned reinforcements from Istanbul, Sfakia declared union with Greece and a trickle of foreign volunteers arrived. The insurgents forced a whole Turkish army to surrender in the plain of Apokoronas. But the *palikares* were too irregular and too disorganised to achieve permanent gains. They set out from their villages with enough food for a few days and when this was finished returned home. It is said that during this rising the Sfakiots attacked their own Cretan allies from the rear in pursuance of a quarrel. The revolution began to lose ground.

Then late in 1866 the Turks attacked the handsome, fortified monastery of Arkadi, which the guerrillas were using as a strongpoint. It fell after two days of ferocious fighting. As the Turks entered, a defender put a torch to the powder magazine, blowing up hundreds of women and children, Christian defenders and Turkish assailants. (Much of the monastery still survives, however, including the façade of the church. This is the most ornate piece of Venetian architecture in Crete and well worth a visit. The museum helps to evoke the heroism of the *palikares*, and the bones of many of those killed in the explosion are preserved in a fly-blown monument.) News of the explosion at Arkadi rang round the world, drawing support and admiration for the Cretans from such diverse figures as Garibaldi and Victor Hugo. Algernon Swinburne wrote a poem about it. Yet despite the international sympathy, a Turkish army was able the next year to devote five months to systematic destruction in the White Mountains.

Twelve years later Crete rebelled again. This was a smaller conflict but well known, at least to readers of fiction. Nikos Kazantzakis (1883–1957), that very considerable Cretan writer, made it the subject of his most powerful novel, *Freedom and Death*, setting out to capture, through figures deliberately larger than life, the elemental aspects of Crete's long battle for liberty. It is not a realistic novel, yet it conveys a strong sense of the heroic aspirations of Christian Crete. It also conveys a forceful impression of Cretan landscape and weather, portraying the revolution as born not only out of terror, obduracy and pride, but equally out of the hot wind which blows up from the south, falling on women like a man and on men as if it were a woman. The sea rubs its breast against the sea-wall, and the repressed eroticism turns into savagery. There are powerful scenes showing the panic among the Christians in the towns as country Muslims come flooding in for refuge – while the Metropolitan lives night and day in his long robes so that he will be fittingly dressed for martyrdom. When the action moves to the countryside, the revolution is shown to consist largely of random violence and foolhardy self-sacrifice. It is hard to make out what attitude Kazantzakis himself takes to his story – to the cruelty, the imposition on women, even to the Cretan ideal of self-sacrifice. But one of the characters speaks of freedom as a seed which must be nourished with blood. It was this belief which drove on the Cretan freedom-fighters throughout the nineteenth century.

Crete had been an international question since 1821 and its final fate, as the Ottoman empire tottered towards dismemberment, lay with the Great Powers. Each revolution helped to remind them of this trouble-spot, and from time to time they compelled the Turkish authorities to promise reforms which were in practice seldom carried out. Britain consistently blocked Cretan union with Greece and must bear the greatest blame for the hardships endured by the Cretans.

During a final revolution in 1896, a Greek force landed in Crete while the Greek crown prince attempted a blockade with six torpedo boats. War broke out between Greece and Turkey, and the Powers imposed a settlement. The French took responsibility for Sitia, the Italians for Ierapetra, the British for Iraklion and the Russians for Rethimnon. All four looked after Khania while a joint fleet lay in Suda Bay.

The Turks did not care for the reforms now imposed. In August 1898 fourteen British soldiers and the British consul were murdered during a Turkish upheaval in Iraklion. The British admiral allegedly trained his guns on the city; the Pasha caved in. The Powers sent the last of the Turkish troops packing and ordained that Crete should become independent under the nominal suzerainty of Turkey. Prince George, the heir to the Greek throne, was appointed ruler of the island. Union with Greece seemed to be only a step away.

In fact, there was a delay of fifteen years. This irritated the Cretans but at the same time produced the most notable leader of modern Greece – Eleftherios Venizelos. This handsome, well-educated, immensely ambitious lawyer came from the west of Crete. He soon declared that Prince George was not pushing hard enough for union and that this should be achieved by force of arms if necessary. In 1905 Venizelos convened an illegal, revolutionary assembly at the village of Therison. According to Venizelos, who told Sir Harold Nicolson, who told Xan Fielding, a copy of *The Times* was smuggled to him daily during this period by the British consul in Khania. As the drift towards union continued, Venizelos's stature grew and in 1910 he became Prime Minister of Greece itself. The union of Crete with Greece followed in 1913 and it seemed that the island could now settle down to peace. There followed twenty-eight peaceful and fairly uneventful years, though the Turkish story was not quite finished.

Inflamed by the 'great idea' of recovering Constantinople, the Greeks engaged in various attacks on Turkey. In August 1922 they were shatteringly defeated outside Smyrna (now Izmir); this large city with a Greek population was sacked and looted, and the Greeks who survived had to escape by sea. This was a great humiliation for Greece and led to an enforced exchange of populations the next year. All Greeks were expelled from Turkey, all Turks from Greece.

A small number of Cretan Turks had decided to stay on the island under Greek rule. They departed with great bitterness and their houses and property were taken by Greeks from Asia Minor. M. Elliadi, the British vice-consul in Iraklion, captured some of the sadness of the event in a little book he wrote for British visitors:

I was deeply impressed on the eve of their departure at seeing many Mussulman families visiting the extensive cemeteries on the outskirts of the town, taking leave and kneeling down, offering prayers to their dead. I noted also their farewell looks at their monasteries ... and the freshwater fountains scattered here and there, with their inscriptions in Turkish, cut in the stone, inviting the thirsty to drink.

Sad, certainly; but Crete at least has been spared the sufferings which Cyprus still endures on account of a mixed population.

6. The pity of war

The Allied cemetery is by Suda Bay; the Germans are buried above the airstrip at Maleme, west of Khania, on one of the hills where so many of them died. Crete herself lost uncounted men, women and children during the desperate battle for the island in the spring of 1941 and during the years of German occupation after it. Sometimes, as above Chora Sfakion, you will come across memorials of the later days, glass-fronted shrines containing an untidy heap of bones and skulls with bullet holes in them. These are a testimony to the methods of the occupying forces and to the spirit of the Cretans. An astonishingly high proportion of Crete's people refused to acknowledge that they were beaten and fought back as best they could, covertly at first and later openly, often at the cost of their own lives. One might say, perhaps, that the island's history equipped it admirably to engage in one of the most determined of all World War II resistance movements; equally, one must acknowledge that its dreadful consequences were all of a piece with much of Crete's modern history. Surely, one thinks, Crete had the right to live without further need for blood and heroism.

The preliminaries to the Battle of Crete were disheartening. Late in 1940 Mussolini attacked Greece. His troops were met and held in the wintry mountains of Albania by Greek forces armed more with courage than with the conventional weapons of modern warfare. The Cretan division fought there, sent to the front after threatening a hunger strike unless it went. But it was clear that Greece could not contain the Germans as well as the Italians.

Despite Greek doubts, the Allies dispatched an expeditionary force to Greece, moving back on to the mainland of Europe for the first time since Dunkirk. But when the Germans attacked, Greeks and Allies were forced to retreat. A second desperate evacuation took place, this time from the Piraeus. The Allies now decided to stand and fight in Crete.

The British had already had six months there in which to carry out instructions from Churchill to turn the island into a fortress; the idea was that the navy, operating from Egypt, would repel seaborne invasion, while the garrison of Crete would deal with attack from the air.

Unfortunately, this formulation left out of account the overwhelming strength of the *Luftwaffe* and its total control of the skies. It also ignored the fact that astonishingly little had been done to improve the defences of Crete. The island had had seven commanders within four months, one of them twice, and Wavell, hardpressed at his headquarters in Egypt, had failed to give Crete enough of his attention. Preparations had been sloppy and half-hearted. But nobody knew this, last of all Churchill. He was determined to hold Crete for both strategic and political reasons and on the general principle of opposing his will as stubbornly as possible to that of Hitler.

During the retreat from the mainland, late in April 1941, Crete was used as a transit camp. Thousands of battle-weary troops, poorly armed and organised, were landed by ships which hurried back to fetch still more. They set up camp among the olive groves round Khania and Suda, on the edge of that fertile country so praised by William Lithgow and other travellers. And then, for a week or two, nothing happened. As the troops, mostly Australians and New Zealanders, recovered from the effects of endless pounding from the air, a carnival atmosphere developed. The soldiers did not know that even while the last of the evacuations were taking place from the mainland, the Germans were building advance airfields for the attack on Crete. And so the men enjoyed the bright spring weather, bathing by day and dealing with the chill of evening by means of the excellent local wine.

The people of the villages round Khania helped as best they could. Theodore Stephanides, a Greek-born doctor serving with the Allied forces, recalls in his book *Climax in Crete* that the troops received many presents of such precious commodities as eggs and oranges.

But there was an unpleasant side to this period of holiday, for many of the Australian troops passed from exuberance to licence and disorder and what had begun as simple relaxation now seemed to contain the seeds of possible disaster.

Wavell arrived on 30 April for a few hours. He swiftly picked General Bernard Freyberg, the leader of the New Zealand armed forces, to conduct the defence of the island. In World War I, Freyberg had been one of the party who carried Rupert Brooke's body to his grave on Skyros. He had won a reputation for gallantry in leadership during the same war, not to mention the Victoria Cross. But now, as he surveyed the island's defences, it was clear that the situation was difficult, if not desperate. He had perhaps thirty-six planes, without camouflaged pens to protect them, against the thousand-odd fighters and bombers available to Germany. All Crete's ports, airports and serviceable roads were on the north coast of the island. Nothing had been done to construct north–south roads or to improve the ports in the south. This meant that to supply the defending forces the navy would have to sail up from Egypt and then, as it were, round the corners of the island, passing either east or west through narrow straits immediately accessible to German aircraft. The island's existing garrison was small. It had never been intended that the troops in transit from the mainland should help to defend Crete. Now it began to appear that they would have to; but they were miserably armed. Nor, despite the express instruction of Churchill in 1940, had anything been done to arm the Cretans. (For centuries it had been a tradition for Cretans to bear arms but, shortly before the war, the Greek dictator Metaxas, alarmed at the island's Venizelist tendency, had done his best to call in weapons. Many Cretans had complied.) The Cretan division had been shattered in Albania and most of Crete's young men were already dead or captive.

But Freyberg immediately recognised that the remaining islanders abundantly possessed the will to fight. This realisation was helped along by a letter from one of the Cretan gaols. 'We wholeheartedly put ourselves under any service, dangerous or not,' wrote the prisoners, 'provided that the cause of the Allied effort is fulfilled.'

Among the many supplies which Freyberg requested were rifles for the Cretans.

Interestingly, the Allied officer up to then most eager to arm the Cretans had been the archaeologist John Pendlebury. He had enlisted, become a captain and returned to Iraklion, during the early months of the war. Here, since Greece was still neutral, he was officially described as a vice-consul. His real job was to enlist the help of the Cretans against the day when it might be needed. For a few months he rejoiced in this role, making huge walks to establish contact with likely guerrilla leaders throughout the island. His new associates were known to the British as 'Pendlebury's thugs', and he himself, when engaged in particularly brigand-like pursuits, made a habit of leaving his glass eye on his bedside table, setting out for the mountains with a black patch.

Pendlebury calculated that with ten thousand rifles the Cretans would be able to make a decisive contribution to the defence of the island. Now, when Freyberg asked Wavell for the rifles, it was already too late.

However, Freyberg made one move that was to prove extraordinarily effective. He took the few Greek forces on the island, bringing in raw cadets from the Cretan training college, and divided them into eight 'regiments'. To each of these makeshift units one or two Allied officers and N.C.O.s were assigned; and they were given sectors to defend. Nobody at the time thought much of their capabilities.

The battle for Crete began in the middle of May with intense air attacks. Casualties were light, but the troops were battered in body as well as in mind. 'The continuous noise and concussion made one feel sick and rather dazed,' Theodore Stephanides wrote later, 'yet every nerve was on edge as in a nightmare.' Hour after hour, day after day, the raids went on, stopping only at night.

Early in the morning of 20 May, all round Khania, Suda and Maleme, the bombardment became extraordinarily fierce, even by the standards of that grim week. As usual a pall of smoke hung over Suda Bay where Allied ships were burning. Then suddenly, without apparent logic, the noise ended.

Crouching in slit trenches among the olives, the defenders were at first too stunned to comprehend that enemy gliders were landing among their own positions. Some of the gliders crashed; others got down safely and spilled out their troops. But by now the Allies were shooting frantically.

Then all at once the sky was full of noise again as a vast fleet of transport planes came up over the defenders from the landward side. They left behind them a sky full of parachutes, bulging and blossoming in weird and appalling concentration. For a moment the Allies watched dumbfounded; then once more a frenzy of gunfire began.

Parachutists were killed in scores while still in the air and more were shot down as they tried to free themselves from their 'chutes. Here and there a group survived and struggled desperately to establish a position. Because they had landed among the Allied positions it was from the first moment a necessity to kill in order to avoid being killed. I. McD. G. Stewart, the most comprehensive historian of the battle, wrote:

Man stalked man among the olives, through luxuriant gardens of scented jasmine and mimosa, from wall to wall across the narrow fields of barley, and from behind the rocks and boulders that littered the terraced hillsides. Almost every encounter was mortal. The cold of the morning had turned quickly to blazing heat. From a cloudless sky the sun blazed down upon the sweating soldiers who quickly came to exhaustion as they struggled up and down the steep ravines or dashed for cover among the rocks. And the wounded grew desperate for water.

In the coastal villages around Maleme, the Cretans came out of their places of shelter and fought the Germans with shotguns, knives, clubs and anything that came to hand. The Germans were astonished, having been told in their briefings that the Cretans were friendly and would join them in the fighting, identifying themselves with the code-words 'Major Bock'. Under the assaults of Allied troops and the Cretans, great numbers of Germans perished.

But outside the main battle area, where the river Tavronitis joins the sea to the west of Maleme, some thousand German parachutists got down safely. Lieutenant-Colonel Andrew, another New Zealander with the V.C., was in charge at Maleme, perched on a hill above the airfield. But his three forward observers on the western flank did not survive long enough to bring him news of this landing; nor had they, in the chaos of the time, a wireless set. The thousand German parachutists therefore landed unreported; and though Andrew found no great difficulty in commanding the airstrip, throughout the day mysterious attacks developed from the west. He asked for reinforcements, but the wrong and misleading reply was that the troops available were heavily engaged.

British intelligence before the battle had accurately predicted the form of the attack, stressing that the main German objective would be the airfields. The critical areas for the defence were thus Maleme with its single strip; another, very poor, strip at Rethimnon; and the much more elaborate airfield at Iraklion. Both Rethimnon and Iraklion were attacked during the afternoon of 20 May, but the German assault had got out of phase and in both places the parachutists landed in scattered waves, to the great advantage of the defenders.

In Rethimnon, the young Australian officer in command – Lieutenant-Colonel I. R. Campbell – fell on the parachutists with great verve, though he was heavily outnumbered. Within an hour,

Campbell had committed his whole reserve force, reasoning that if further drops were to be made, every parachutist surviving from the first drop would add greatly to his later difficulties.

Some Greek forces under his command, inexperienced and short of arms, at first showed a tendency to panic but were rallied and brought back into the fight. Meanwhile the Cretan police, unaided, were holding the Germans back from Rethimnon itself.

At Iraklion, as at Rethimnon, the Allies held the airfield confidently; but the situation in the town was much more difficult. The Germans forced an entry through Greek and British positions in the west, and during the night, despite the resistance of townspeople as well as the defending troops, they fought their way to the harbour. They drove in front of them some thirty British troops who in due course found themselves retreating along the Venetian mole which Morosini had once so valiantly defended. Finding boats tied up along the mole, they put out to sea in the blackness and were lucky enough to encounter a British destroyer.

One man who died at Iraklion was John Pendlebury. It seems, according to evidence assembled by Dilys Powell, that he was caught by parachutists on the west of town as he attempted to join potential guerrillas on Mt. Psiloritis. Rallying a Greek machine-gunner and shooting with his pistol, he killed several paratroopers before himself being shot in the shoulder. The Germans carried him to a nearby house and that evening he was treated by a doctor. But the next morning, German troops came for him. They put him outside the door of the house and demanded information. When he would not reply beyond a cry of 'No, no, no,' they killed him.

The profit and loss sheet for the first day showed Rethimnon and Iraklion holding fast. At Maleme, Colonel Andrew was in trouble. There was also trouble in a large valley with a prison in it – and therefore dubbed the Prison Valley – lying south-west of Khania and due south, though set apart by hills, from Maleme.

Intelligence had warned of possible landings here and the valley was defended – by an Australian force and by the Greek 6th and 8th regiments, these last two stationed at opposite ends of the valley from one another. The German parachutists duly landed and quickly dispersed the Greek 6th. This regiment had received ammunition, but it had not been distributed to the men, and during the fighting its colonel was shot by the New Zealand 19th battalion, in the belief that he was throwing grenades at them. As Stewart points out, the Allies were at this time ready to see fifth columnists everywhere:

> And certainly there were individual Greeks who sought to help the enemy. But in Crete there was confusion enough to account for almost any mistake or failure. Today, any such accusation of treachery at once becomes suspect in the light of what is now known of the stoic gallantry of Greek behaviour as a whole.

There were reports that the Greek 8th had been dispersed. In his headquarters in a quarry on the Akrotiri peninsula near Khania, General Freyberg was informed that the Germans were constructing a makeshift airstrip in the Prison Valley. This was untrue; it came on top of fallacious stories that the Germans were landing troop carriers all about the countryside. The result of this misinformation was that the defence of the airstrips began to seem less important to Freyberg. Why concentrate on Maleme if the Germans could land on the beaches or build an airstrip in the Prison Valley? This line of reasoning was the second in a fatal series of Allied errors.

The first had been the failure to send help to Andrew at Maleme. That night, having lost contact with his forward companies and wrongly assuming them (again because of lack of wireless sets) to have been annihilated Andrew decided that his position was untenable without reinforcements. Accordingly he pulled back off the top of the hill. At that moment Maleme was effectively lost and so was Crete. There were several opportunities for retaking the hill, but each of them was missed.

The irony is that Maori troops arrived on the hill during the night, found it empty and went away again. Andrew's forward companies also sent men back to the hill to re-establish contact. Discovering that they had been deserted, they too withdrew. Thus for several hours during the night Allied troops wandered unmolested on the hill where Andrew had refused to stay. Meanwhile his superior officer, Brigadier Hargest, made no move to counter-attack. This was the third fatal error in the defence of Crete.

Morning broke on 21 May to reveal that the Germans had discovered the situation and moved quietly on to the hilltop. Though Allied positions could still fire on the airfield from the eastern side, German troop carriers from Athens simply ignored the reduced fire of the defenders and came in to land at Maleme. Some crashed, but many more got through the curtain of fire. Little by little the Germans began to enlarge their enclave and little by little the balance of power round Maleme began to change in their favour.

General Karl Student, sitting all that first night at a brilliantly lit table amid the opulent baroque décor of the Grande Bretagne Hotel in Athens, had realised that he was in the gravest danger of losing the battle. He had spread his forces too widely and too thinly and Maleme was the only point at which a chink of light shone through. Accordingly he decided to accept almost any risk to reinforce there. And as the day wore on it was apparent that the gamble had paid off. Meanwhile the Allies held on in Rethimnon and Iraklion. There were accusations in Iraklion that the Germans had been advancing behind screens of women and children; these incidents ceased after the local Greek commander threatened that any repetition would mean the death of German prisoners. Remarkable events were also taking place in the Prison Valley, scene of the phantasmagoric airstrip construction. A young English lieutenant named Forrester, blond and thin, hatless and wearing a jersey which came almost to the bottom of his shorts (to one observer he seemed like a P. G. Wodehouse character), had succeeded in rallying the Greek 6th and other supporters. A New Zealander reported that he had seen Forrester charging at the head of a 'crowd of disorderly Greeks, including women; one Greek had a shotgun with a serrated edge bread-knife tied on like a bayonet ...' The Germans fled before them.

The Greek 6th fought prodigiously. At the other end of the Prison Valley, the Greek 8th, reported dispersed on the first day, in fact continued to hold the ridges where it had originally been stationed. Though Andrew had withdrawn from Maleme, this Greek contingent, cut off, outgunned and without hope of success or even survival, fought on.

That night the British fleet, patrolling the north coast, encountered an invasion flotilla of caïques and destroyed them totally. Freyberg's greatest worry had been attack by sea on top of parachute landings and he clearly appreciated the importance of what he had seen. 'It's been a great responsibility, a great responsibility,' he was heard to mutter.

With the threat of a sea-landing removed. Freyberg had a supreme opportunity to counter-attack in force at Maleme. Uncharacteristically he missed it. Certainly an attack went in, but with too few troops; and it began far too late (through administrative muddle) to have any hope of achieving much.

This force, made up mostly of Maoris and including some freelance Cretans, fought its way to the perimeter of the airfield and was blasted out at dawn by air attacks. At dawn too, another part of the British fleet, pursuing a second invasion flotilla north into the Aegean, was obliged to break off action because of the danger of air attack. As it raced for Egypt it sustained fearful losses.

That day, 23 May, there was a further Allied withdrawal in the Maleme sector, supposedly to a more easily defensible line. Iraklion and Rethimnon held. The Australians were fighting hard and skilfully in the Prison Valley, while to their south many villagers had joined the Greek 8th, arming themselves as best they could from fallen Germans. Little was known about this battle until German evidence became available after the war. Then it emerged that parachutists in the Prison Valley believed they were up against four thousand men, not the mere one thousand who opposed them.

There is a story from about this point of the battle of an old man and his grandson throwing rocks at the Germans until they managed to find weapons. Another story, from Rethimnon (recounted in

Christopher Buckley's study of the battle but not, to my knowledge, otherwise confirmed), has a Cretan boy dropping a swarm of bees down the chimney of a cottage held by Germans and a priest picking off the Germans with a rifle as they ran for refuge from the bees.

It seems that nothing so deeply enraged the Germans as the resistance of those they attacked, and on 23 May an ominous note was struck in a notice put out to troops by the German 5th Mountain Division:

> The murder of a German airman on 22 May has proved that the Greek population, in civilian or German uniforms, is taking part in the battle. They are shooting or stabbing wounded to death and also mutilating and robbing corpses.
>
> Any Greek civilian taken with a firearm in his hands is to be shot immediately, as is anyone caught attacking wounded.
>
> Hostages (men between 18 and 55) are to be taken from the villages at once, and the civilians are to be informed that if acts of hostility against the German army take place these will be shot immediately.
>
> The villagers in the area are to be informed that 10 Greeks will die for every German.

One point here is that since the Cretans were not regular soldiers they were not covered by the Geneva Convention. The Germans felt they could do what they liked with them. As the prospect of Allied defeat came closer, the more bleak became the position of the Cretans – and the harder they fought.

The question of mutilations has remained contentious, and clearly requires examination. One can arrive at some understanding of the kind of thing that happened by considering events in Kissamou Kastelli.

Kissamou – today a sleepy little town largely ignored even by tourists – lies in the far west of Crete, some fifteen miles beyond Maleme. In May 1941 it was defended by the No. 1 Greek regiment, with forty Cretan policemen, volunteers from the local villages, ten New Zealand N.C.O.s and three New Zealand officers, the highest ranking among them being Major T. J. Bedding, a physical training instructor.

Bedding put this force through some elementary training in a dis-used factory, but the gesture was an optimistic one since many of his men had no rifles. Some were untrained cadets. Quite early in the battle, however, they defeated a parachute force of seventy-four men sent against them. During this encounter, the parachutists were in many cases stalked by men without firearms who killed them, when they could, with knives or improvised clubs. Cretan casualties were high, largely because the men were too inexperienced to take cover. The few German survivors were rounded up and Major Bedding locked them in the town gaol. The victors gave themselves over to a rowdy celebration but sobered down in time to meet a second detachment which shortly attacked them.

This time they were not strong enough. The Germans took the centre of the town and the prisoners escaped after a direct hit on the gaol. But it took the fresh German force another three days to reduce Kissamou Kastelli, even though they were blasting the defenders from house to house with anti-tank guns.

The attacking Germans, finding the bodies of parachutists with knife wounds or crushed skulls, assumed that these injuries had been inflicted on disarmed Germans after capture. It is possible to say categorically that in most cases they were wrong – misled, because they fought with guns, into thinking that others would be doing the same. But this mistake came on top of and reinforced rumours of bodies with genitals hacked off and eyes gouged out. There were even stories of crucifixions. A German tribunal sitting later was able to establish to its own satisfaction only half a dozen cases of mutilation at Kissamou Kastelli (with another two or three at Rethimnon and about fifteen scattered elsewhere). It seems beyond doubt that some incidents of this sort took place. But far more horrifying was the German reaction. When Kastelli fell they assembled two hundred men and butchered them.

Meanwhile another drama of great importance to the Greeks was being acted out. The Greek king, George, and his (Cretan) Prime

Minister, Mr. Tsoudheros, had been staying in separate houses a short distance behind Khania. The king's was nearest to the town, but the day before the German landing he moved further back to stay with the Prime Minister. As the battle opened, a contingent of parachutists landed in the garden of the house he had vacated. Hitler had identified the king as his principal enemy in Greece and it was now decided to evacuate him from Crete. As the landings continued, the royal party, with an escort of New Zealand soldiers, set out to cross the White Mountains on foot for the south coast. It was a hard, nerve-racking journey.

Right at the start they had to fight off parachutists. Soon another group of parachutists landed within a few hundred metres – but moved off in a different direction. Time after time the king and his companions had to fling themselves on the ground to shelter as best they could from German aircraft. Sometimes they could even see the faces of the strafing pilots. They were also fired on several times by confused local patriots. 'Can't you see we are Greeks?' the king's cousin called out to one group of assailants who held them pinned down from a ridge above. And back came the reply: 'Germans also speak Greek and wear Greek uniforms.'

The party slept near the snow line, the New Zealanders suffering in their shirts and shorts. Next day they descended with bleeding feet into the gorge of Samaria. From Ayia Roumeli, at the mouth of the gorge, the king and his men were taken off on a British submarine. The New Zealanders walked straight back over the mountains to rejoin the battle.

By now, though, that battle was thoroughly lost. The gradual retreat eastwards from Maleme continued, the Allied commanders persisting in pulling back their troops despite a desperately bold counter-attack to recapture the village of Galatas.

The Germans bombed Khania with increasing fury, finally setting the old town on fire. Theodore Stephanides, still without instructions as to what to do if his contingent encountered Germans, tended the wounded in a haze of fatigue and watched the stricken city burn. For many local villagers, he reflected, this was the only town they knew and its burning must have seemed like the end of the world. 'Some of the men had tears streaming down their faces and shook their fists and cursed the Germans.' Only the old quarter round the harbour survived.

Rethimnon and Iraklion still held, but the retreat round Khania was turning into a rout. The last act was the withdrawal of the front line by Brigadier E. Puttick, during the night of 26–27 May. A force sent to relieve him, finding no front line, marched on and on towards the Germans. Finally, they took up a position in which they were effectively annihilated the following morning.

Freyberg now tried to evacuate his men from Sfakia on the south coast. This meant a march across the mountains and a final descent across a bare and roadless mountainside. Mercifully, the air attacks were thinning out as Hitler regrouped his planes for the assault on Russia. But conditions were desperate enough. Men threw away their arms, fought for places on the few lorries, abandoned dignity and courage. Evelyn Waugh tells the story with the bitter accents of truth both in his diaries and in *Officers and Gentlemen*, the second novel in his World War II trilogy. The best account of all, perhaps, is in Theodore Stephanides's book.

What nobody could know at the time, however, was that the evacuation was made possible by the Greek 8th regiment. Without regaining contact with their allies, these men fought on for six days south of the Prison Valley. In doing so, they delayed a south-eastwards flanking move by the Germans which would otherwise have cut the Sfakia road before the fleeing Allied army reached it. Yet all over the island the Greek forces were now simply abandoned. No Greeks were taken off during the evacuation.

Psychologically, the key point on the retreat was the pass over the ridge of the mountains and down into the Sfakiot valley of Askyfou. Here an Australian force held off the Germans, while troops were being taken off far below at Chora Sfakion. The defenders of Iraklion were taken off at dead of night by British naval vessels which raced round the eastern corner of Crete for Egypt. Losses on the return journey from Iraklion were hideous. And now Admiral

Cunningham had to send his tired sailors into Sfakia night after night, always fearing that they would be caught again by air attack. The navy came three nights in a row, but Cunningham refused to sanction a fourth. As a result, five thousand men were left behind. There were ugly scenes in Sfakia on the third night. Guards with drawn bayonets were posted on the beach to ensure priority for the men who had borne the brunt of the fighting. Even so, those likely to be left behind before the end swarmed on to the beach and jetty so that there was no way through for the Australians when they came down from Askyfou, marching in a daze of exhaustion after their last long fight. They arrived to hear the hawsers rattle as the evacuation fleet weighed anchor.

Next day the Germans came down to accept the surrender of the troops left behind; at this point a last and horrifying air-raid took place. North in Rethimnon Lieutenant-Colonel Campbell, through mischance, had not heard of the evacuation. But he realized that his position had become impossible and on the same day he surrendered. The Allies had lost Crete and in doing so had destroyed the finest of Hitler's airborne troops. Now the resistance lay ahead.

The spirit of the resistance is exemplified by an encounter between Theodore Stephanides, trudging up towards Askyfou, and an old man riding down on a pony against the flow of the troops. He was on his way, he said, to shoot 'one of those German pigs, even if it's the last thing I'll ever do'.

The battle for Crete laid foundations for a (temporarily) implacable hatred of the new conquerors. The guerrilla bands that came into existence during the battle did not melt away as one might have expected. One band which originated in May 1941 survived in central Crete until the end of the war. The Germans were still recapturing their own weapons around Kissamou Kastelli as late as 1944. And near Khania Baron von der Heydte, who had been commanding a German force in the Prison Valley and had then accepted the surrender of Khania, was sent one day to investigate a rumour that Greek troops were hidden in a monastery in the

Akrotiri. In his book on the battle, *Daedalus Returned*, he records how he and a fellow soldier were interrupted in their search and brought in to see the abbot.

'In a monastery,' said the abbot with severe dignity, 'one should seek God, not human beings – and you are in a monastery. Here there can be no soldiers. There can be only human beings seeking God, even if they stand in the guise of soldiers.'

Von der Heydte and his companion crept away shamefaced – only to learn later that over one hundred heavily armed Greek soldiers and guerrillas had been hiding all about them.

Ordinary village people were involved from the beginning. Of the six thousand or so Allied troops left throughout Crete, some thousand evaded capture and took to the hills. These men were sheltered and fed by the local population, despite the danger of reprisals. Some were captured and a few were turned in to the Germans; but hundreds were in due course gathered secretly together under the auspices of the abbot of Preveli in his lonely monastery above the south coast. Most of these were taken off by British submarines during August 1941. But there were still hundreds of Allied troops on the island as autumn began and the weather grew more severe.

One of the earlier escapees was Jack Smith-Hughes. Captured by the Germans at Khania, he had escaped and then been helped across the island by a Cretan colonel named Papadakis who owned a threadbare country house high in the White Mountains, and who told him of plans to establish a resistance. Smith-Hughes returned in the autumn to set up a wireless station and co-ordinate, with Papadakis, plans for resistance. Soon another agent was sent into east central Crete to make contact with two guerrilla bands already in existence there. This was the Hon. C. M. (Monty) Woodhouse, who later took charge of all S.O.E. operations on the Greek mainland. He is the leading English-language historian of the Greek civil war; and he was for many years Conservative M.P. for Oxford. In due course these first two British agents were withdrawn and their places taken by a group of three. (All arrivals were at night. The agents came ashore from an odd variety of craft, never sure whether to expect death or a warm welcome as they landed.) In the west was Xan Fielding, a tough and determined man who later wrote in *Hide and Seek* an excellent account of his experiences. The centre was in the care of Tom Dunbabin, archaeologist and fellow of All Souls, Oxford. Away to the east was Patrick Leigh Fermor, now known, though he has written little about Crete, as author of some of the most perceptive books on modern Greece. His original role in the east was later filled by A. M. (Sandy) Rendel, a *Times* journalist whose *Appointment in Crete* makes a good companion to Fielding's book.

It was, I imagine, accidental that so lettered a group of men were involved in the Cretan resistance. They brought their own distinctive personalities to the job and discovered in the Cretans an element of nobility, courage and self-sacrifice to which they responded and in which they shared. There seems to have surrounded them in their dangerous occupation a curious atmosphere of schoolboy daring, of chivalry and of intellectual excitement.

The original aims of the British operation were to collect and pass on to Cairo as much useful military information as possible and to help create an organised resistance ready to spring into action when the moment was ripe. But Colonel Papadakis at first managed to frustrate these objectives.

A man by turns hectoring and cringing, he appeared to Xan Fielding to be interested exclusively in establishing a political position for the post-war years. He had formed a Supreme Liberation Committee, recognised mainly by its own members, and tried to prevent the British from making contact with other resistance groups.

This impossible situation was resolved when Papadakis accepted a crafty offer of evacuation for himself and his family because of the growing danger to the latter. The departure itself was a sinister event. Apparently suspecting a trick, Papadakis ensured that Fielding was covered by two tommy guns all the time that he was signalling out to sea, as prearranged, to call in the navy from the blackness. The rendezvous was missed on the first night, so the dangerous

charade was played out again on the following night. But once Papadakis was gone events at last began to take a more positive turn.

It was a strange life, for Cretan helpers and Allied agents alike.
At first they sometimes lived in villages, protected by the community. But there was always the risk of accidental discovery or
betrayal by an informer, of sudden raids which would end in the
burning of houses and the rounding up and brutal interrogation of
the village people. This became more frequent as German counter-
intelligence improved.

Generally the highlands were safest. In the lowlands the population was both less unanimous and less eager to take quixotic risks.
Reprisals were also easier for the Germans because of the terrain.
But a great many people even here were always willing to work with
the Allies. Nicholas Skoulas, the mayor of Khania who had surrendered the city to Baron von der Heydte, became the secret head
of E.O.K., the non-communist resistance party. In the end he had
to take to the mountains. (E.A.M., the communist group, which
the British were always trying to outflank, was led by General Man-
dakas, who lived in mountain encampments with all the ceremony
of an earlier century of brigandage.) In lowland Iraklion, the leading
agent was Micky Akoumianakis, the lawyer son of Evans's overseer
at Knossos (the father was killed during the Battle of Crete). There
were other successful intelligence gatherers in Rethimnon, Neapolis
and Ierapetra, some of whom paid for this activity with their lives.
And in many lowland settlements there were houses where British
agents could always find a welcome.

But perhaps the place where the resistance fighters felt most at
home was in the high valley of Amari. Here their undercover visits
became a signal for general and generous celebration – even during
the first hard winter of the occupation when Crete was gripped by
famine. The people survived – just – on snails, *horta* and a kind of
bread made from the sticky, sugary carob beans that were usually
reserved for animals. Cretans old enough to remember speak with
uniform horror of that winter of 1941.

With the improvement in German intelligence, the resistance

groups abandoned the villages. Sometimes they sheltered in the little cheese-making huts among the mountains; more often they set up home and wireless stations in caves, living in damp and dirt and cold as Cretan outlaws had done for centuries, and suffering, like Cretan outlaws, from hunger, lice and fleas. They could never linger anywhere; and communications between the different groups, the collection of intelligence and the constant shifting of wireless stations involved endless night marches over the mountains.

Many of the communications between Allied hideouts were carried by Cretan messengers. Of this notable tribe none was more renowned than George Psychoundakis.

Psychoundakis had been a boy of eighteen or so at the start of the war and was left without livelihood when his family's sheep were stolen. Papadakis took the young shepherd on as a messenger, then quarrelled with him and threatened to shoot him. Psychoundakis transferred his allegiance to Fielding. He was, and remains, a quick-witted man, with a natural flair for words and with a gay charm overlying melancholy. But his fame during the years of the resistance was for his speed across the mountains. According to legend, he more than once pressed himself so hard that he fainted on the path. But there is no mention of this in his book *The Cretan Runner*. This is translated and introduced by Patrick Leigh Fermor and annotated by Leigh Fermor and Fielding – and is one of the most singular documents to come out of modern Crete. Though a very personal book, it describes the resistance on behalf of Cretans, and incidentally passes judgements on individuals, which Leigh Fermor for the most part endorsed as strikingly shrewd. The story is told with a direct simplicity and lack of self-consciousness that seems to exemplify some of the finest aspects of Crete. I can do no better than to recommend it.

The long years of resistance were touched both by comedy and tragedy. One of the funniest episodes must surely have been Xan Fielding's first trip to the extreme west during which, for reasons of secrecy, he was represented as a deaf and dumb cousin of his

companion, Pericles Vandoulas. Vandoulas introduced him everywhere with the words, 'You must forgive my poor cousin; he hasn't
been quite the same since the bombing of Canea.'

From time to time the tension was relieved by trips to Cairo,
though the Cretans, finding themselves at first under conditions of
maximum security there, on occasion concluded that they had been
duped and were in captivity. But finally, bereft of their tell-tale
cummerbunds stuffed with daggers and pistols, they were let loose
on the pleasures of the town. It was marvellous to discover a world
where a man could eat and drink and be merry without apprehen-
sion. George Psychoundakis tells how, when asked during the journey to Egypt what he would like for his dinner, he replied, 'Bring
me something of everything and lots of it.'

These trips were preceded, of course, by secret evacuations from
Crete; and since footwear on the island was in desperately short
supply, it was etiquette to take off your boots as you embarked and
pass them back to someone who was staying. Often, with rendezvous
missed and German patrols on the alert, it took weeks to get off
from the island. Landings continued to be agonising. On one
occasion a party putting ashore in western Crete were terrorised
by loud bumping noises in the blackness. The source of the noises
turned out to be sheep in a cave and they all cheered up – only to
find, when dawn broke, that they had been covered all night by the
guns of villagers who thought they had found an isolated party of
Germans.

Supply was a constant worry. R.A.F. pilots did their best to parachute necessities by night to prearranged spots marked by fires. But
given the nature of Crete, with its gullies and ravines and seesaw
countryside, the results were often farcical. The addressees, as it
were, might find themselves better off to the tune of a canister of
powdered milk while shepherds for miles around were set up with
batteries, useless to them but vital to the wireless stations. By the
end of the war the number of locals out and about in the hills would
increase dramatically if there were rumours of a forthcoming drop.

This had its lighter side, but there was nothing entertaining about the occasions when somebody involved in the resistance was captured by the Germans. Usually these unfortunate people were beaten around for weeks before they were executed and it was fair to assume that they would talk before they died. Thus none of the survivors could tell whether they had been implicated and their families placed at imminent risk. A Cretan wireless operator was swept up by the Germans and also the capable secretary of what had been Col. Papadakis's group. The informer said to be responsible died in his own house, close by a German billet, with seventeen knife wounds in his body. At Alones, the son of the parish priest was captured with an incriminating letter on him and led away to death. His father insisted that this was no reason for himself and his other sons to abandon the struggle. 'God is great,' he said, inviting his friends to drink with him to the toast. 'May the Almighty polish the rust off our rifles.'

Courage is the common component of almost every story. A New Zealand sergeant, 'Kiwi' Perkins (later to die in a German ambush), was hit by a bullet which entered his shoulder and travelled some way down his back. None of his Cretan companions knew what to do; but Perkins induced the reluctant guerrillas to cut it out, with the jibe, 'Haven't any of you killed a sheep before?' This incident, coupled with great bravery in action, earned Perkins a reputation that lived after him. Under his *nom de guerre* 'Vassilios' he was accorded the Cretan status of Captain; in 1951 a photograph showing a small girl about to lay a wreath arrived from Crete. On the back of the photograph were the words: 'Grave of the most fearless of fighters ever to leave New Zealand, known to all Cretans as Captain Vassilios. Killed over 100 Germans single-handed during the occupation. Led a guerrilla band and fell from machine-gun fire in February 1944, near Lakkoi – the last gallant Kiwi killed in Crete. This man is honoured by all Cretans.'

The military intelligence sent from Crete was at its most useful about the time of El Alamein. On receipt of a message from Tom Dunbabin, a flight of German transport planes from Crete was intercepted and destroyed over the North African coast. At the very end of the war the Allies bombed some German installations on the island on information supplied through their network. Beyond this there was nothing very concrete to show.

In the fostering of bands capable of armed uprising the British were clearly more successful – though the decision to re-enter Europe through Italy and not through Greece ultimately robbed them of their purpose. Strong bands under strong leaders grew up north of Psiloritis at Anoyia – the leader here was Michael Xilouris – and to the south of the same massif at Kamares. Here the leader was Captain Petrakoyiorgis, the comfortably placed owner of an olive-crushing plant and a man much admired by the British.

Somewhat further east matters were less satisfactory. This was the territory of a gang which had originated in the Battle of Crete, and its leader, Manoli Bandouvas, on that account enjoyed a good deal of prestige. But, unlike Xilouris and Petrakoyiorgis, he had no strategic sense, no broader aim than immediate personal success. This led him into serious quarrels with the British over weapons from parachute drops, and his combined failures as a leader led in due course to a Cretan tragedy. It happened like this.

Eastern Crete was occupied by the Italians, who had come creeping in from the Dodecanese in the last days of the battle. When the Italian war effort collapsed, Patrick Leigh Fermor undertook the dangerous task of contacting the Italian general in Crete and spiriting him off the island – an enterprise which he accomplished successfully. Part of the plan was that the Bandouvas guerrillas should attempt to take over the Italians' arms before the Germans could. They were therefore sent a supply of weapons and promptly and prematurely fell upon a combined Italian and German patrol in the Viannos area in the south-east, killing about one hundred men. Under the orders of the German commander, General Müller, many villages were burnt in reprisal and some four hundred Cretans were taken from their homes and shot.

At about this time the Germans rounded up the villagers of Koustoyerako, a White Mountain village above Souyia in the south-west. Xan Fielding had been closely associated with this village; it was also the home of a family named Paterakis. The half-dozen brothers of this astonishing clan all figured in the resistance, some very prominently. On the occasion of the Koustoyerako round-up, the men of the village had been sleeping out of doors for safety. Now, aghast, they watched from a distance as the Germans lined up the women and children for execution. At this point Kostis Paterakis took aim and from four hundred yards shot the German commander through the head. The Germans fled and the whole village took to the hills.

Not long after the evacuation of the Italian general a plan was hatched to kidnap the German general in charge of Crete and to remove him by the same means. This improbable concept led to perhaps the most celebrated propaganda coup of the entire war. The story is well known and it would be wearisome here to do more than remind readers of its outlines – how Patrick Leigh Fermor and Stanley Moss, with Manoli Paterakis, Antoni Zoidakis and others on the night of 26 April 1944, held up the German general's car not far from the Villa Ariadne where he was living. They passed through over twenty routine road blocks in Iraklion. Finally they abandoned their car so as to suggest that they had left by sea and set off with the general on foot up the slopes of Psiloritis. But it was eighteen days before they escaped from the island with their prize – eighteen days of fearful night marches, of lying up in ditches day after day in pouring rain, of sleeping in cramped caves, of cold, fatigue, illness and mortal danger as the German cordon time after time closed round them. But in the end, with sang-froid unimpaired and with courageous help from Cretan villagers everywhere, they succeeded in their mission.

Analysis of the event today, however, raises questions which few cared to face clearly at the time. First, it was not the much-hated General Müller who was abducted but the more humane General Karl Kreipe. He had replaced Müller while the operation was being planned. When it succeeded, Müller returned to Crete. During one terrible week of reprisal in August the Germans set about the Kedros side of the Amari Valley, killing any men whom they could find and burning and blowing up the villages. While George Psy-choundakis watched from Dunbabin's cave high on Psiloritis, the Germans destroyed Yerakari, Kardaki, Gourgouthi, Vrises, Smiles, Driyies and Ano Meros. I have met people in the Amari Valley who took part in the resistance and now think the likely consequences of the abduction were so great it should not have been risked.

But the question is a complicated one. If there was to be a resistance at all, its success would inevitably be measured in blood and flames. The Cretans have always known this. What they did, although they may now forget it, was of inestimable importance to people in many countries. But to make this point is merely to open a more complicated debate about all wars.

Throughout this period and particularly in the areas devastated after the Bandouvas reprisals, the communists had been gaining ground. One of their leaders was a man named Yannis Podhias, sus-pected of psychopathic tendencies by the Allies, just as they felt that Bandouvas suffered from megalomania. Relations between communist and non-communist guerrillas now became exceedingly difficult. This was happening elsewhere in Greece and those with foresight must have had a premonition of the civil war that was to follow Germany's withdrawal. In Crete, the British agents tried to hold the ring while denying arms to the communists. They had in fact become overtly political and were interfering in Crete's inter-nal affairs just as they were subsequently to do, with decisive effect, on the mainland during the civil war. One result was many un-pleasant scenes with justifiably resentful communist leaders.

Sandy Rendel tells a more cheerful story of a large peace-making assembly in the eastern mountains. 'My own friends used to say', he wrote, 'that the bands got on among themselves just as well as a brace of pistols.' But now Rendel was deeply struck by the romantic and brigand-like appearance of the throng of two or three hundred men, armed with an extraordinary variety of weapons and looking as extravagantly fierce as the *klephts*, the brigand-like sol-diers of the War of Independence. In what must have been a delicate speech, he advocated unity, then left the meeting.

But matters grew worse and worse. With the Germans by now heavily on the defensive, the Allies launched raids into the island, on one occasion destroying a petrol dump at a German airfield near Kastelli Pediados. An American officer, Bill Royce, set about infiltrating demoralising propaganda into the German positions – some of it luridly erotic, designed to raise doubts as to how German wives were getting along at home with Italian labourers. Assailed on all sides, the Germans by turns drew in their horns and then paraded themselves about the lowlands with minatory violence. As a withdrawal began to look more and more likely, the rival bands gathered themselves for the race to fill the power vacuum.

In October 1944 the Germans finally pulled back to Khania, which they continued to hold for another seven months. In Rethimnon there was a brief flicker of fighting between communists and non-communists. Iraklion seemed likely to be the flashpoint.

Allied officers and bands of partisans came tumbling into town before the Germans had even left. Petrakoyiorgis arrived in a captured German vehicle; Yannis Podhias came down on a reluctant horse with a garland of flowers round its neck. Sandy Rendel, who had already been in Iraklion for some time, appeared in British uniform, a fact which embarrassed both himself and the Germans he encountered. Bill Royce rode into town from the airport – in the hope of minimising incidents – sitting beside the German adjutant at the head of a column of German vehicles bound for the west. Meanwhile the people of Iraklion thronged the streets waving Greek flags at the departing garrison. Celebrations became general and, extraordinarily in view of the political situation, remained entirely cordial. Somehow Crete never slipped over the edge into civil war and so the island was spared the fresh horrors that awaited the mainland. But it was a close-run thing. Yannis Podhias and his men went into Ierapetra where they murdered a dozen right-wing refugees from Albania. They in their turn were chased into the mountains, and Podhias was shot dead among the branches of a pine tree into which he had climbed for refuge. There were violent incidents round the gorge of Samaria, though this was a question as much of brigandage as of political quarrelling. And that was as far as it went. Except for Khania, still in German hands, the shattered island began slowly and dispiritedly to pick up the pieces.

From this last phase one or two little anecdotes stand out as archetypically Cretan. A British pilot, returning from a raid on German positions at Khania, passed over Iraklion, so I have been told, just as a wedding party was at its height. The guests were blasting off so joyfully with every weapon they possessed that the pilot reported that he had encountered anti-aircraft fire over Iraklion. Away to the east at Ayios Nikolaos, according to a Cretan tale which must be apocryphal, the Allies now took up the mines planted by the Germans. But they found that the local fishermen had already helped themselves to the explosives; for it has long been a deeply regrettable characteristic of Cretan fishermen that they throw explosive – despite fearful legal penalties – at anything moving in the water.

The war is over; but it is not forgotten. In 1974 two communist guerrillas emerged from the mountains where they had been in hiding for thirty years. As for the Germans, the Cretans seem to bear little resentment. There is a huge German memorial just outside Khania; and since many Cretans now work in Germany and many German tourists visit Crete, mutual tolerance has been established. What lingers is the memory of death, destruction and hardship, bitter to think about but accepted without blame, much as a natural cataclysm, an earthquake, say, or a tidal wave.

Because the island is small one still comes across people whose names became famous in those days. In 1972, shortly before his death, I glimpsed Captain Petrakoyiorgis, old and immensely dignified, as guest of honour on a visiting British warship. He sat in a wicker chair under an awning, his sons and grandsons standing behind and British officers paying court in front.

One of the Paterakis brothers still keeps the little café-restaurant at Souyia, cooking skarus fish in the time-honoured manner of the region, leaving the guts entire and nicking out the gall-bladder through the gill. I have eaten there among a company of Greeks to whom he was still a man to be venerated.

My oddest encounter was in the German cemetery at Maleme. Wandering on the sad hilltop with my family, I fell into conversation with two grave-tenders. They turned out to be George Psychoun- dakis (now hard at work translating Homer into Cretan) and Manoli Paterakis. We were led away, with laughter, to drink *raki*, and heard that both men had recently had an agreeable rendezvous with General Kreipe in Athens. That these two men were now looking after the graves of their former enemies seemed a perfect illustration of the uselessness and pity of war.

7. Town and country

A traveller landing in Crete today, more than three thousand years after the end of the Minoan era, might fairly expect to find an island strewn with fragments of its past, showing copious signs of former glory and of former devastations. But if this were the total of his preparation, modern Iraklion, the island's capital, would come as a severe shock. The fifth city of Greece, despite its gigantic Venetian walls and the harbour fortress that withstood the twenty-year siege of the Turks, despite its rebuilt Venetian loggia and its one or two old and lovely fountains, seems to be built entirely of reinforced concrete. It is a place of tatty modern buildings lacking grace and form, grey and dour, common denominator construction. On a summer's day, at noon, there is a smell of grit and dust. At night corrugated iron shutters are rolled down across the shop fronts so that the roads become so many defiles flanked by what seems an endless procession of lock-up garages. Even in these times of comparative prosperity for the city, the first thing you notice is a look of desolation. The second is the noise. Iraklion clatters and bangs at you from early in the morning – lorries roaring, brakes yelping, men in workshops hammering away at bits of shiny tin. Even at the dead hour of the siesta a solitary motor bicycle racing through town from the Khania gate to Eleftheria Square can stir such a clamour that you imagine thousands of sleepers stirring in sticky beds and turning over to compose themselves again.

On the first day, one knows beyond contradiction that Iraklion is one of the least pleasant cities of the Mediterranean and nothing to do with that splendid imagined Crete of mountains and mountaineers, ancient palaces and tiny churches rich in paintings. Some people later change their minds about it; and I am one of them.

It becomes possible to like Iraklion, I discovered – only people born there actually love it – when you get to know it well enough to pick out fragments and concentrate on them. It is a personal business. Once, for example, from a hotel bedroom, I noticed a building covered in little grey domes, a former mosque, perhaps, or a public bath from Turkish days. I had not seen it from the street, and as I tried to work out which its façade must be, a black cat with white paws materialised on the edge of the roof. Slowly, delicately, the cat marched up one side of a dome and down the other, then gave a little leap to land among the concrete roofs of nearby houses and disappear. Now I took note of washing lines and big square tin cans, whitewashed and luxuriant with plants. Though it was winter and the roofs deserted apart from the cats, I recalled similar scenes in Iraklion on summer evenings, with old men taking the air in their pyjamas and chatting to one another from house to house, safe from the hubbub of the street. I was surprised to find that rooftop Iraklion had become as much a part of my image of the place as the general ugliness from street-level.

Then there are little corners which are positively attractive. Here, for example, is a sultana-processing plant covered in a bushy creeper. There you may find a few old houses standing together but threatened by the approach of apartment buildings. One little district, north of the main through road and about three hundred metres into town from the Khania gate, is all old and all agreeable, with winding alleys and little enclosed wooden balconies from which Turkish ladies once peeped out. It is a part of town which is particularly memorable for me since here I was once entertained to coffee in a boot shop by an Argentinian free-style wrestler. Of Iraklion's Turkish balconies, my favourite is in Kazantzakis Street, just across the road from where Kazantzakis was born (an apartment building

Turkish-style wooden balcony.

marks the spot). From outside, it is a little wooden box of not much distinction protruding from the side of a dilapidated house; but inside, when I saw it, it was surprising and delightful. The room of which it formed part was occupied by a trio of young architect-engineers who had decorated the room as if to express gaiety and idealism – water tank picked out in blue, rays of light in poster paint on a bright blue door. Photographs of Cretan buildings lay about in piles, there were Greek ballads coming from the record player and everywhere a pleasant smell of coffee. The box balcony began at hip height to the room, so that it was more a reclining bed than a floor, made for lying in among a pile of cushions from whence to engage in a covert survey of the street's activity. I lay among the architects' pleasant clutter, imagining these windows to have inspired the lattices from which that tantalising catalyst of tragedy, the wilful Circassian wife of Nuri Bey, looked out with carnal longing in Kazantzakis's *Freedom and Death.* How much it had changed from Turkish days, I thought.

The liveliest place in Iraklion is the market, a slip of a street closed to traffic and lined on either side with a higgledy-piggledy array of stalls – a barber next to a vegetable shop, lambskins next to socks, sides of beef, capons, piles of pigs' trotters, a thin home-made sausage called *loukaniko* wound round and round like a primitive hosepipe. Best of all to look at are the fruit and vegetable stalls. The lovingly displayed fruit is mostly familiar – piles of oranges, plums, quinces: you can tell at a glance what is in season. But the vegetables are constantly intriguing. There is always some new variety of *horta* to admire, anything from a peculiarly tasty variety of dandelion to the leaves of horse-radish. Connoisseurs dwell over them as they might over local wines.

There is also good restaurant eating, of a simple kind, in the market, in a little side-alley where each establishment has a charcoal grill and great pots of beans and trays of stuffed tomatoes. Here many country people in town for the day eat lunch at eleven or twelve in the morning.

Drama is as abundant in the market as foodstuffs. Every little dispute attracts a crowd for whose benefit all passions are portrayed five times as large as life. One day, at a grocer's stall, I saw a man accused of theft by other customers. He had in his hand a plastic bag containing a pair of Cretan knee-boots that were not his own. His story was that he had inadvertently put down his own plastic bag full of meat and vegetables, picking up the bag of boots in error. Not so, said an angry woman in a black headscarf. The boots were

worth far more than the amount of meat that would fit into a plastic
bag. How wrong, how wrong, cried the grocer to a crowd of about
forty, his hands raised above his head like a Byzantine saint's,
why should anybody *buy* meat if he was planning to *steal* boots?

The market is always vivid. But the greatest pleasures it has to
offer are to be found in a cool haven down among the butchers'
stalls. Here, behind what appears at first to be a simple stall selling
cheese and yogurt, there is a deep cranny with shelves along both
sides and hooks along the ceiling; and every inch of space is
crammed and jammed with swelling mounds of herbs. As you walk
deeper inside the shop the herbs press at you, at first delicious to
smell, then suddenly so strong and pungent you feel you will be
overcome. After a while, you begin to accept this astonishing odour
as perfectly natural.

There are three kinds of herbs in the shop – medicinal herbs,
herbs to flavour food and herbs for drinking in a tisane, or tea. Some
are easily recognisable – dispirited sprays of eucalyptus, branches
of thyme, rosemary and oregano. There is basil, cinnamon, bay,
coriander, cummin, pepper, camomile, most of them from Crete.
Others are mysterious – a skeletal mass of fibres turns out to be the
inner parts of a gourd. The most notable is dittany, the magical
dictamus of classical times. It grows only in the island and is known
locally as *erontas*, a Cretan variation of the word for love. Ibex
wounded by hunters were supposed to pluck it from the crags,
achieving an instantaneous cure which almost always enabled them
to elude their hunters. In sober fact, it was collected in historical
times by men swinging on ropes over desperate gorges – a trade as
dreadful as Shakespeare's samphire gathering. Nowadays it is also
cultivated and the tea it makes is highly valued as a restorative and
cure-all.

All this Christos Tsitopoulos, the shop's owner, explains lovingly; but it is over the medicinal herbs that he is most fascinating.
His customers treat him with the respect they would give a doctor,
consulting him quietly over the cheese counter and going away
clutching a little packet. Once, for an upset stomach, Christos Tsito-

poulos gave me tea brewed from a mixture called *saranda dendra* –
forty trees. The idea was that even if thirty-nine of them did nothing
much the fortieth was sure to cure me. It worked a modest miracle.
But some of the remedies are more surprising. Tsitopoulos recom-
mends rosemary for diabetics, saying it reduces blood sugar levels.
(The Greek word for rosemary is *dendrolivano*, but the Cretans call
it *arismari*.) Ivy and laurel seeds, boiled up into a potion in which
you wash your hair, are remedies for the onset of baldness. Then
there is a terrifying herb called *apiganos* from which hot poultices
are made for piles. Henna, once used by Turkish women to tint
the soles of their feet a delicate pink, is now sold to redden hair.

Other herbs are as remarkable for their names as for their supposed action – for skin trouble, *chrysohorto*, or 'golden herb'; for
heart disease, the 'hare herb', *lagoudohorto*; for the stomach, the
'bee herb', *melissohorto*. For dissolving kidney stones there is a
variety of remedies – *kyparissaki* (little cypress); *gorgoyannis* (the
name carries a suggestion of mermaids); and the marvellous *skorpid-
hohorto*, or 'scorpion herb', allegedly found in scorpions' nests.
Tsitopoulos declares (going, I am afraid, beyond the bounds of
credibility) that some Cretans eat scorpions, nicking off the poisonous tail and frying them like shrimps.

It is not surprising that in a town with a shop like this, some of
the older ways survive. I was led once by a friend through a semi-
basement door in what I thought a totally familiar street. I found
myself in a long, dark chamber thick with smoke. As my eyes got
used to the gloom, I saw that a number of middle-aged men were
sitting round the edges of the room puffing away at narghiles. In
theory the place was a café, run by an aged couple who had come
from Smyrna in 1923; in practice it was a club, a meeting place.
'I am not learned,' said one of the members, a heavy, friendly man,
a senior clerk, perhaps, or a businessman in a small way, 'but I like
to talk things over. For me, this is a university.' What he loved most
of all, he said, was to find the roots of words. The narghiles in the
dark room are a rare survival from Turkish days; but the attitude
to conversation is deeply Greek. For older Greeks, in particular,

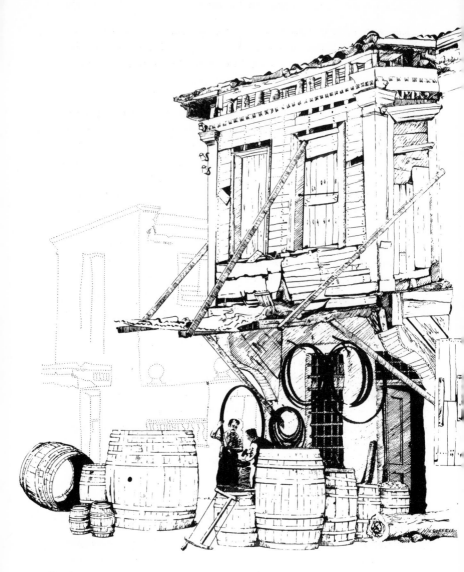

Coopers at work near the old harbour, Iraklion.

conversation is the main medium through which they expect to learn and teach and live. Each summer evening in Iraklion you will see what looks like half the population sitting out at the little café tables of Eleftheria Square, their purpose to see, to be seen and above all to talk.

Many interesting activities are to be found in Iraklion. The simplest way to begin a visit is to stroll through the market or to make the obligatory tour of the town's monuments, but keeping a sharp eye open as you move from one to the next. You could begin, for instance, at the Morosini Fountain with its carved mermaids and exhausted lions, then stroll down August 25 Street – named for those killed on that day in 1898 by the Turks in the prelude to independence – leaving on your right St. Mark's, the rebuilt Venetian loggia and the lovely stone façade of Ayios Titos. After a while you will reach the port and the fortress out on the harbour mole. Its battlements are splendidly, romantically thick; and there are fine views back into town and up into mountains to the west. You will see, no doubt, a cluster of fishing boats and most probably a cruise liner or two, for Iraklion has become a fixed point in most cruise itineraries in these waters. This is because of the proximity of Knossos – though shore-dwellers with a car can reach it in about an hour from either Rethimnon or Ayios Nikolaos. Cruise passengers and package tourists are also lugged in great numbers round the Archaeological Museum in the corner of Eleftheria Square. But other monuments and places of interest are usually less well attended – the icons in the Sinaiite Church of St. Catherine or the rather disappointing exhibition of (reproduction) frescoes in St. Mark's just by the Morosini Fountain. The Historical Museum is better than most of its kind, taking you pleasantly through recorded time with Byzantine, Venetian and Turkish stonework, with icons, oddments, Cretan interiors, marvellous woven cloths, and gold-braided uniforms from the days of Prince George. There is also a replica of Kazantzakis's study; but his most moving memorial is his burial place in a flowery bastion of the city walls. It looks north over the roofs of Iraklion and south to Mt. Youktas, tomb of Zeus.

The epitaph for this most Cretan of writers is taken from one of his own works: 'I hope for nothing; I fear nothing; I am free.' Cretans were always ready to pay a high price for liberty.

Some sixty kilometres due west from Iraklion lies the little port and country town of Rethimnon, a world away whether you take the new road through the magnificent, gaunt hills that line the coast or twist and turn inland past the conical giant of Mt. Strumbulas and over the foothills of Psiloritis. Near Strumbulas beehives stand on the herb-laden slopes and oleanders flower profusely in the dry stream beds of summer. Rethimnon, in contrast to Iraklion, is a gentle, delicate place, tired perhaps, dilapidated certainly, but entirely and always full of charm. It possesses the same peace as the hills that lie behind it, with their huge, twisted trees and rocky little gorges full of bird-song. Rethimnon is not a town that you would wish to shout in.

It stands across the broad neck of a promontory, with on its seaward side the sleepy walls of the huge Venetian fortress. Inside these walls are thistles and pines, ruined official buildings – memories of a citadel that proved in the end notoriously insufficient. Though I have known people enthuse over the fortress, I do not care for it except at a distance. But the town is a very different matter.

Behind a curved and sandy beach, which is protected east and west by harbour moles, there stands a long row of ample houses, their lower storeys inclined outwards at the base to form a buttress in the Venetian manner. At the east end, incongruous but pleasant, stands the little modern Xenia Hotel. The town and its tourists bathe on the beach here, retiring afterwards to the restaurants and cafés which occupy the ground floors all along the front. In the evening their tables and chairs spread out to cover most of the esplanade, taking precedence over traffic. The town also enjoys a reputation for its cakes and honey-dripping Levantine pastries; some of the best patisseries are along the front.

Just by this esplanade, but hidden round a corner, there is a little fishing harbour. The boats are beautifully painted, though the old

Venetian houses at
Rethimnon, one of them
remodelled in reinforced concrete.

Venetian houses – here the ground floors are fish tavernas which smell, deliciously, of frying calamares – are in a state of calamitous decline. Next comes the harbour proper, with small cargo ships moored along the high sea-wall.

It is a varied and appealing front. But the true Rethimnon is tucked away behind, a maze of little streets to wander in with constantly renewed delight. Many of the houses and shops have stone-built Venetian doorways, and peering inside you can sometimes see that other tell-tale sign of the Venetians – stone arches holding up the ceilings. There is a handsome little loggia, now a museum, and many other echoes of Venetian empire. But the dominant architectural feature of the town is the great number of Turkish-style balconies. They float out over the streets feather-light, their ancient woodwork pale and delicate. Some are carved, some plain, some supported on elaborately shaped beams, others on plain bits of wood jutting out uncompromisingly. All of them are beautiful, if seedy; they give an ethereal effect to alleys which are otherwise in summer as stark a meeting place of light and shade as the backstreets of Seville or Cordoba.

In the middle of this part of town there is a nondescript little square, the centre planted with eucalyptus and a bank of oleanders and other shrubs. At one end a mosque stands partly hidden, blank masonry, locked door, prettily fluted minaret. At the other end, also half-hidden, is the Arrimondi Fountain, built in 1623. It is a cool place with columns and Corinthian capitals, beside it the remnants of arches that once roofed it in. This square, with its conjunction of styles, under the invisible walls of the citadel and with the graceful little alleys radiating out from it, is the spiritual centre of Rethimnon.

There are fine views of the town and citadel from high on the Spili road; from here you see how tiny Rethimnon is. It comes as a surprise to think that this fragile little place can be the third city of anywhere, let alone of so challenging an island as Crete. Perhaps the most obvious aspect of its character can be read in its reputation for producing doctors, writers, scholars, university deans – meditative men; and Rethimnon has been chosen as the site for Crete's projected but long-delayed university.

But this is by no means a sufficient account of character, for Rethimnon people have time and again proved themselves heroic, sometimes excessively so, in action. Arkadi, the monastery blown up with patriotic abandon in 1866, is only twenty-four kilometres away and many of the most determined resistance fighters of World War II were from the province – the men of Psiloritis and the villagers of Amari. The people are frank, friendly, unabashed; the area is particularly rich in song and inherited tradition; local arts are vigorous. The virtues which seem peculiarly Cretan flourish abundantly in Rethimnon and its province.

The finest of Crete's towns is Khania, fifty kilometres further west. Iraklion is stridently masculine, Rethimnon is gentle and feminine; but Khania is a satisfying mixture of the two, offering gentle blandishments and vigorous assertiveness. There is something peculiarly stimulating about the town.

The sense of headiness begins with a first glimpse of the mountains. They rise a few miles south of Khania like a long wall, from almost sea-level to eight thousand feet, snow-covered half the year above their low, green foothills. In summer the bald limestone of the peaks still shines white above slopes now tawny-grey like the rest of Crete. The best view of them will be from Suda Bay for anyone arriving by sea; they grow slowly as one's ship approaches. But if you come from Rethimnon along the coast road you see them all of a sudden as you enter the Gulf of Georgioupolis. In either case, the effect dwells in the minds of visitors – Pashley is typical. Opening the account of his travels on 8 February 1834, he writes:

'On entering the gulf of Khania I was struck with the grandeur and beauty of the White Mountains, which well deserve the name bestowed on them by both ancients and moderns. ... The fame of the Cretan Ida is greater than that of these snow-clad summits, and I had some difficulty in persuading my companions that the majestic forms before us were not those of the loftiest and most celebrated mountain in the island.'

There is always the feeling in Khania that this splendid range lies just behind. The shops are full of the things that people take with them to the mountains – steel water-bottles on leather straps, binoculars, boots, shotguns. A fair proportion of the people in the streets have mountain faces – craggy, kindly, but with eyes fixed on objects more distant than those of townspeople. Often they still wear Cretan costume – not the huge baggy breeks of Turkish days, but riding breeches with high Cretan boots, perhaps a cummerbund and waistcoat and very often the little black turban with a fringe of small black beads. Underneath their shirts, winter and summer, they wear thick jerseys of untreated oily wool to protect themselves from sudden changes of temperature. Osbert Lancaster referred to the impression they create as one of 'elegant ferocity' and in towns the effect is rather startling.

The vigour of the mountaineers matches the new parts of town, slowly rebuilt after the fire-storm of 1941. Building for building, it is not distinguished, but there are big shops full of bales and barrels looking as if each could supply a village single-handed. There are woodworkers carving church screens into a rich profusion of grapes and heraldic birds: boot- and shoemakers; knifemakers turning out big clasp-knives with serrated blades – all kinds of small-scale manufacture and larger-scale supply.

One of the most enjoyable places is the market. It occupies a cruciform building modelled on the market at Marseilles, a cool and lofty hall glowing with fruit and vegetables, stacked with cheeses and hung about in quite an orderly fashion with sausages. Near carnival time – just before Lent – there are piles of hideous masks in the toy stalls; and all year round, in one of the transepts, a little restaurant specialising in hooves and the dishes that can be made from them. A barrel of hot water simmers in the doorway while a huge man in an apron is trying to break an ox's shin across the stone doorstep. The fish stall almost next door has a painted sign which shows, as

if to prove that popular painting is not dead in Crete, a maiden
seated astride a huge fish which peeps out lewdly from between her
thighs.

For centuries Khania was the capital of the island. Today it has
lost that position, but it is a town of nearly fifty thousand, the centre
for the agricultural activities of a large part of Crete and the business
centre for much maritime coming and going, even though the port
is now at Suda, a few kilometres to the east.

One of Khania's disadvantages has been the presence of Greek
and American naval bases at Suda. The long blank wall behind
which their affairs are conducted creates a disagreeable impression.
You often encounter groups of sailors on the beaches of Akrotiri,
the peninsula north-east of town, and the Akrotiri mountaintops,
like some of those in the east and near Iraklion, are liberally
decorated with radar equipment – great bowl-shaped scanners and
spiky masts. It is a way of keeping off the evil hour a good deal
less appealing than the Minoan peak sanctuaries which are sometimes
hacked away to make room for them.

The old town of Khania helps you forget the modern military
presence. Like Iraklion, Khania was built within Venetian walls.
Of these only the long battlement in the west remains intact and
a modern hotel has been erected on top of this, so the accent is on
the old town itself and the harbour round which it rises in venerable intimacy.

The harbour is delightful. Its inner recesses are backed by a row
of splendid Venetian arsenals, great vaulted sheds for building and
mending galleys in, now used, spasmodically, for storage only. (A
very nasty hotel, all concrete balconies, was erected here in 1973.)
But the best part of the harbour is the little three-quarter circle by
the sea entrance. A Venetian-Egyptian lighthouse stands on the
mole. Fishing boats ride on the landward side, made fast to the edge
of a road which is backed by houses more beautiful still than those
at Rethimnon. Few modern buildings have so far intruded and the
style is unmistakably Venetian. There is a lovely stairway rising to
first-floor level on the back of a half-arch – an architectural feature

often found in Greece. At one end of the harbour circle stands a purpose-built mosque converted into a tourist information office and shiny restaurant; at the other end, restored and painted a deep puce, a mansion which houses a naval museum. It is a child's paradise, full of models of ships, real bits of torpedoes and portraits of the bearded admirals of Greece's modern wars. Between these two extremes are restaurants serving the best food in Crete. Most of this comes from the sea – red mullet, octopus, calamares and sea urchin salad. The sea urchins come in dripping from the boats, black and spiky in baskets, bales and boxes. Cleaning them is a minor industry. Fishermen on chairs in doorways split the shells with knives, then deftly remove the black goo to extract the strips of orange roe beneath. The salad itself consists of a heap of these roes, drowned in oil and sharpened with a little lemon. You eat it on bread, a teaspoonful at a time, savouring the strong tang of the sea.

In summer the crowds sitting outdoors at the restaurants add to the interest of the eye – bearded German youths in mountain boots, Americans chewing chops; but above all, outnumbering even the foreigners, deftly securing service out of turn, enjoying the view, the sea air and the commotion, the burghers of Khania.

On Sunday evenings the whole town parades here for the *volta*, that massed stroll which is such a feature of Mediterranean life. In Khania first comes a military band, then files of soldiers, sailors and airmen. When they have gone past, winking at the girls and often out of step, all Khania saunters behind.

The district on the little hill above the maritime museum – only a few steps from the harbour front – consists of alleys often not much wider than an armspan. The houses rise high, reminding one of Naples, and, as in Naples, everything is peeling and misshapen. Pink and ochre-painted plaster crumbles overhead. The corners of the first floors are carried out a little way on wooden beams, their undersides clad in planking. There are ground-floor windows with heavy iron grilles, handsome Venetian doorways, fine stone buttresses holding up the lower courses, stone balconies on delicate wrought-iron supports, chimneys built as little pointed towers with lancet windows. Theotokopoulou Street, named for El Greco and running along the top of the hill, is a living museum of wrought iron, with balconies and lights above front doors all covered in a great variety of designs ranging from simple rosettes to pairs of confronted griffins, Byzantine style. Doorways and balconies are full of plants and there is a multitudinous chirruping of canaries hung outdoors in cages.

Neoclassical residence, Khania.

This part of the town is mostly Venetian; and so is the church that houses Khania's Archaeological Museum, a pleasant, gloomy place with a courtyard full of shrubs and statuary and fountains. East from the Museum, in a district named Splanzia, you come across mosques in little squares, then remnants of the city walls and new hotels, and after a while you reach the sea again. The district that lies behind the front on the eastern extreme of town is, or was, a lovely place for anyone with a taste for the neoclassical. For Halepa was the fashionable suburb when Prince George ruled Crete at the turn of the century and many handsome residences were built here. They stand among big gardens with palm trees through which you sometimes catch a glimpse of snow on the mountains behind. Plaster caryatides pretend to hold up the eaves, double stairways curve up to flaking doors.

Unfortunately, Halepa is much threatened by apartment buildings and part-destroyed in favour of a new road to the Akrotiri – all the more pity since scattered among the neoclassical buildings there are earlier echoes. One fine Venetian fountain in a backyard stands out in the memory, together with a roadway vaulted over for ten metres or so and one or two big houses with upper storeys clad Turkish-style in planking. There is something peculiarly attractive about the effect of Cretan sun on wood. The sun makes it seem fragile like bone-china and in the bright light cracks in the wood throw little black shadows fierce as knife blades.

Beyond Halepa lies the Akrotiri, a lobe-shaped peninsula with its airport, military installations, fine monasteries and one or two agreeable beaches. Venizelos's tomb is here on a hill looking down across Khania.

Though there are good reasons for the traveller to spend some time in each of Crete's main towns these should perhaps be thought of equally as gateways to another and in the end a more rewarding Crete – an island of far smaller towns like Sitia or Palaiochora; of mountains, orchards and olive groves; an island above all of villages.

There are eight hundred of them and much of the life of Crete resides among their little alleys and houses.

To make the most of the villages, I have learnt slowly, you must first come to accept a number of unpalatable facts. The most important is that, outside the coastal plains, things are not well with rural Crete. Mostly the land is hard, water is short, payment for produce low and wages in the city more attractive. The population has been draining away to the Cretan cities and tourist spots, to Athens, to Germany and Australia. Houses stand empty and crumble in the winter rains, adding to the ruins of war. You may not immediately come across this aspect of the island since visitors, contributing their own wealth, move by definition mostly among the more prosperous districts. But it exists; and it is as well to know it at the outset. Those who find the sight of a hard life insupportable or who feel that to look at it at all is prying or patronising might do better to keep to the towns and coastal plains. My own feeling is that one should be aware of this aspect of Crete without letting it come to dominate one's thoughts, for what is most remarkable is the way village people retain their good humour and kindness despite the difficulties. The emotions one feels most often turn out to be admiration and gratitude: if you linger just a little, men with trenched faces may insist on your drinking with them; women, no matter how poor they seem, press on you gifts of fruit and cakes. This is the aspect of Crete I failed to see at first, but it is certainly there. No stranger, they believe in many villages, should go away empty-handed and in remote places a visit sometimes turns into a modest carnival. The Greek word for it is *philoxenia* – love of strangers. It is a form of feeling and expression to which Cretans in some parts of the island have held fast since the Bronze Age and which they are conscious of as a strong element in themselves.

For the visitor, it helps to have some sense of the activities of the countryside, if only to reduce by a small fraction the sum total of mysteries. I say small fraction because, though we may *see* Cretan agriculture, it is probably impossible for people from industrial societies to understand what it *feels* like to be a Cretan village farmer.

Village scene, Lassithi plateau.

The rhythms are closer to medieval or biblical times, even to those of neolithic culture, than to the mechanised smash and grab of northern European or American agriculture. It is partly because of the mechanical lag that life is still so hard in Crete; but the slow country ways of the island reflect attitudes, even though they may be dying, which we have sacrificed and now regret.

The olive tree makes a good starting point. The yield from each tree tends to be high and the oil is generally of good quality. But the olive, lovely as it is, makes rather an awkward master. Young trees take so long to mature that they are only planted in very stable periods – you do not see many young trees in Crete at present. The hardest task is the collection of the fruit.

Olives grow on the tree in summer, ripen during the autumn and are ready to bring in from about Christmas. The Cretans use sticks to beat the olives to the ground, letting them fall on nets spread out on the fresh winter grass. A good tree takes several hours to clear, and usually this is a family activity. Out among the groves you may come across a group of trees with two or three harvesters perched in each, beating away and calling to one another like so many birds – a scene also to be found in classical Greek pottery. The work is tiring but often conducted in a festival spirit. Spring flowers are out before the last olives are in, and the snow lies on the mountains – making it a most attractive season.

Many of the little pointed leaves come down with the olives, and these are winnowed out like chaff from corn. The winnowers pick up the olives in scoop-shaped wooden spades, then fling them high and far so that the leaves fall out before the olives arrive on the growing pile. Now the olives are put into hessian sacks and carried to the presses – by donkey, in the boots of taxis, any way you can think of. Most villages have an olive press, known by the Italian word *fabrica*, and here, after the sacks have been delivered, the village people stand chatting round the doorway, like American farmers at a cider pressing. The difference is that the trees here have been tended for several thousand years.

Inside the *fabrica*, the olives are ground to pulp by huge stones revolving vertically round a column. This mush is stuffed into flat, round baskets and squeezed in the press until the black oil comes trickling out. Hot water is used to help loosen the oil, so there is a fire to heat it, glowing orange in the gloom. Later the water is separated out and often goes flowing black and rancid into local stream-beds. The whole process is smelly, with an acid edge. But it is a productive kind of smell and, as with the pig, none of the olive goes to waste. The residue is turned into soap, into animal feed and into *pyrina*, a fuel made of crushed olive stones. As in most Mediterranean countries this is burnt in little metal bowls that stand on the floor, the dead-looking grey ash glowing most prettily when it is raked.

After the olive, the grape is perhaps the most characteristic fruit of the island. The vines still grow quite generally and most districts have their own wines. The best of these are red; they come from Sitia, Kissamou and, as in Venetian times, from the district of Malevisi between Iraklion and Phaistos. Here the broad valleys are as full of knobbly, tight-pruned vines as the Moselle and curiously reminiscent of it. Some of the cheaper Cretan branded wines are beginning to acquire a nasty chemical taste, and it is better to buy, if you can, straight from private barrels in the villages. Another change is that retsina, until recently a rarity in the island, is now being manufactured in Crete.

There are also many – and delicious – eating grapes, and sultanas are produced near Iraklion and round Sitia in the east. The vines are pruned in spring at the time when the bright yellow *martolouloudia* or March flowers bloom in huge profusion all about the vineyards. The clipped branches of the vines are carried home by donkey to be stacked on flat roofs or in courtyards as firewood for next winter. The grape harvest begins in the middle of August and this is another time of great activity in the countryside. When the vines have been stripped, the wine grapes are pressed, often, still, by foot. The sultana grapes are dipped in a solution of soda to drive out the moisture, then spread in the sun on big flat patches usually made of concrete. Finally, they are washed and packed and most of them exported.

This can be paralleled in other parts of Greece; but in one important way Crete remains different. This is that vineyard owners are allowed to distil *tsikoudia* (or *raki*, as it is often called), a fierce liquor made, like marc or grappa, from the stalks and skins of grapes left over from wine pressing. Cretans, who are not so abstemious over drink as other Greeks, consume *tsikoudia* copiously in little glasses, clinking them together with fierce joviality so that everyone drinks at once and nobody is left behind. But it is very rare to see anyone drunk to the point of sickness or collapse.

Oranges grow well in western Crete. There are bananas round Maleme, at Malia on the north coast and Arvi on the south; but, if one must speak true, the potato is rather more widespread – and it brings its own attraction in the shape of the little windmills used to hoist water from the wells for irrigation.

The corn harvest in many parts of the island owes little to mechanical invention; and here one sees how hard people have to work in economically backward districts. The corn or barley may be cut and gathered by hand, then threshed on the old circular threshing floors of ancient times. Donkeys or oxen plod round and round, dragging behind them a kind of sled which the driver rides on and which, with his weight, has the effect of breaking up the ears. Afterwards, on the corners of windy hills, the winnowing takes place. The chaff flies high in the air, catching the sun like copper filings in a fire. It is backbreaking work and I do not believe that anyone enjoys it, however attractive it looks to alien eyes.

The milling of cereals, though, is efficiently mechanised and this change has produced some of Crete's most splendid ruins. The old corn mills were huge affairs, big stone towers rounded on the windward side. Bereft of sails they stand in gaunt honey-coloured rows along the crests of hills or at the heads of valleys. Many of the finest are near Ayios Nikolaos – on shoulders of hills up by Neapolis and on the ridges between Elounda and Fourni. There are other fine mills on the way up to Lassithi. Strong and empty now, they carry a symbolic value quite different from that of forts and watchtowers.

So too, of course, do the shepherds, engaged in an occupation unchanged for centuries. They graze their flocks of goats and sheep on open land, particular areas belonging by ancient usage to particular villages. In winter the flocks are kept close to the village; but in the summer months some shepherds move to the high hills, living in twos and threes in small stone huts called *mitatos*. They come down only from time to time for supplies and it is often a very long walk indeed to the womanless existence of a shepherd's summer pastures. Each year fewer shepherds make the trek. It is sad or not, depending on your attitude, but it is only to be expected.

Perhaps the one surprising aspect of Cretan agriculture is the most recent development. Farmers round the little south-eastern town of Ierapetra and in the Mesara have found that they can take advantage of the long hours of sunlight by building greenhouses of plastic sheeting on simple wooden frames. Here they force early crops of fruit and vegetables, moving on from tomatoes and cucumbers to melons and watermelons as the season advances. Row upon row of these greenhouses behind the sea create a curious effect, as if there were two seas divided by a beach. Unfortunately the sun destroys the plastic by the end of summer. The wind strips it from the frames and it goes blowing about the coast in desolate streamers.

Much of the activity of Crete goes into producing food and drink for the home. In a reasonably fertile district each family will have, by inheritance, a number of little plots, each like an allotment, and called a *kipos* – literally, a garden. There are no paid jobs in the village for ordinary folk. The only people who draw salaries come from somewhere else – the priest, the policeman, the passing postman or visiting doctor – and those without enough land are virtually forced to move away. Curiously, few Cretans adopt the customary Greek remedy of going to sea.

The villagers work in unison, each man pruning his vines or bringing in his corn at exactly the same time as his neighbours. And working hours are identical, as if there were security in common action. Cretan farmers and their wives rise early, have perhaps a rusk and a tiny Greek coffee, saddle their donkeys, call up the dog and ride out to the fields by half past six or seven. In unsettled weather most people sling an umbrella on the saddle, putting it up at the first drop. Donkey riders under raised umbrellas create an odd effect, as if of pageantry.

Work in the *kipos* goes on till eleven or twelve. Then, if a family finds itself near the village, all its members may go home for a mid-day meal. Otherwise they will picnic from the bright little woven

At rest outside the *kafeneion*.

bags that everybody carries in the country. These are laced round the top with a cord that also goes over both shoulders like a knapsack. After lunch it is back to work again until four or five o'clock. Then, well before dusk, men, women and children, donkeys and mules, goats, sheep and dogs, begin to flow slowly homeward. This is one of the loveliest hours in Crete, a time when the closer you are to a village the busier are the roads and paths with little caravans converging as they come back from the fields. And now, while daylight lasts, the women, who generally work harder than the men, prepare the evening meal. The men repair to the village coffee-shop (or *kafeneion*). Sitting on little wicker-bottomed chairs round tin-topped tables, they play cards or chat with absorption over a *tsikoudia* and the small snack that accompanies it. Women do not go to the cafés. But it is not a long evening. By nine o'clock most people have had their evening meal and are in bed asleep.

Cretan villages are tightly packed. The fields end at a well-defined point and there the village begins as it means to go on, houses

Some Cretan village houses. *Left*, Sfakia; *centre*, Rethimnon; *right*, Dikte massif.

running beside the lanes in unbroken, higgledy-piggledy terraces. From far away, being compact, they often look beautiful, up on the shoulder of a crag, perhaps, or in a cup formed by the hills. At night, high above in the mountains, they ride mysteriously on the dark like floating islands or ships at anchor with portholes glowing.

When you get near you may at first be disappointed. There is no strongly insistent architectural style as in the Cyclades or Dodecanese. Everything is somehow ill assorted and every vista tends to have a telegraph pole in it, or a ruin, or a pile of rubbish. There can be an air of seediness even in the prosperous villages, which people passing quickly by will often take to be the whole story. In fact, if you approach the villages slowly, dawdle over a coffee, fall into conversation with one of the old men, you will see that you were partly wrong about the architecture, even if not about the messiness. There is not one style, but several, all woven together with different elements predominating in different places. In the

east, for example, almost all the roofs are flat. The walls are plastered and whitewashed, but usually there is a pleasant frame of stonework around windows and doorways. Most doorways are arched. With a shuttered window on either side, the effect of a house of this kind – in good condition – is simple and pleasing.

A few villages in the remoter places are built in the same way but entirely in rough stone except for the frames around the doors and windows. Generally they have retained their natural warm brown colour, despite an attempt by the authorities during the 1930s to get all the country's villages whitewashed.

So there are two kinds of eastern village, white and brown. There are also all kinds of little variations to catch the eye. Door knockers all over Crete are attached to frail metal discs decorated with random perforations. Sometimes the doors are double with a raised central plank which may be elaborately carved. The front doors in the mountains south of Lassithi are like stable doors except that only a top quarter can be opened by itself, not half. Sometimes the houses stand right on the street, but often there is a little courtyard (or *avli*) full of washing and pot plants in square, whitewashed tins. Many of the old houses have outdoor ovens, humpy whitewashed domes recognisable also by their blackened mouths. The fire is lit inside the oven and the smoke allowed to escape from time to time by unplugging a small hole. When the heat is intense, the fire is raked right out and the bread popped in to bake in the hot air.

Detail of weathered wooden door.

As you move westwards in the island the incidence of pitched roofs slowly increases, until in the province of Rethimnon it becomes unusual for a house to have a flat top. Often the roofs slope one way only, falling from a high wall on one side to a low one on the other. Rethimnon houses are sometimes long and narrow with the front door in the end. There are many remnants of Venetian houses in the foothills of Rethimnon and Khania, reduced perhaps to one or two storeys in Turkish days and finally taken over by the village. Usually the pattern of inheritance has split them into three or four so that it is hard to see just what belonged to what. You may encounter a handsomely sculpted escutcheon over the doorway of what seems a simple village house or find a family in tiny rooms, once perhaps sheds or storerooms, around the cobbled courtyard of a vanished mansion. It is a little dispiriting. In some places the houses interconnect so that you can enter one and emerge from another forty metres away – a reminder of the subterfuges by which village people kept alive during the unpredictable tyranny of the Turks.

In Sfakia it is all change, for here the old houses have a wide arch in front and the door is in the deep shadow under it. The roofs are flat and houses are almost invariably free-standing.

There are, of course, some kinds of house which can be found everywhere in the island; the prettiest of these are the modest, single-storeyed neoclassical buildings put up in many villages from the turn of the century until about 1950, with plain exteriors almost always painted some bright colour, and steeply pitched roofs. One or two villages are built almost entirely in this style.

There is one last style about which it is impossible to find a kind word. Reinforced concrete has dealt the richer villages of Crete a devastating blow since 1950. Because it is simple to use and relatively inexpensive, people have gone mad with it, to a greater extent even than elsewhere in Greece – right angles everywhere, rigid metal fences and balcony railings, concrete pillars often painted puce in honour of Knossos. Inside there are reconstituted stone floors and a brisk impersonality. These houses are in many ways more efficient than the old ones – though they fail in the essential function of keeping out extremes of heat and cold. One must regret also how little the possibilities even of reinforced concrete have been exploited; one seldom comes across a new stairway that has been shaped sculpturally like its predecessor, or a rounded wall, or any feature that shows the old feeling for plastic form. Another unattractive feature is the customary door of glass and steel with gilded bars across the glass. These are installed in old houses as well as new and, unbelievably, in many of the Byzantine churches.

The pity of it is equally obvious when you begin to look inside the old houses. Many of the interiors are delightful. The Venetian-style arches are the most striking feature, springing up in a great hoop from floor-level to support the ceiling. The bigger arches give a surprising sense of loftiness to single-storey houses and they are extremely graceful. In the village of Mourni near Lake Kournas I saw one which was just over five metres wide and nearly four metres high, with one big room on either side of it, each divided up for different uses. Here, when the family wanted more space, instead of demolishing the old house they had added a modern room on one corner. It could have been an object lesson for the rest of Crete.

But some aspects of the old houses are quite unsuited to their modern inhabitants. In the village of Sklavi south of Sitia I once visited a house which had no chimney. It was tiny – so tiny that the chairs were hung up on the walls after use – and the smoke came billowing out through the front door. In Kalogerou in the Amari Valley I enjoyed an excellent *raki* in a house where the animals used the same front door as the family. Though there was a certain pleasing oddity in meeting a donkey on the threshold one could scarcely argue for the perpetuation of the arrangement. But equally it would be a grave loss to Crete if all the oddities were to be ironed out and a suburban sameness spread over mountains and valleys.

Government grants have recently been made available to modernise old houses. For the point is that many of the old houses can be made at least as comfortable as a new house and for far less money than it takes to build one. But those who sell reinforced concrete have persuaded village people to be ashamed of their own homes. For five thousand years it came naturally to Cretans to build their houses beautifully, but today scarcely a house goes up which is not offensive to the eye.

One feels also that the days of the vast clay storage jars (*pitharia*) are numbered. Many of the old houses have a row of them, usually whitewashed, holding all kinds of staple foods which keep well in the even temperature they provide. But few, if any, *pitharia* are made today, and people turn naturally to steel barrels and refrigeration.

Everyday life in Crete nevertheless retains its closeness to the rocks and soil and, even more important, to the roots of society. To experience this last quality, you have to abandon the town as

completely as possible. Once, I remember, I decided to walk from
Sitia to the little monastery of Faneromene a few miles to the west.
It was a spring day and as I climbed the hill above the little seaside
town the barking of dogs and the hammering from building sites
grew faint behind me. There were marguerites on the hill and, more
sparsely spread, the gaunt, upstanding asphodel. After a while I
found myself following a line of cliffs, the water below a thrush-
egg blue. Then I joined a dirt road, encountering a young man
named Nikos who kept a *kipos* out by the monastery. He walked
there daily, an hour each way, carrying his lunch done up in a che-
quered cloth. We strolled together through the spring landscape,
until a passing pick-up truck gave us an unsolicited lift. Now our
progress was headlong, even if upwards, until we came to a corner
where a tethered donkey had crossed the road, stretching his rope
waist-high behind him. We slithered to a stop in time and pulled,
pushed and prodded him to safety.

In a moment we were at the monastery, an undistinguished
cluster of buildings. Nikos and the two men from the pick-up
accompanied me into the church, kissed the icons and lit candles.
But really it was nothing much to look at – a screen, a totally blackened ceiling which had once had frescoes, a cluster of little silver
plaques hung on a string as if on a washing line. These plaques are
found in almost every church. They usually represent a part of the
body and are left behind in hope of a cure by worshippers afflicted
in that part. Plaques showing babies are distressingly common.

Had it not been for Nikos and the driver I would have missed
the essence of the place. They led me to a tiny cave, behind the
church, perhaps two metres deep, shaped like the blade of an axe
driven into the rock. Its floor was covered with a dirty rose-pat-
terned oilcloth, on which stood many oil-lamps, made of soft drinks
bottles with a twist of cotton for a wick. Then there were little
pewter-coloured saucers full of the ashes of incense. And on the
walls of the cave, in every crack and crevice, there were tens upon
tens of icons, framed and glazed and all in the worst chocolate-box
style. The place was tatty and sacred-seeming all at once, a tender

evidence of the human regard for divinity. It reminded me most strongly of the cave of Eileithyia, goddess of childbirth, a neolithic and Minoan shrine near Amnisos where the votive offerings were equally frail and moving. To see the Faneromene cave by accident, on a spring day, with people who believed in its sanctity and eagerly led me to it, was profoundly moving.

After the monastery Nikos took me to his *kipos*, where he had a plastic greenhouse. He loaded my arms with prickly cucumbers and pointed me along the path for home.

After a kilometre or so, in a valley full of the sound of water, a big old man in a forage cap stood up from pruning vines a hundred metres downhill.

'Where are you from?' he called to me.

'From England.'

'Where are you going to?'

'Sitia.'

'Where have you come from now?'

'Faneromene.'

And then, his voice ringing above the running water, he told the story of the monastery. Long ago an icon of the Virgin Mary miraculously appeared in the cave. A church was built for it. But the Virgin preferred the cave and shortly reappeared there – another miracle. This happened once again, and on a third occasion when the icon was removed to the village of Skopi. There was yet another miracle associated with the church. During the nineteenth century two Turks tried to burn it down and succeeded only in making a mess of the frescoes before the Lord struck them with a sudden and fatal sickness.

I thanked the old man warmly for the story and went on my way with the cucumbers, feeling that the countryside about me was merely the temporary and visible expression of an almost unlimited past.

This same sense assails you all over Crete and usually in a journey of any length you will see more layers than I encountered that spring day. Let us take, as an example of the complexity you might experience anywhere, a trip from Ayios Nikolaos to Ano Viannos, due south but cut off by the Dikte massif. To get around the mountains you travel east on the easy corniche road round the Gulf of Mirabello. First you pass lime kilns, then a *pyrina* plant, and after that a place marked by trees and rushes where huge quantities of precious but brackish water flow out underground into the sea. Passing delectable swimming coves, you come after twenty minutes' driving to Gournia, the Minoan artisan town beside the sea. Soon you turn south across the isthmus of Ierapetra, the big Sitia Mountains dropping in a sheer rock wall to the left, at one point split by a breathtaking crack with a church at its base. All the way, Dikte climbs up in fits and starts to the right. At the village of Episkopi, half-hidden by the road and probably escaping notice, there is a curious little church. One half is surmounted by a Byzantine dome, the other is in Venetian style. The Orthodox community worshipped under the dome, the Catholics under the arch. Next stop is Ierapetra, originally a Dorian state. It became important in Graeco-Roman times and in this century has contributed a headless statue to an Iraklion square. Ierapetra was later the seat of a Byzantine bishopric, and the remains of a Venetian castle can still be seen. Today it is becoming a tourist town, popular with young foreigners in winter and remarkable for a barber's shop as full of sea-shells and sea-monsters as the cave of Faneromene with icons.

Now the road turns west along the coast through the great sea of plastic greenhouses and past the hill at Mirtos where Peter Warren excavated an important Minoan site in the 1960s. Next it climbs into facsimile Wild West country among near-vertical clumps of hill. Then it goes higher still and passes a string of villages – Ayios Vasilios, Simi, Pevko, Krevata, Kefalovrysi, Kalami, Vakho, Amira and others – burnt by the Germans after the Bandouvas episode.

Ano Viannos is almost a town and has a number of painted churches. A mountain stream has been channelled to drop down through a series of little stone towers in each of which there was once a corn-mill. Two of them were still in use when I visited

Viannos, and made a pleasant conclusion to a day's journey through time.

Usually in Crete you have to recover from the shocks induced by the landscape before you can concentrate on human affairs. A good example is the Amari Valley, with Kedros and Psiloritis always ready to impose themselves on your interpretation of everything. But Amari, also, demonstrates how inextricably past and present are bound up together.

Take, for instance, the classical inheritance. On the site of the modern village of Thronos there once stood a substantial ancient Greek township named Sybritos. It is comparatively high and local shepherds taking their flocks to summer pastures still speak of 'going to Sybritos'. Then there is the mosaic, recalling early Byzantine glory, and the paintings, to evoke later Byzantine days.

Just down the road is Genna, a hamlet inhabited almost entirely by Greeks from Turkey who replaced Turkish inhabitants in 1923. The atmosphere is somehow more cosmopolitan. A little down the valley is a monastery, visited by Pashley, and now an agricultural college. Its huge pigsty is built like a European cathedral with a high central nave and low aisles. Thumbnail-sized oranges named *cum kwats* grow here, bitter and delicious, and there is one of those vast plane trees that so often stand at the centre of Greek villages.

In Meronas at the head of the Amari Valley I was offered almonds the shape of candle flames and drank *raki* with an old man in a room full of photographs of his grandfather and father, his own wedding-day and those of his sons and daughters now spread out from Chicago to Melbourne. He couldn't retire, he said, because there was no one to help him with his land. The village of Nefs Amari has, I learnt, a tradition of sending its sons to Africa, whence they return in old age to lay their now wealthy bones in Orthodox soil. Here too I drank much *raki*, though I managed with difficulty to say 'no' in Vistagi, a village which is almost entirely neoclassical. A little further south, almost within sight of the coast, lies Ayia Paraskevi, a spiritless little place with a lovely church and otherwise remarkable only for having produced Stylianos Pattakos, right-hand man of the dictator Papadopoulos in the regime of the Colonels from 1967 to 1973. Even though Pattakos had fallen when I went there, the village was still extremely proud of him and had, who knows why, a brand-new asphalt road of surprising width. The country around is beautiful, full of little conical hills dotted with trees. These same hills, lit by a mysterious light and inhabited by huge partridges, were a favourite subject of a primitive painter named Markakis, one of the wardens of Phaistos.

The countryside of Crete, for those who care to unravel its secrets, is full of remarkable sights. As one travels, notebooks and memory become loaded down with minor wonders. In a gorge near Rethimnon there is a beautiful and entirely deserted village named Milo. The rocks hanging over it account for its desertion and its architectural purity. At Mates, a ruined village behind the Gulf of Georgioupolis, there is a chapel said to date from the fourteenth century, built inside the roots of a giant carob tree. Near the Dorian ruins of Lato I found a shepherd's hut with a segment of an ancient column in use as a table. Then there are the caves and gorges, the beaches, the high mountain plains. One could spend a very long time in Crete without managing to see every place of interest or natural beauty.

Most of Crete can nowadays be reached by road, posing the problem of whether to go by car or bus. There is a lot to be said for the latter. The buses are great raucous creatures that go swinging along the mountain roads, horns bellowing, piloted by stern-looking men whose tender side is expressed by the decorations in their cabs – framed photographs of film stars, mothers, sisters, wives, bunches of fresh and plastic flowers, and almost always a medallion of St. Christopher and another of the Virgin. Inter-city buses run east and west along the north coast all day, but the village buses come into town in the morning and go back in the evening, the wrong way round for visitors. So often enough one finds oneself obliged to travel, if one can, by car.

There are, however, some parts of Crete where the traveller must still go on foot. The most famous of these is the great gorge of

Samaria, a cleft which runs down from the centre of the Lefka Ori
(the White Mountains) to the Libyan Sea and is worthy of its reputation, even though an ever-thoughtful Ministry of Tourism has
installed litter bins and metal trays for stubbing out forbidden
cigarettes.

To reach Samaria you first travel to Omalos, a high, flat plain
celebrated in folksong. It takes a bus from Khania two hours
of huffing and puffing upwards. Here you disembark and perhaps
spend the night – there is a Tourist Pavilion, at which it is wise to
book in advance – and in the morning plunge over the lip of the
gorge, down, down and down, almost six thousand feet, descending
through pines, past gushing springs, while the mountains rise higher
above you. At the bottom the path winds more sedately downwards
among abandoned olive groves, cypresses and chestnuts. A stream
runs with you, sometimes invisible under the big, round pebbles,
sometimes breaking out, suddenly noisy, to form pools big enough
to swim in; this is in summer – in winter the gorge is an impassable
torrent. You pass, at a particularly lovely point, the little cluster
of houses from which the gorge takes its name. This was the old
stronghold of the Viglis family, descended from the Archontopouli,
that imported Byzantine aristocracy.

Finally the vast walls of rock close in until they are only a few
yards apart. This strange, forbidding place is called the Sideroportes
or iron gates. Soon after it you walk through a straggling village
and finally reach the sea at Ayia Roumeli. No swimming is ever
so good as here, no beer so refreshing.

The walk is sixteen kilometres; it takes four to five hours and
is pleasantest if started in the very early morning. From Ayia Roumeli you go on to Sfakia by boat, tiny under the awesome coast,
and on again to Khania by bus. The way not to do it is with one
of the organised tours that in recent years have begun to march their
chattering clients down this trail, once one of the loneliest in Greece.
Tours save time by providing instant transport at either end. But
there is no guarantee that your companions will not complain of
blisters all the way; and it is too beautiful a place to enter under

someone else's orders. Despite the metal ashtrays this is, without doubt, one of the most beautiful walks in Europe.

If you have an appetite for solitude you will find it almost anywhere else in the Lefka Ori by the simple expedient of walking out of sight of the road. Here the only people on the hills are shepherds. One should, however, look before leaping. The paths, such as they are, are hard to distinguish from animal tracks and usually there is no water. This being said, the country is magnificent and poignantly desolate.

The same sense of remoteness lies over many of Crete's numerous offshore islands. Some are uninhabited and seldom visited, like Dia, north of Iraklion where Jacques Cousteau has claimed a Minoan find, or Gramvousa. This last, with the crumbling ruins of a Venetian fortress, is off the rhinoceros-horn peninsula of the same name in the extreme north-west of Crete. Then there is Spinalonga, another fortress islet, across from Elounda in the east. Here the ruinous lion of St. Mark presides; but at the foot of the fortress there is an empty village used until 1955 as a leper colony. Tourists are now taken there by boat, making an extraordinary spectacle as they wander in bright and scanty summer dress through alleyways that almost seem to smell of human wretchedness. The island is beautiful – beautiful and repugnant.

South of Ierapetra is Gaidouronisi – Donkey Island – long, low and tempting. In the Gulf of Timbaki, where the Mesara runs down to the sea between Psiloritis and the Asterousia range, there are the shoe-shaped islands of Paximadia which sometimes feature in the paintings of Markakis. But to my mind the best of the Cretan islands is the most distant – Gavdos, forty kilometres south of Palaiochora, alone in the Libyan Sea.

A big caïque trundles to and fro about twice a week; but often local people only are allowed to go on it, the risk being that, if visitors were stranded by bad weather, supplies on Gavdos might run perilously low. For Gavdos is threadbare and, until the tide of tourism finally reaches it (this year, next year, sometime, never), has barely enough to sustain its three hundred or so inhabitants. But the people, as I found when I visited Gavdos with my wife and an English sculptor whom we had encountered by a happy chance (before the travel ban), are as gentle and courteous as anyone could wish to meet.

The journey began well, for it was apparently the habit of the skipper of the caïque, Captain Emmanuel Bikakis, to brew up fish stew for his passengers. We ate it eagerly, shading our eyes and watching Gavdos grow bigger across the brilliant sea. Skipper Bikakis told tales of war, of fearful storms and splendid fishes. Finally we drew near Gavdos, chugged past a wide beach and round a headland, to drop anchor in an undistinguished cove. From this apology for a harbour we walked across the headland and down a prickly valley to a beach. Here a caïque was being built, the ribs in place and waiting for the planks. With absolute trustfulness the carpenter had left his tool kit spread out on a cloth beside the wooden skeleton. That evening, after we had climbed the hour-long path to the main village, we were welcomed not with any overbearing exuberance but with politeness and real consideration for our wants. The three of us were given seats on the customary wicker-bottom chairs in a general store stuffed with the cheapest version of everything that might prove necessary. Here we were engaged in grave conversation. Who was married to whom? How many children had we? What work did we do? We for our part inquired about Gavdos – where did its children go to school? Was there a doctor? Did the men leave the island? It grew dark quickly as it does in Greece; a lamp was lit; more and more people crowded into the store to join the quiet conversation. Though the answers to our questions were not entirely happy, a sense of peace spread out as if from the lamplight and stayed with us long after we had returned to the mainland.

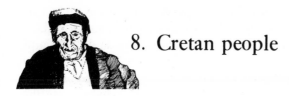

8. Cretan people

As elsewhere, so in Crete: history and landscape are, in the end, of less importance than the people who spring from them, and the depth of one's response depends on the friends and enemies one makes. Enemies are hard to come by – unless one gives offence by ways of behaviour that a deeply conservative society cannot tolerate. But friends are easier to find. The warmth of the villages is often paralleled in the towns – even in the tourist towns where one might least expect it. All that is needed is a willingness to find it. So great on occasion is the cordiality, the *philoxenia*, that one sometimes wonders if it can have much personal meaning. Even so, one can only experience it with pleasure. But where genuine contact is made and loyalties exchanged, no friend is likely to prove more long-lasting than a Cretan. Full of notions of *levendi*, the *palikare*'s attitude of gallantry, Cretans do not call friendship into question once it has been given. Whether this makes people more honest in business dealings than elsewhere in Greece or less likely to claim they will perform what they plainly cannot, I doubt very much. But certainly Cretans preserve the ideal of honour in friendship; and for this one is bound to feel admiration and gratitude.

There is also the question of how greatly people differ in different parts of Crete. Many writers profess themselves as having found a special geniality in the people of the east and a closed-in obduracy among the Sfakiots in the south-west. The Cretans themselves believe that this is so and perhaps subconsciously act out the belief. They also credit each city with its own characteristics – Khania for arms, goes the old saw, Rethimnon for learning and Iraklion for drinking. There is a fourth line, not repeated quite so often, which credits the people of Sitia with 'making love like swine'. I am not sure about Iraklion as a special preserve of the bibulous; nor that Sitia, agreeable as it is, is laxer in its *mores* than other parts of Crete. Khania, on the other hand, has aspects that appear to betoken resolution and Rethimnon undoubtedly possesses a tradition of learning. But however true or false the rhyme, it seems to me a great pity to spend too much time on fitting people and places neatly together.

People in Crete, as anywhere, may be typical of this or that, but unless one sees them as individuals one sees virtually nothing. And it is in these terms that one must write of them. Here I shall simply describe a number of differing people and incidents: a Sitia family with whom I lived for a while, and some of their friends; a journey, only moderately happy, with shepherds in the Lefka Ori; and conversations with a doctor in Rethimnon.

George Nikolarakis (almost all Cretan names end with the diminutive '-akis') is a barber in Sitia. He was in his early forties when I got to know him and a man whose ruling characteristic was good nature. I have seen George in many situations and though he may have been miserable at the turn of events or angry at somebody else's action I have not yet seen him fail in face-to-face kindness. It is tempting to describe him simply as a good person and to extend the same description to his wife Katina – big, sighing Katina with the lovely singing voice and sloppy slippers.

Their house is high on the hill in Sitia and from a parapet on the road in front of it you can look down over the town – now a quiet, moderately pretty little place of no great note – and across the bay to the mountains opposite, grand at all times, green in spring and dotted with ivory-white chapels. The house itself is fairly new and simple – a tiny basement entered from the street, useful for parts of motor cycles and broody turkeys; above that is a floor with a fair-sized living-room, dark little kitchen, indoor lavatory and three bedrooms, all very cold in winter, with cement floors and green-washed walls. Above again there is a floor to let out to summer visitors, for tourism is fast becoming the main summer business of Sitia. I stayed in the house one year as winter shaded into spring, enjoying a friendliness that never faltered and which has been unquestioningly renewed on other visits. Much of my time I spent with Katina, idly watching as she prepared the great meals around which the day revolved and discussing the welfare of her huge family of sisters, uncles, aunts and cousins or her own two children – Betty, then aged fifteen, and Ritsa, a shrill, mercurial nine-year-old. But very often I was out with George, taking part in his intricate daily programme. For as well as barber he was a hard-working smallholder, keeping himself extremely busy even when the town was empty of tourists. With the barber's shop due to open at eight in the morning, he would set off for his *kipos* at half past six; and frequently we went together.

The journey was a shattering event for we travelled in George's *mikani*, a machine like a three-wheeled motor scooter with a little cab of blue fibreglass to sit in and at the back a carrying space like a miniature pick-up truck. The cab was so close a fit that, when

The *mikani* – a favourite form of transport.

we were both inside, one of my arms had to go round George, the other out through the window. The doors had a tendency to fall open going round corners, the foot pedals were worn to stubs and often had to be jerked by hand. In front of our noses as George drove, images of St. Christopher, St. Nectarios the healer and the Holy Virgin swung with wild abandon. Behind, and more especially when George was in the cab, the *mikani* sagged so much it seemed to scrape along the ground like a dog with worms. But the most remarkable aspect of this machine was the noise it made – a hooter like a pig in a slaughter house and an engine which effortlessly undermined any idea that discord and disturbance might bear some relationship to the size of their point of origin. Our early morning progress down through town and out along the coast road the other side was one of the more notable events in the daily life of Sitia.

George's *kipos* is about a kilometre from town. It begins with a piece of salty earth backing the road that backs the sea – unusually for a *kipos*, this is big, the size of a football pitch, and its value as a building plot may yet make the family's fortune. This tract is backed in turn by a summer cottage with a flower plot and rich little vegetable garden, two ramshackle sheds and a patch of vineyard. The cottage, when I first saw it, had just been done up, and here the family proposed to spend the hot months (while their own rooms in town were let) hidden away behind the astonishingly high bamboo fence with which the cottage was tightly ringed.

At that time George kept in his sheds one fine young pig, a goat with a wicked golden eye, two sheep, a turkey, two ducks, three chickens and almost fifty inquisitive little grey rabbits. All of them lived permanently indoors, except the sheep and goats. These spent the daylight hours tethered to stakes about the *kipos* or on neighbouring grass verges; and they needed to be moved to fresh grass two or three times a day.

I particularly remember one day on the *kipos*, a day like any other but marked by the fact that George had trodden on a nail and went down to the animals with one foot slippered, the rest of him neatly clad in polished black shoe and his town clothes. We had brought a pail of pig swill with us from the house and a bag of old greens. George, one shoe off and one shoe on, pig swill in one hand, greens in the other, dotted through the little flower garden, then through the French beans. Arriving at the sheds, he wiggled a stick to free the decaying chicken-wire gate. We ducked in under an old car spring that exercised some obscure function in holding one or other of the sheds together. The sheds themselves were built of old planks, old barber's shop signs nailed in upside down and twisted branches doing duty as uprights. There was a lot of rotting wire about and pieces of old machinery lay on top of the sheds. The little passage-way between the two was deep in mud and variegated droppings. George had laid out bushy branches of thyme to keep his feet dry and now, in shoe and slipper, he hopped from one tussock of thyme to the other until the pig, catching sight of him, squealed in eager-ness. This jaunty animal wore a collar round its neck and lived in the semicircle defined by the full extent of the rope that tethered it to the wall. By rooting out with its snout along the circumference of the semicircle it had built up a rampart around its territory. George tipped the swill into a big, battered saucepan. Next he fed the rabbits, destined one day to make meals for himself and his family. For them he broke up dull red carob beans – from trees on a plot belonging to relatives – and gave a bit of this to the sheep as well. During the worst period of the German occupation the young George and his family were reduced to eating carob beans.

Rabbit feeding finished, George leant through the door of one of the hutches. 'My children,' he said, 'my children,' fondling them. Then he banged down the door and muttered the word 'Dachau'. There is a mordant edge to perception everywhere in Greece.

Next he dealt with the kid – four days old and wobbly on its legs. Its mother had died at the time of its birth and George had decreed that one of the sheep, which had itself lost a lamb, should act as foster mother. But the sheep had set its narrow face against this plan.

First George had to catch it. Then, the struggling sheep in the scissor grip of his legs, he lunged hopelessly in the direction of the kid. After four or five tries he managed to get it. Holding the kid by the scruff of the neck, he now bent over the back end of the sheep and with his spare hand seized the udder between its legs. With a last heave, he accomplished a conjunction of sheep's teat and kid's mouth. And now the real excitement begins. The sheep wriggles and bucks between George's legs, the kid sucks and butts and George struggles to assert his will over both. After a while he pats the kid's belly much as he pats his own and swings his leg over the sheep's back to give it its freedom. It goes off like a demented bronco while George pops the kid back into the wooden box which is meant to provide some of the warmth of its missing mother. Then he goes out behind the shed among the decrepit vines. He looks for ducks' eggs and relieves himself. A little dog which lives tied up in a tin drum in the next door *kipos* begins to bark at him. (Most of the plots have a dog to keep off rodents and, being bored, they bark a lot; but they are almost always tied up and present no threat even to the nervous walker.) George goes back in to fetch the sheep, and tethers them among the vines. He tethers the goat to a stake in the salty ground behind the beach.

George's pleasures are mostly domestic ones and his devotion to family is what seems to animate him in his hectic double life – a treble one in summer when the rooms in his town house are let. And if I have understood him rightly, he sees his family's needs most vividly in economic terms, often revolving in his mind new ways of making money to meet the mortgage payments on his summer cottage and the extra floor of bedrooms in town. There is also the problem of security. His big dream – one that would put an end to all these worries – is to build a shiny new hotel on the salt flat in front of the *kipos*. The hope of sudden wealth through tourism lies at the back of many minds in Crete, rather like the possibility of winning the football pools in Britain.

George's economic approach is a good deal more flexible than his attitude to family. As a father he is the final and unquestioned court of appeal in all disputes; and though he is softer with the children than many Cretan autocrats his ways are rigid by American or

British standards. The girls get little visible liberty and George, like the rest of Sitia, supports the ferocious edict from fifteen-year-old Betty's school that no child is to be out of the house after half past seven at night. He wishes his daughters to make the best of themselves and this means that they must be orderly and disciplined. At the same time the house is an emotional one and the children love him with a heady passion which quickly turns to anxiety if he is late home – which happens seldom. George does not usually drink; he does not play cards; and though he is of a quick and humorous turn of mind, conversational days in the barber's shop seem to reduce his need for outside social contacts. Apart from his money worries, his only other continuing anxiety is the clash of social values experienced by everybody in Sitia who has to deal with foreigners.

George's ideas are firmly rooted in his family upbringing and in the concepts of conduct that stem from Greek Orthodoxy; yet, all summer long, Sitia, not to mention his own home, is full of people who laughingly think and act otherwise. It is George's tendency to like the people he meets when he first makes their acquaintance; but he is often disillusioned later by standards of decency which do not conform to his own, long hair being the supreme symbol of a moral decay. Only his good nature sees him through this continually perplexing situation.

At eight o'clock, just as the school bugle was blown for the start of lessons, George would roar up to his shop which was then on the leafy harbour front. Andreas, his gentle assistant of that epoch, would be there before him, setting out on the pavement the multitudinous canaries which were his special pleasure. Passers-by would often pause to listen to them sing. Across the road, the fishermen would be mending their bright yellow nets, passing them over stockinged toes to find the holes. A couple of bright caïques might be moored along the harbour wall with a small steamer from Athens picking up wine or sultanas.

There were pleasures for the eye inside as well. Andreas, a lover of beauty, had reared four splendid ivy plants in big tin cans. Their strands went circling round the barber's shop so perfectly that you would think they were made of plastic. The walls beneath them carried decorous pin-ups.

All morning the two barbers worked side by side, both with their off-white, once-white jackets buttoned tight across swelling stomachs. Both men constantly interrupted work, to rock back on their heels, their normally quick hands still, as they made an elaborate conversational point. Or, while a customer sat there all shaving soap, they would strike up a conversation with somebody waiting his turn. Everybody smoked much of the time, the barbers puffing in all directions, customers in the chair carefully inserting their cigarettes between soapy lips and holding their breath a moment before blowing out.

Apart from the ivy, the telephone is the other great feature of the shop, even though rather inactive and generally kept locked to deter pirate calls. But there is great excitement when it actually rings. George picks up the receiver. 'Yes,' he says, 'good morning, Mrs. *So-and-so*,' pronouncing the name with special emphasis so that everyone will catch the name and be able to share the fun. 'Yes, yes, I will see if I can find time to bring the medicine for your *nephew*.' Calls have been known to come from as far as Athens and when George puts down the telephone they are eagerly discussed. Sometimes, when she is out shopping, Katina finds a telephone and calls George just for the fun of it.

Mostly Katina is at home. She does not care for housework, setting about it without benefit of any obvious method. Her real vocation is cooking. All round the table, when the family sit down at midday, to hugely heaped plates, there arise little murmurs of 'Eat, eat, it's good, have some more'. And so they do. Katina's generation knew hunger in childhood. Now she and her contemporaries in the towns (but not the villages) are making up for it.

Lunch might be stuffed vine leaves, stacked high over the rim of soup plates, eased down with a pure tasting yogurt and accompanied with huge chunks of bread. Then there might be *feta*, a fresh clean cheese, extremely tasty if eaten in good condition; and more yogurt and more stuffed vine leaves. A lot of pasta is consumed, Italian style, and there is a dish named Cretan macaroni which resembles pellets of wholemeal bread in tomato sauce. Katina is good with fish, achieving a tasty crispness with small varieties and very often boiling larger fish to serve with oil and lemon. Her chicken and rabbit stews are famous among all the branches of her family and she is an expert at preparing *horta*, the wild mountain vegetables, which are served cold and in deep pools of oil. Most meals end with fruit, cucumber being assigned to this role and sliced not horizontally but lengthwise. To enjoy this style of cooking to the full you have to like huge quantities of everything and particularly olive oil. Saying 'no' is uphill work.

George's favourite dish is one which I find hard to look at though I am prepared to eat it – just. The main ingredients are the hooves and guts of kids. Waiting to be cooked the severed hooves are a pathetic sight, while the guts give a pale, uncanny tinge to the green plastic bowl in which they lie curled up. Katina cleans them with painstaking care, cold water and a skewer, then guts and hooves are brewed together in an egg and lemon sauce. It is a somewhat gelatinous dish, and the taste and texture drive George wild. But finally he is eaten to a standstill. He sits, hoof in hand, white streamers hanging down from either side of it, exhausted pleasure on his face. This is Katina's moment.

Her father came originally from Zakros, marrying a girl from Piskokephalo, near Sitia. The bride had a house and *kipos* as her dowry so that, as often happens in Crete, the young husband abandoned his village for hers. Here he became a butcher and in his own turn worked to provide dowries for three daughters. Unfortunately, he had no son to help him.

Now, though his life's work was done, he still sat late each night in his simple butcher's shop, at a rickety little desk beside the hanging goat carcasses. He didn't hear very well and he didn't talk very much, but the good nature of his smile was one of the pleasures of Piskokephalo.

One Thursday afternoon, during my stay in Sitia, when both his shop and George's were shut for the half-day, the old man came down by donkey to prune the vines on the trellis in front of the Nikolarakis summer cottage. He was wearing a grey cloth cap with peak, a brown jacket whose pockets were stuffed like a small boy's with useful things, khaki trousers and the short black zip-up boots into which the Cretan knee-boot has degenerated at this end of the island. To prune the vines he balanced teetering on an upturned tin can while George passed him lengths of string with which to train the remaining stems. George's role was an advisory one and he found it boring. But soon there was a diversion.

A big old car had broken down on the coast road just across from the cottage. A knot of people gathered round in the excited manner which is customary in Greece on such occasions, arriving after a while at the consensus verdict that the situation was hopeless without a real mechanic. George, ever eager, engaged to take the driver the half mile to Sita by *mikani*. The two men disappeared with a satisfying roar. An hour later George trailed back on foot, the *mikani* having experienced a puncture. Through all this the old man worked on unswerving. He grafted and pruned and trained while all around him on the little plots others were doing the same. All the way to Piskokephalo the valley was full of bent backs bobbing up and down like those of snorkellers as smallholders tended the low vines among the ubiquitous marguerites and the brilliant yellow *martolouloudia* that battle for dominance all through early spring.

The big festival of this time of year is the Apocrea, the carnival before Lent. Its last day is an occasion for eating tremendous quantities of meat. George, brought up after the death of his own parents by an uncle and aunt from one of the villages in the high Sitia hinterland, invited them to town for the feast. He also slaughtered a pair of rabbits and acquired half a kid from his father-in-law.

Uncle Manoli arrived first, a thin, elderly man with a mild face and self-deprecating smile. Aunt Calliope came down next day by bus. I was in the barber's shop when she arrived. A shadow, not a very big one, crossed the threshold, followed smartly by a hobgoblin of an old woman, no bigger than an eight-year-old. She had on a thick black dress and a black head-scarf. The skin of her face was soft and brown and thick-looking, with deep pink wrinkles. Her lower jaw came firmly up towards her nose. George when he saw her exploded with smiles and mirth, abandoned his customer, darted across the shop, showered her with kisses and cries of, '*Thia, Thia* – aunt, aunt.' Calliope comes up to George's second to bottom rib. But despite being so tiny, and totally unlettered, she is both the ruling force and the ruling intellect on this side of the family, shrewd, tolerant and acquainted with the full range of human weakness. Uncle Manoli draws on her strength as if from a deep well.

The night before the feast was itself a festive time. Neighbours dropped in and out and Manoli had brought down with him from his village of Chandras a liberal supply of his own thin red wine. Sunday morning was vivid with racing clouds and expectation. George, Katina, Calliope and the girls idled pleasantly about. But Uncle Manoli and I had been invited out – to the *kipos* of a retired policeman with a voice as old and dry as parchment and a yellow vest which always seemed to me to be at least half an inch thick.

The appointment was for ten sharp and we set out far too early, walking among the bright yellow flowers, past tethered donkeys and goats and young men in pairs carrying between them back to Sitia huge baskets of freshly gathered animal fodder. Uncle Manoli was wearing a white shirt buttoned up to his thin neck, a dark grey suit, grey cardigan, a pair of extra black dark glasses, bright black town shoes and a formal raincoat draped over his shoulders and flapping as he walked like the wings of a dispirited chicken. The effect was decidedly an odd one for nobody could mistake Manoli for the townsman implied by his outfit, least of all in so rural a setting.

The little chicken-guarding mongrels barked at us from every *kipos*, the more furiously each time we stopped to ask the way. Eventually, lifting our feet high as we traversed a patch of deep and dewy grass, we came to a little hollow surrounded by banks of flowering shrubs. Why Manoli and I had been asked for ten precisely remained a mystery, for Vassili was pottering without purpose, the short white bristles on his head glinting in the sunlight. There were five beehives on top of his decayed shed while in the dark interior he kept rabbits, doves and rubble.

Vassili set out chairs beside a little blossoming apricot and too near for comfort to the beehives. Manoli and I looked round anxiously at the many insects in the air while Vassili pulled his chair closer and began to talk, his old voice dusty in the clean air. He carries in a pocket deep among his many layers of clothing a certificate from the French navy praising his father's zeal as a ship chandler. Another, dated 1916, states that the father was entitled to work as an interpreter for the French armed forces and gives his nationality as 'Grec-Crétois' – a definition more apt than either simple Greek or Cretan.

The voice crackled on and on, rising and falling above the hum of bees in the blossom-laden secret garden. Vassili was telling us of the civil war of the late 1940s. From time to time Manoli would lean forward and with the serrated blade of his clasp-knife cut off the stem of an artichoke plant. He trimmed these carefully, then cut them into three, a piece for each of us to munch. As Vassili's Macedonian tales continued the sun rose higher in the sky and fresh flowers opened about us.

But suddenly a cluster of bees landed on Manoli's face. He dashed them off and drew back his head into his raincoat like a tortoise. Then, quick as a young boy, he was on his feet and running out of the garden – followed with equal verve by the author of these pages. Vassili laughed and Manoli, safe in the flowery meadow beyond the hedge, called out as though nothing had happened, 'Thank you, Vassili, thank you very much, I have to go now.' We looked at one another a little bit ashamed.

While the Nikolarakis family were tucking into their great Apocrea lunch, I was doing the same at the house of George Mathioudakis, one of Sitia's schoolmasters. This George is a big-hearted man with a voice to match his heart. His back is straight as a door and he carries himself with the dash of a mountain brigand, though always wearing a smart city suit. He and I had become particularly friendly, making many expeditions together in his bright blue pick-up, visiting monasteries, examining sultana processing plants, calling on friends and former pupils in many of the villages.

The Apocrea lunch at the schoolmaster's was a triumph, revolving round half a stuffed kid in a bed of rice and roast potatoes. One of our fellow feasters was a Mathioudakis uncle who had worked for many years as a waiter in Boston. Now he had retired to his home village to enjoy his savings and to worship in the manner appointed by the Greek Orthodox Church. He had spent nearly three hours in church already that morning and was full of proofs of the loving-kindness of the Lord, not the least being that since he had already eaten after morning church, this was his second lunch of the day.

The first event after lunch was the arrival of the tenant of the upstairs flat in the schoolmaster's modern house – a lawyer with an elegantly striped shirt, grey hair swept back over his ears and an insatiable appetite for etymology, worrying away at words like a dog at a bone. He came into the room playing his guitar and singing:

May there be no cracks in the stone of which this house is built,
May husband and wife live here happily many years together.

Then there was a toast addressed to 'the man who loves his wife'. The religious uncle muttered something about it being more suitable to toast the man who loves someone else's wife. Nobody heard him properly and he refused to repeat it. Then he turned his attention to a fresh supply of kid and rice.

In the evening the children of Sitia paraded on the front in carnival clothes and after that it was a kind of Greek Hallowe'en, with nasty surprises for grown-ups and small boys firing six-shooters from every corner. The Nikolarakis family got one of the biggest shocks of all. Ritsa was already in bed, when outside in the street there came pathetic sounds of wailing. A broken little voice cried amid sobs, 'Mama, Mama, Mama,' George and Katina looked at one another in surmise. Their eyes travelled together to Ritsa's bedroom door. Then, in unison, they sprang to the street door on which tiny fingers could now be heard scrabbling.

As it opened a child came bursting in, wrapped in a blanket, string bag over its head, the whole surmounted by a top hat. The unrecognisable figure continued to emit low moans so that, even though it was plain a carnival act was going on, the tension in the room was still acute. And then the voice turned gruff and with little growls and barks the child darted first at one person, then at another. A little hand reached up to pluck off the top hat and we saw that the hand was old and rough and the child itself none other than Aunt Calliope. To me the whole incident seemed curiously unnerving; but George and Katina were delighted. They got Ritsa out of bed and dressed Calliope up again to do a round of the neighbours. The rest of us crept behind to join in the laughter at each house as she was unmasked.

The next day – Pure Monday, Kathara Deftera – was the first of Lent and the last day of the festival. This is a day for picnics and from quite early in the morning cars, taxis and motorcycles went streaming out along the coast road as those who had a distant *kipos* made for it and those who hadn't made for restaurants, cafés, beaches, anywhere they could hope to find food, drink and a crowd.

At George's cottage a splendid picnic was spread out, including *laganes*, big flat sesame-covered loaves made specially for Kathara Deftera. Then, after lunch, neighbours started to drop in. Hosts and guests sat on little upright wooden chairs ranged round the edges of the room, the women accepting spoonfuls of sweet preserve, the men a glass or two of *tsikoudia*.

After a while George Mathioudakis, the schoolmaster, came by to sweep me up with him; we dashed on in his pick-up to a beach along the coast. The atmosphere was like an English country fête, with many people standing around on bright green grass waiting for something to happen. Here and there groups were clustered round a man playing the violin or the penetrating three-stringed Cretan lyre. The schoolmaster had a guitar, the manager of the Piskokephalo sultana plant a violin; backed by their own music, the two men sang antiphonally in rhyming couplets.

These verses are called *mantinades* and there is a huge stock of them, handed down orally from generation to generation and adapted by the singer for the occasion. At a party one may suddenly hear one's own name incorporated into a heraldic verse of welcome – a thoroughly moving experience, the kind that brings you out in instant goose-flesh.

After the *mantinades* the two musicians played waltzes. The schoolmaster's wife and I danced together on the bright green grass, the elegant lawyer from upstairs danced close to his young wife. Some boys were playing football nearby and the sea shone behind a row of trees.

When it began to get cold the crowd of friends, swollen to nearly thirty, moved up to a big café in the nearest village, taking me with them. We ate octopus straight off the coals of the pot-bellied stove and then the serious business of the day began.

The schoolmaster and the sultana manager sat on little chairs in the middle of the floor and struck up a Cretan dance. Soon a line of dancers, hands joined, was winding its way round them, doing the complicated steps that everybody knows. The best dancer was a young bank clerk from Rethimnon, a biggish man, all in black, with black hair and black eyes and a fierce black moustache. He glowed and glowered as he led the line of dancers. Sometimes his movements were sultry and athletic; sometimes he expressed simple delight. Mostly, however, it was pride. All the line moved forward a few steps in unison; and then the young man whirled away in front of them, arms raised sideways, making fast and complex steps. Suddenly he leapt – waist high, it seemed – his body inclining sideways in the air as he fetched his right hand down to slap both his flying heels in the same movement. Once he leapt straight on to a table, landing on one foot and holding his balance. A bottle of beer toppled slowly over on to a girl's lap and everybody went mad applauding.

When the schoolmaster got rid of his guitar and danced it was quite as beautiful. With his straight back, his swift and graceful movements, it was hard to believe that he was nearly fifty. He leapt, he pirouetted, he danced out of delight and pride, always impeccable in his city suit. When he sat down at last he stuck a finger inside his collar to let in air. 'How I could dance when I was twenty-two,' he said.

The next day Calliope and Uncle Manoli returned to Chandras and I went with them on what turned out to be the first of several visits. The road snaked up and up, the air got colder as the bus climbed. Manoli and Calliope crossed themselves each time a church came into view, and Calliope was thoroughly glad when the journey was over. Like many Greek village women, she expects to be sick each time she travels.

Chandras seemed at first an undistinguished little place, with little colour except for the Agipgas sign above the grocer's door, the lovely green- and black-striped dragons at either end of it looking back over their shoulders at one another. In fact, the village is quite important locally, a small administrative centre with junior and secondary schools, four teachers, a resident doctor, two ordinary police officers and two agricultural policemen. There are two cafés and several churches. One of these is notably bigger than the rest and here, it being Lent, the village priest held long services each evening. The doors stood open during the service and as the people came in on their donkeys from work they could hear the ritualised Byzantine chant ring out, rich with hundreds of years of history and unquestioning devotion.

Manoli's house, which came as part of Calliope's dowry, is along a little foot-and-donkey lane which runs between whitewashed houses and animal sheds. First there is a chin-high wall with a rickety blue wooden gate and behind that a tiny courtyard, meticulously swept, with a stack of vine clippings for firewood. There is a stone sink outdoors here for washing up – the water runs away down a channel in the middle of the lane – and an outhouse with a tiny but effective flush lavatory. One of the assets of Chandras is running water.

The house itself stands just behind the courtyard, with a low flat roof, a small and sunken front door with a window on either side. The first room you enter is tiny, with a little eating table, a dresser with crockery and a small plastic bust of Byron. The diminutive chairs are set with their backs to the wall in the style of Greek cafés. There are two sleeping rooms to the left, one in front, one behind. This back room has no windows; but there is a skylight covered with a sheet of tin from which a wooden pole hangs down. To open the curtains, as it were, you jerk the piece of tin sideways with the pole. The roofs of all the rooms are held up on beams of straight and slender cypress alternating with twisting olive branches. Between the beams and the roof itself, a layer of bamboo cane is laid crosswise for insulation. Though the rooms are small, the bamboos help to create a light and airy effect.

The part of the house directly behind the little entrance room is the hub of activity. This is an old arched chamber, kitchen on one side of the arch, storeroom on the other.

The storeroom, in Minoan fashion, holds Manoli's wealth – seven *pitharia*, massive in the half-dark, filled variously with oil, olives and the dark brown everlasting rusks, named *dakos*, which are an important part of village eating in the east. There is a tank with a single drainage hole where Manoli each year treads out his wine grapes. Then there are the barrels of wine and a cask of *tsikoudia*. In among the *pitharia* and barrels are little piles of lemons and eggs, strings of garlic and onions and all sorts of bits and pieces – buckets with perforations for dipping sultana grapes into the soda solution, an ancient gourd used as a wine bottle, and oddments left over from the days when all the women spun: a spindle and brushes with steel bristles for carding. There is real grandeur in the profusion of the storeroom.

The kitchen is a less remarkable place – two little gas rings, two tiny chairs, a tiny horseshoe hearth before which the old couple sit. This is where they pass most of their spare hours at home.

The house also has an animal shed giving directly on to the street. Here, in the rich-smelling gloom, Manoli keeps a donkey, three chickens and a fawning little dog. Both dog and donkey are respected members of the community, Manoli, like his nephew, being fond of animals. He calls them 'Dog' and 'Donkey', greeting

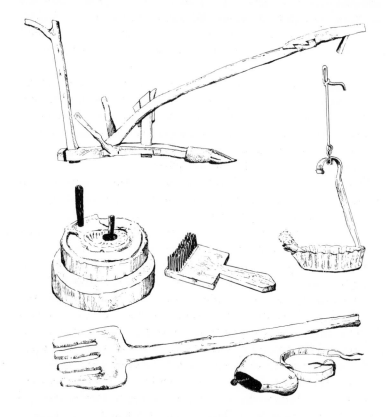

Still to be seen in Cretan villages though seldom now in use –
wooden plough, grindstone, wool carder, tin oil lamp, wooden fork
and cowbell.

them quite formally. There is also an outrageous cat, a predator
living on the edge of the circle. Manoli is proud of this louche and
slinking beast and once or twice in Sitia I had heard him telling
strangers that at home in Chandras he had a very fine cat indeed.

That first day in the village there was a wicked wind. Low red
clouds blotted out the crags around the plateau, and as I accom-

panied Manoli and Calliope to their vegetable plot, red dust coming up from the south stung our eyes, blocked our noses and felt like gravel on the tongue. This, said Manoli, was the taste of the Sahara over three hundred kilometres to the south.

Our path was through irrigation windmills. These come into use as summer begins and the land dries out. Now it was only March and their canvas sails were packed away, leaving whirligigs of wire and iron on top of the iron frames. Some of these whirligigs had not been tied down and spun madly like catherine-wheels. Others swayed and trembled without spinning. All of them made wild metallic noises, some whirring and whizzing, some creaking, some groaning, some yelping as if in agony. A weird cacophony rose from the allotments behind Chandras in the red mist.

Their *kipos* was fifty metres long and fifty wide. It had a few rows of cabbage-like greens, some eating grapes, artichoke plants and quite a lot of young barley. This is grown as hay for the donkey, the young green shoots being plucked by hand before the grain has ripened, bound into sheaves and laid aside for winter. That makes room for the summer crop – vegetables of many kinds and potatoes. There were also two peach trees, two apples, an almond and a quince. Manoli walked up and down as Calliope gathered greens for the evening meal.

Later I went with him to inspect his cornfield and substantial vineyard of wine grapes. But we could not so easily visit the olives on which his domestic economy was dependent. One of the problems of Chandras is that it is too high for olives and most of the villagers' groves are far down among the lower slopes. The Chandras olives are clustered together in particular spots so that effectively the village owns various substantial tracts of lower-lying land. These are dotted with hamlets which are empty eight months a year but used during the winter olive harvest by their Chandras owners.

There was no work to be done that first day of my visit. Calliope cooked a Lenten meal of potatoes and greens in olive oil. Manoli and I whiled away an hour or two in the dusty café. The three of us later sat before the tiny hearth; and by eight-thirty we were all

Old couple at home. Plain of Lakonia.

in bed. From the front room I could hear the old couple moaning and tossing in their sleep.

Calliope had bad rheumatism, Manoli a stomach complaint. Both were often in pain and bore it stolidly. But it was clear that their physical state reflected the hard conditions of their daily lives. I had taken Calliope for seventy and was astonished to find her fifty-five. Manoli, too, looked far older than his age. The life-style of a peasant community is increasingly hard with increasing age.

Perhaps it would have been different if Manoli and Calliope had had children; but their one baby was stillborn while Manoli was away in Albania in the bitter action against the Italians in 1940. His consolation for the subsequent emptiness of life had been conversation and his own red wine. Calliope, on the other hand, had shaped her earthly life in hopes of reaching heaven. Like most Greek countrywomen, she is passionately devout, exposing herself, for instance, to the full rigours of Lent. For forty days now her only protein was to be oil and snails, a permitted Lenten food. To me as an outsider it was strange to see such self-inflicted deprivation in a woman whose cupboard was on the bare side at the best of times.

Lacking a child, the couple had allowed their affections to focus on George and Katina; and George's episodic visits on his *mikani* were eagerly awaited.

On one occasion, after I had gone back to Sitia, George and I went up together. But we made so many diversions on the way that it was long after dark when we arrived.

First we visited a village where a Nikolarakis cousin owned an oil press, then, for my sake, another where we looked at some particularly ancient houses. Here, as everywhere in Crete, each division of a road or path is likely to be marked by a wayside shrine, a little box of tin or stone, set head-high and with a glass front through which you see perhaps a small icon and a little oil lamp, almost always made of a soft drinks bottle. These shrines, and the chapels perching on many of the highest peaks, are a most distinctive part of Cretan scenery.

Our third stop was the substantial village of Lithines where we ate walnuts and, in my case, sipped *tsikoudia* in the modern kitchen of a cousin who drives a bulldozer. We had with us a big plastic container which the cousin's wife filled with wine. Soon we were on our way again; for, on entering Lithines, George had compacted with a friend he saw on a street corner to meet him half an hour later in the café by the church. Only a quarter of an hour had passed in the cousin's house, but it was now George's pleasure to walk from café to café inquiring for his friend and when he wasn't there to mutter, 'Strange, strange, I had an appointment with him.' In this way he created as much confusion as a man could wish, unearthed two more cousins and drank coffee with another group of friends. They were complaining about long hair and the number of young men in Germany. 'Greece is where good Greeks should stay and work,' George said angrily.

After a while George decided on a visit to the church where his uncle had been priest until his recent death. Going into the two-naved building – one nave old and full of frescoes, the other modern and full of wrought iron – we encountered the new young priest from Ierapetra. By now we were a party of half a dozen or more. The priest stood near the altar, George and supporters half-way down the aisle. When the priest had finished a polite speech of welcome directed to me as a foreigner, George told us the story of a miracle that happened to him here when he was a little boy. It seemed that he had uttered an unseemly word in church and, going over the hill on his way back to Chandras, he was seized with total paralysis. George's father hurried back to the church with the suffering child and prayers to the Virgin quickly released his limbs.

The story went down well. George's friends, who knew its every word, listened with bated breath. The priest murmured 'True, true,' at every pause in the narrative. And who was likely to doubt it? The Virgin of Lithines is held in extraordinary respect locally, her icon hung about with literally thousands of the little votive simula-cra people offer up when hoping for a cure. Katina says she has seen the icon weep real tears. It is also a fact, George told me, that fresh meat carried too near this church goes bad. So if you see anybody in Lithines making a detour with a package you will know he is on his way home from the butcher.

After Lithines we took the dirt road to Chandras towards Manoli and Calliope. It passes first through Etria, a village of great poverty with a fine Venetian ruin where George and his childhood friends played castles. The next stop was Armeni, just next door to Chandras. Here we popped into the school – two busy little classrooms full of the children's art work and portraits of the Cretan heroes. The schoolmaster gave George a bunch of Sweet Williams for Katina. Next we visited George's 'wealthy' aunt in her bright new concrete house, accepting a gift of the local wheat considered indispensable for Cretan macaroni. Then we went a round of the village, calling at friends at quite a dozen shops. Like Robert Pashley's guide, Captain Manias, George seemed to know and be eagerly welcomed by everybody. During the course of that memorable day we declined invitations to upwards of thirty meals.

Our visit to Armeni ended with a great-aunt, an exceedingly old lady discovered in the corner of a one-room house reeking of old age and poverty. She was cradling somebody's baby on her lap, but when she saw who her visitor was, she handed the baby to its mother and began to weep great bitter tears, calling out the names of sons, grandsons and great-grandsons who had gone ahead of her to the grave. George wasn't a bit put out by this – seemed, indeed, to take it as his due.

Finally we reached Chandras for the visit to Manoli and Calliope. It was not a long stop because it had grown so late, but it was the most loving and the most lovingly received. George picked up a little olive oil and a few olives and after a while we went back down the hairpin bends to Sitia, equipped now with flour, olives, oil and wine. Katina and the girls were sobbing in case we had had an accident, but the schoolmaster's Sweet Williams helped to cheer them.

A week or two later I had the use of a car and set out with Manoli and Calliope on a visit from Chandras to their olive hamlet, Azali. It was a long way and reached by a road which made me glad that Calliope had said a longish prayer before our departure.

Azali turned out to be a charming place, belonging to another century and another country. You would never guess you were within thirty kilometres even of so small a town as Sitia. It stood, one church, a cluster of tiny stone houses and sheds, on a steep slope in a hidden valley without electricity, piped water, café, lavatory or any public building except the church. All around there were olives and bird-song and the sound of running water. Below the village, plumed bamboos grew high and graceful in the stream-bed. There was even a little palm tree.

Calliope and Manoli made first for the little church. Katina had sent up a shampoo bottle of oil for the lamps and the first job was to get them filled and lit. Next, Calliope lit a pewter saucer of incense and waved it under each icon, kissing the appropriate spots on the pictures as she did so. Then she waved the saucer from the church door, leaving little trails of blue smoke in the still air. All this time

Intricate stone carving on the apse of a country church.

she was murmuring prayers and sobbing with religious intensity, a tiny black figure overcome with love of God.

After that the couple went to their own house, opening the door into its one small room with a key the size of a hammer. It is a dear little room and Calliope adores it. 'If I weren't married,' I have heard her say, 'I'd live in Azali the whole year round. For me, it's better than Paris.' There was no glass in the windows, only steel bars and shutters in the old-fashioned Cretan manner. The floor was packed earth and when Manoli had drawn water from the communal spring Calliope sprinkled a few drops to settle the dust.

The hearth was much like the one in Chandras, but the sleeping arrangements were quite different. Here, Manoli and Calliope had a platform of branches, rather like a raft 'floating' at waist-level, and covered with straw-stuffed sacking on which a second layer of palliasse was spread out at bedtime. It was reached by a short ladder of untrimmed branches. The three chairs in the room had high backs, but their cane seats were only inches off the floor. One of them, made of walnut, was boldly carved and notched and, so Manoli asserted, a full two hundred years old. To me it looked far older, but it is one of the consequences of the Cretan climate and the many episodes of destruction that there are few objects of vast antiquity in everyday use.

The little house had four of the giant storage jars. One contained rusks; two were full of winter clothes and bedding. The fourth held the big black nylon nets that are spread out under the olive trees before the beating of the branches.

In Azali Manoli had another vegetable garden, a number of plots with olive trees and other individual trees of various kinds. These holdings were dotted about the slopes, their apparently random position reflecting the pattern of inheritance in Crete. Land is divided among all the children, so every substantial piece of property – of which there are few – constantly diminishes. Most people have tiny plots in several places. This sounds all very fine and egalitarian, but it means that Cretan peasant farmers spend a huge proportion of their time travelling from one plot to another.

That particular day in Azali the weather was too lovely for Manoli to worry unduly about the vegetable patch. Leaving Calliope at the house, he and I wandered away uphill to check that all the trees were well. The olives did not preoccupy him since they are extraordinarily hardy. But he wanted to take a look at his chestnuts, at an infant walnut tree, a mandarin and a lemon that had once yielded fifty kilos of fruit in a single season. We walked up through the stony olive groves, setting our feet down carefully among marguerites and wild orchids. There were no sounds at all but those of natural origin – until from high above we began to catch a distant sound of goat bells. And this too was a cause of satisfaction. For Manoli explained to me that he owned the grazing rights on that particular stretch of mountain and had let it out to a goatherd for six kilos of hard white cheese a year.

We stopped to rest at a little stone hut built to shelter olive harvesters from winter showers, then slowly made our way down again, here sampling a fruit, there straightening out the crumbling bank of a miniature irrigation channel. Down below Calliope had been cleaning weeds from the irrigation channels at the vegetable patch, tearing at them with her quick little hands. We ate in the sun, then loaded armfuls of firewood for Chandras. The bending caught Aunt Calliope in the rheumatic hip joint. 'Ah,' she sighed, 'work is a tyranny, a terrible tyranny.'

It has sometimes seemed to me that there was an inevitability about the lack of understanding between myself and George Kopasakis – a barrier to communication as definite as a river too fast to cross or a wall without a door. But I did not see this at the time and was puzzled and slightly wounded throughout a journey I made with him and other shepherds in the summer fastnesses of the Lefka Ori. Perhaps the trouble lay in the way it all began.

I had made the steep climb up from the coastal village of Loutro to Anopolis, one-time home of the Sfakiot hero Daskaloyannis. Anopolis lies in a broad and comparatively rich hollow, one high ridge behind the sea; out of its valley on the other side the Lefka

Ori go climbing towards the sky, the pines and cypresses of the lower slopes giving way finally to the bald peaks. Passing the café, where two young men were throwing down cards with astonishing ferocity, I joined a knot of older men making shepherds' crooks in the shade of a huge tree. You take the stick – preferably, in Crete, a knobbly one – heat it, bend one end round a rock and bind it there with wire until it has set. After the conversation had run awhile I mentioned my hopes of making a journey up into the mountains. A country policeman sitting in the group announced that a shepherd from Anopolis was going up next morning and a small boy was dispatched to fetch him.

The shepherd turned out to be George Kopasakis, one of the violent card players. He was shortish, handsome-featured, clean-shaven and wearing a neat white shirt. He looked trim and fit, not at all rough and ready like some of the older shepherds. His clothing made no concession to Cretan costume.

When the country policeman suggested that I should accompany him to the mountains he agreed, with a good grace, to take me. I said I would only go if truly welcome. 'How could you not be?' all replied as one. But the expedition would leave at four in the morning, so I had better go down to the coast to fetch warm clothes, then come up again to sleep at Anopolis.

I did all these things, regaining the village square – with aching legs – as darkness fell. An extraordinary change had taken place in the atmosphere. The old men were sitting in a wide semicircle in front of a café. George Kopasakis was alone on a bench by the café wall. He beckoned me to join him and went straight on with the conversation he was engaged in. When this lapsed I said I had brought no food with me since there was nothing on sale at the coast. What would he advise I should take with me? '*Xero ego*,' he replied, a phrase which means 'How should I know?' but which carries, when spoken with the contempt of George's delivery, the additional meaning 'and nor do I care'. After a few moments I went into the café, where I bought two tins of fish and a kilo of squashy tomatoes. I was about to ask for bread when Kopasakis dashed in, ordered what turned out to be the last loaf and then dashed out again. I bought four unappetising rusks instead. When I came out with my purchases, Kopasakis stood up and marched off into the darkness. I waited, uncertain, in the pool of light by the café door. 'He's gone to bed,' somebody said at last. Then somebody else said, 'He's not going up the mountain tomorrow.' A third voice said, 'Pavlos here is going, you can go with him.'

By now I was so mortified at my unknown crime, whatever it might be, that I made a long speech saying it would be better if I didn't go. It occurred to me very forcibly that perhaps George Kopasakis had simply been unable to say no to the country police-man and that I might be as much an embarrassment to Pavlos as to George. But all the circle began to insist that I would be the greatest asset on Pavlos's mountain tour. Still uncertain, I decided once more to go ahead and arranged for a bed at one of the cafés. Pavlos said he was taking up a young boy as well as me, and that the expedition would depart not at four in the morning but at three. He would knock on my door to make sure I was up. At this point one of the old men intervened. He said I shouldn't worry about food since the shepherds would share their meals with me. He also insisted that I would get nowhere without a torch. I added one to my purchases, not realising how much I was to owe to this piece of advice.

Before going to bed (I was sharing a communal bedroom with the bus driver and an explosives expert working on a nearby road) I inspected my feet and found them puffy but still serviceable after the double ascent to Anopolis. I laid out my clothes in the order I would need to put them on, so that I would be ready on the instant when my call came, and slept lightly to the snores of the explosives expert. At half past three I heard a sound of hooves and a light tap at the door. I leapt out of bed thinking it was Pavlos, but the hooves, a lot of them, went on uninterrupted into the distance. I lay down again to wait.

Five minutes later the café proprietor came bursting in.

'Didn't you hear them?' he said. 'They've gone.'

Oh for heaven's sake, I thought, once more inwardly abandoning the expedition.

'Hurry and you'll catch them,' said the café man. 'That's the road.'

'They don't want me,' I replied.

'How could they not?' he said. 'Go quickly and after a while you will hear them. But if you miss them, don't try to go up the mountain by yourself.'

All right, I thought, I'll go, and by God I am going to catch them. I plunged into my clothes, hefted my rucksack and dashed into the night, following the circle of light wafted ahead by my Hong Kong torch. I raced down the track for a quarter of an hour, came to a divide in the road, opted for the left on no evidence other than the need, induced by fury, to make an instant choice. After another quarter of an hour I was sweating profusely and concluding that I had been made a fool of in several ways at once. Then, through the darkness, I made out the shape of a mule and rider and a voice called to me from a path near the road.

'Didn't you hear me knock?' asked Pavlos.

I now saw that as well as the mule there were three donkeys, two of them with riders and one laden with sacks. Out in front there was a smaller figure, a walker, presumably the boy who was accompanying Pavlos. I moved towards the head of the file and took a place behind him. Then we went on. The pace was steady, and soon we began to climb. The leader never eased up, never looked back no matter how steep the going. He had, so far as I could see in the dark, a short-stepped rolling gait, like a sailor at the start of a Saturday evening on the town. The quick aggression of his walking was rather beautiful. At times, though, I found it hard to follow him, for now we were climbing steeply and continuously on rough ground in the dark. The path wound up in zigzags, but the leader took short cuts, jumping upwards from rock to rock, from corner to corner of the path. Sometimes he held his crook across his shoulders, one hand hanging on to either end of it. Sometimes, among the rocks, he used it to balance with. There was a piny smell

from the thin forest on either side of us and a strong, hot wind blew
in our faces; I sweated copiously, my mouth tasted fouler and fouler.
Soon we were far ahead of the animal train. After an hour the figure
in front of me turned. I was hardly surprised to find it was George
Kopasakis, my first intended comrade.

'Tired?' he asked.

'No,' I replied untruthfully.

'Good,' he said, 'now let's sleep.'

He flung himself down in a cavity of the rock, the only comfortable spot, while I perched on a sharp edge trying to rest my feet
and thighs. I think he was actually asleep when the animals came
up with us.

He now rode one of the donkeys and again I continued on foot,
but with a new walking companion, a sixteen-year-old boy with
huge ankles and wrists.

We came quite soon, still in the dark, to a big rainwater cistern
from which the shepherds drew a few buckets of water. These they
tipped into a trough for the animals. I drank from the bucket.

As day broke the smell was still glorious, the wind still hot and
strong and my new walking companion even swifter on the steep
short cuts. I decided to walk the full length of the path at donkey
speed while the young shepherd dashed ahead, gaining enough time
to feign sleep. Once we found him lying full length along a pine
branch, his heavy legs resting among the copious clumps of needles.
He was a most engaging youth, Damoulis by name, and he spoke
of the pleasures of partridge shooting and his love for the clear and
exciting air of the mountains.

Soon after daybreak, and though it was August, there came a bitter cold. By now we had climbed out of the forest and the trail led,
still upwards, through a long limestone valley, bare and desolate,
under the highest peaks of the Lefka Ori. The sun had still not
reached down into this cratered and forbidding piece of country
when at about seven o'clock, we came down a steep incline to
another cistern and beside it, half under a rock, a one-room house,
small but stout and rendered with fresh cement. We watered the

animals and retired into the hut. It was dark and dirty inside with
a few blankets spread out in one corner and a pile of firewood outside
the door. We were to breakfast here, and as the shepherds unpacked
cloth bundles from the bags they carried with them, I made to open
my rucksack. But I was prevented by George who said there was
food for all and that I must eat heartily. In this respect he was an
outstanding host. In the half-darkness of the hut, the cold beginning
to numb me as we crouched there, we feasted on fresh fish out of
a little plastic container, cold soft-boiled eggs, tomatoes and bread
cut in large chunks by the knives which each man carried. Damoulis's
was so sharp he opened a tin of fish with it. On the floor beside
the bed of the hut's absent occupant we left our eggshells, fish-bones
and the bad bits of tomato we spat out.

The next leg of the journey was through a still more awesome
countryside. Nothing at all grew here; we walked on solid rock or
rocky rubble; on either side there were huge limestone pits and the
bare peaks, now not so very much higher than ourselves, clustered
round us threateningly. Damoulis pointed out to me a pit he said
was fifty metres deep. About twenty metres down was a pillar of
perpetual snow – dirty, dusty now, shrinking away from the rocky
walls to stand on its own like a piece of mouldy confectionery. In
the old days invalids were carried up here by mule in summer so
that the icy snow could help to cool their fever. Finally we made
a steep climb to a high and windy ridge.

Here Pavlos dismounted from his mule and set off by himself
across the wilderness of broken rock. He had sheep to attend to on
the slopes of Pachnes, the highest mountain of the group. Watching
him lope down into a deep valley, then traverse the rough slope
on the other side of it, I abandoned the theory that George Kopasakis had been testing me out during the first part of the walk. I
even began to wonder whether he had been going specially slowly.

Now, after a descent of a little over an hour we began to make
out below us a little flat valley with three stone huts and sheep pens
made of dry-stone walling. We were arriving at the summer pastures
of the Lefka Ori.

A big yellow dog ran out barking, saw that it was George and came bouncing up to him with the top side of its muzzle wrinkled in a snarl of adoration. He ruffled the back of its neck and then, as if it were part of the ritual of welcome, the dog cocked its leg and discharged a yellow stream into the horse trough.

We walked up to the huts to be welcomed by George's brother Yannis. He was twenty-one years old, thin, stubble-bedecked and wearing a duster tied round his head, with one triangle sticking up in front like an Indian war bonnet. He had a slightly dotty laugh and an impediment in his speech that held him up for a moment each time he spoke so that when the words were ready they came out in a childlike rush. Like his brother, he was limber and graceful as a trained athlete.

Most of the animal train went on to a more distant encampment while George Kopasakis, Damoulis and I remained behind. As well as brother Yannis there were two young boys, Kopasakis cousins spending their summer holidays in the mountains, tremendously proud of their admission into this man's world. The shepherds' little round huts were in some disrepair. Originally they seemed to have been vaulted over in dry-stone like some Minoan tombs, but the tops of the vaults had caved in and been replaced by rough planking and heavy Perspex sheets. Inside, they were dank and untidy. Two were used only for sleeping, the beds bunches of brushwood on the earth with a blanket thrown over them. The third hut, which had a rectangular room attached was used for making cheese and yogurt and as a general social centre. There was a little fireplace for cooking on and sitting at and a second far larger fireplace over which stood a cauldron indistinguishable to my eye from its Minoan counterpart from Tylissos. There was no chimney so the smoke from both these fires had to find its way out through the door. From this hut a stench of sour sheep's milk rose into the mountain air. Rotting tins lay in heaps about the front and the lavatory area was about four metres behind. To judge by appearances nobody had given much thought, perhaps for hundreds of years, to comfort, cleanliness or convenience.

We celebrated our arrival by falling to on yogurt which was as pure and fresh as the camp was squalid. To find spoons, Damoulis raked deep in a bowl of what looked and smelled like sour milk. The system was that as you finished eating you threw your cutlery into this bowl and fished it out again when you next wanted it. I didn't care one way or the other, partly because I was tired, and partly because I was already committed, having gulped down pints of green and crawling water from the cistern.

After the yogurt we all lay down and slept for seven hours.

That evening the Kopasakis brothers had a quick and ferocious card game, then disappeared with shotguns. Meanwhile, at the encampment I learned that cheese-making was over now since the ewes were dry. The only work was seeing the sheep were safe and moving them from pasture to pasture. I was also shown the camp's reading matter – an Agatha Christie in translation, a judo manual and a stack of comics. The villain in one of the serials was an English redcoat of treacherous aspect.

The boys and I climbed the hill behind the camp to watch the mountain sunset, hearing, as we did so, one or two distant shots. Yannis returned empty-handed, but George came back after dark, two fine partridges stuffed inside his jersey. We ate tremendous quantities of a stew of wild greens and potatoes and discussed my journey back to Anopolis the following day.

George was of the opinion that I should start well before daylight, but I wasn't confident of finding or keeping the path in the dark. When I suggested that one of the boys, if he had nothing else to do, might come with me for the first hour or so, George replied that nobody was leaving that day. I felt that I had been both rude and foolish though without understanding why.

In fact, it was nearly daylight when I woke. I shook George by the hand that emerged from his pile of blankets and stepped out into the windswept valley. The dogs, which had been sleeping just outside, leapt at me as one, and only a bellow from George saved me. I drank a last cup of green water and ate a tomato. Then, abandoning the rest of my food stock as a tiny act of propitiation,

I set off on the long walk back. The landscape was exalting and I enjoyed going downhill, but inevitably I was troubled by the resentment I felt I had provoked. I still do not know whether to blame myself or Sfakia, a region in Crete where I and my family have otherwise found many friends.

'Can I help you?' asked Dr. Frangedakis, by way of greeting, in the middle of the road in Rethimnon. I suspected he was addressing himself more to my wife than to me, for though he was a very old man he was unmistakably a gallant one.

'No, thank you,' we replied, falling into slow step beside him and continuing the conversation. He spoke slowly in American English (that dialect found so frequently in Greece), announcing himself as a surgeon and physician, now retired. Would we like to take a drink or one of Rethimnon's famous pastries with him? Yes, we said, we would, very much indeed.

The doctor, wearing a Panama hat and leaning on a cane, led us to a table set out on the esplanade in front of a fragrant cake shop. Here, while the heat of the summer morning gathered itself for its daily assault on the beach and the pavement cafés, we began to talk. It was one of those conversations that stop and start, often moving off in new directions, so that those taking part feel as if they were visitors at a flower show, enjoying now this bank of roses, now that display of dahlias on the far side. My wife and I must have talked a good deal of ourselves and our pursuits, but what we remembered afterwards was what the doctor said about himself.

Manuel Frangedakis's memory stretched back to before the turn of the century. He could recall attending the long church services of childhood as one of a congregation made up partly of Russian soldiers. And when he was a child, he said, the city gates still used to be shut up at night.

The doctor was one of a large family, from Vrises in the province of Rethimnon. Like most Rethimnon people, he said, the Frangedakises respected learning and one of Manuel's elder brothers mastered eight languages. Another emigrated to America at the turn of the century and opened a confectionery shop in Lewiston, Maine. Here the young Manuel joined him, working as a confectioner until he succeeded in becoming a medical student. The Balkan Wars of 1913 found him in uniform in Greece and he remained a military doctor right up to the disastrous campaign in Turkey in 1922. He had won a medal for his services to the maimed and dying in the front line, but it was his greater source of pride that he also treated Turkish civilians as the need arose. This was a peculiarly bitter war with much mutual hatred, but Dr. Frangedakis had done his best to be even-handed. One day, as if in recompense, he was invited into a Turkish household where the women set aside their yashmaks for the occasion – an acceptance of him, under terrible circumstances, which he described as 'better than baskets of money'.

Next there came another American period and further medical studies. Dr. Frangedakis was foiled by the immigrant quota system in his attempt to settle permanently. But he did not give in easily. Learning that the authorities favoured inventors, he promptly invented a surgical instrument. But the immigration men remained unimpressed. 'So I told them I would let them know when I invented perpetual motion,' said the doctor. 'Now I have been in Rethimnon since 1929. Every corner of every house knows me.'

He married and set up a little clinic in the main street – the Surgical Clinic of St. Catherine. When he retired almost forty years later, he found that he could not bear to remove the plaque which bore the clinic's name. So he called in a stonemason and had him write 'This was' above the name of the clinic. (We later looked for the plaque; it was no exaggeration.)

But medicine was not Dr. Frangedakis's only avocation. Like most of those who leave, or try to leave, the island, he was a passionate lover of Crete and all things Cretan, especially the language and the songs. The dialect is dying, he said, because of the use of standard Greek in schools. He himself had written four little books in Cretan as an exercise in preservation. As to the songs, he, who had been such a dancer in his youth – the best of all three hundred boys in the high school in Rethimnon – was now a collector. He had listed 12,500 *mantinades* and great numbers of *rizitika*.

To admirers of Cretan song, the *rizitika* are of as much interest as the *mantinades*. The latter, as sung by schoolmaster Mathioudakis and others all over the island, are short, simple, direct and moving. They deal with all aspects of life, but love is the favourite theme. The *rizitika* are longer, mostly in the heroic mould and full of heraldic attitudes. Many of them are striking, though more, per-haps, for the stories they tell than for their somewhat monotonous tunes. Literally, *rizitika* means 'from the roots', the roots in ques-tion being those of the Lefka Ori. The songs, which are mostly from their lower slopes, deal with a semi-fabulous mountain people, their daring deeds and chivalrous behaviour. The subject has been seri-ously discussed in *The Great Island*, Michael Llewellyn Smith's study of Crete.

The *rizitika* are divided into two kinds – those sung on the road at marriages while the bride is being fetched ceremoniously from her own village, and those to be sung at table. Dr. Frangedakis had amassed great quantities of both, not to mention one hundred and fifty funeral eulogies.

By now the heat was insistent as a road-mender's drill. We talked of Cretan costume, of the tradition of learning in Rethimnon; but the doctor was beginning to show signs of fatigue. Inviting us to carry on the discussion at his house that evening he walked away into the noon glare, slow but jaunty under his Panama hat.

In the evening we found him waiting for us on the balcony of his house. After a formal welcome we drank iced lemonade in his study under a stuffed hawk and a tinted photograph of the enormous Frangedakis family. When we left, the doctor presented us with a copy of each of his books, the inscription inside them saying they were for 'my friends...to remember me by and say good luck to them'.

Postscript: Crete and tourism

By far the most important change in Crete since World War II has been the development of tourism, at first slowly, then at an increasing pace under the dictatorship of the Colonels from 1967 to 1973. There was never much possibility of a redeeming expansion in industry or agriculture and tourism was accurately seen as offering the best chance for Crete to break out of the cycle of deprivation. Though the villages are still extremely poor, urban and coastal Crete are far more prosperous now than a decade ago and anybody who wishes Crete well must be glad about this. At the same time it is fair to note one or two serious objections and problems for the future. The first is that Crete is being forced to adjust at an alarming speed to differences between its own extremely conservative lifestyle and the relaxed behaviour of its visitors. Secondly, the money brought in by tourism does not yet seem to be well distributed and price rises due to tourism may actually be making the lives of some peasant farmers harder. From a conservationist viewpoint there have been many obvious mistakes. Hotel siting has been uncontrolled and careless, with many landscapes forced to accommodate quite unsuitable buildings. Welcome improvements to the road system have been accompanied by a brisk brutalism, at its height during the time of the Colonels. But these are errors of the past and there is at least a possibility they will not be compounded in years to come. More important is the question of what kind of tourism

Crete should encourage for the future. Up to now, tourist policy has concentrated on attracting the greatest possible numbers. Development lags far behind Corfu or Rhodes, far, far behind the Canary or Balearic Islands, but experience in these places may well suggest to prudent planners that if Crete is to retain its extremely individual character, then the time to change course, concentrating on quality of development rather than quantity, has already arrived.

NOTES FOR THE VISITOR

From the viewpoint of the visitor, the expansion in tourism means that it is possible to have almost any kind, or combination of kinds, of holiday in Crete – from hotel or rented house to indigenous taverna, from Minoan pilgrimage to water-skiing or lonely journeys on foot among the mountains.

Most of the hotels are on the north coast, either in the towns or dotted along the coastal plain. Ayios Nikolaos, whose pleasant little port is backed by a dramatic, cliff-enclosed sea-lake, has become the island's leading resort, with much summertime activity and accommodation of all classes. Most Cretan hotels are middle-of-the-road package affairs, with, as I write, a few centres of excellence – the Doma in Khania, the Minos Beach in Ayios Nikolaos and the much larger Elounda Beach Hotel a few miles north. Among middle-price hotels, the Xenia in Rethimnon has struck me as being pleasant without pretence to being more than a modest modern hotel. There are *pensions* in all the towns, some of them most agreeable; and people who travel widely will discover small hotels in a number of out-of-the-way places – at Ano (Upper) Zakros, for example, or Kissamou or Palaiochora. There is much to be said for an unbooked ramble out of season when beds will more easily be found. One particularly interesting development in recent years has been the availability for rental of houses in some of the villages and in one case, at Ay Ianni Koutsounari, near Ierapetra, a number of houses in a depopulated village have been restored for holiday letting.

Swimming in Crete is excellent, with beaches along most of the north coast and many delightful coves and bays to be discovered elsewhere. The only snag is the strength of the August wind – a problem which prevails throughout Aegean and Cretan waters. This apart, the climate is excellent for the holidaymaker. Spring and autumn are generally fine without being hot enough to discourage travel. Summer is very hot and a good time of year for taking things easily. In winter there is likely to be rain, but though this may spoil a short holiday it will add visual variety for anyone able to stay a little longer. Winter in Greece can be an exhilarating season, with shifting cloud and changes of light to bring out the best in a land-scape hammered by the sun so many months a year.

Cretan food is much the same as in other parts of Greece, though those who travel to remote places will find that there is little variety in summer. There are no particular problems over drinking water, though in case of doubt it is wise to ask. Often enough in the villages, the water used for drinking will come from a special well or spring and will be offered with pride.

Shops, though perfectly adequate, are concentrated in the towns and many everyday items are unobtainable in the villages. There is, for instance, no chemist shop as such in the whole of the province of Sfakia. It is clearly best to anticipate needs rather than discover them at an awkard moment.

As for transport on the island, the bus network is growing year by year. Services are frequent on the main east–west highway but often at inconvenient times on secondary roads (see p. 195). For those who can afford the considerable cost, a hire car may be the best solution.

On this, as on questions of tour operators, medical facilities and above all accommodation (where the situation changes from year to year), the most up-to-date point of information is likely to be the National Tourist Organisation of Greece. It has branches in most western capitals. In London its address is 195 Regent Street, London, W.1; in New York it is the Greek National Tourist Organization, 601 5th Avenue, New York, 10017; and in California, the

Greek National Tourist Organization, 627 West Sixth Street, Los Angeles, 90017.

One final point. Most future visitors are likely to reach Crete by air; but it remains an intoxicating experience to arrive for the first time by sea, crossing overnight from Piraeus and waking in Suda Bay to watch the Lefka Ori come closer, surging into the sky, rugged and as eternal as anything on this alterable earth.

Lion's head fountain, Historical Museum, Iraklion.

Bibliography

PREHISTORIC CRETE

The literature on Cretan archaeology is voluminous and ranges from the popular to the extravagantly recondite. I have found the following books useful and in most cases readable:

Alexiou, Stylianos, *A Guide to the Archaeological Museum of Heraclion*, General Direction of Antiquities and Restoration, Athens, 1972.

A Guide to the Minoan Palaces, Spyros Alexiou Sons, Iraklion.

Cottrell, Leonard, *The Bull of Minos*, Evans, London, 1953, and Pan Books, London, 1955. A popular account of early archaeological discoveries in Crete and Greece.

Faure, Paul, *La Vie Quotidienne en Crète au temps de Minos (1500 av. J.-C.)*, Hachette Littérature, Paris, 1973. A stimulating study of daily life.

Hawkes, Jacquetta, *The Dawn of the Gods*, Chatto and Windus, London, 1968. A sensitive account of Minoan civilisation and art.

Homer, *The Iliad*, translated by E. V. Rieu, Penguin, London, 1950.

— *The Odyssey*, translated by E. V. Rieu, Penguin, London, 1946. (Homer's incomparable epics contain scattered references to Crete.)

Hood, Sinclair, *The Home of the Heroes, the Aegean before the Greeks*, Thames and Hudson, London, 1967 (in the Library of the Early Civilisations series).

Hutchinson, R. W., *Prehistoric Crete*, Pelican, London, 1962. Stiff in tone but packed with information.

Luce, J. V., *The End of Atlantis*, Thames and Hudson, London, 1969, and Paladin, London, 1970. Learned and speculative.

Pendlebury, J. D. S., *The Archaeology of Crete, An Introduction*, Methuen, London, 1939. Still remains of interest.

Platon, Nicolas, *Crete*, Nagel, Geneva, 1966 (in the Archaeologia Mundi series). A clearly written introduction to the subject.

Powell, Dilys, *The Villa Ariadne*, Hodder and Stoughton, London, 1973. Archaeology and modern Crete come together in this illuminating book.

Willetts, R. F., *Everyday Life in Ancient Crete*, Batsford, London, 1969. Mainly about Crete in classical Greek days.

HISTORIC AND MODERN CRETE

Engaging curiosities and useful sources:

Allbaugh, Leland, *Crete: a Case Study of an Underdeveloped Area*, Princeton, 1953 (Rockefeller report on post-war Crete).

Dapper, O., *Description Exacte des Iles de l'Archipel*, Amsterdam, 1703 (translated from the Flemish). Vast and picturesque volume.

Elliadi, M. N., *Crete Past and Present*, Heath, Cranton, London, 1933.

Matton, Raymond, *La Crète au Cours des Siècles*, Collection de l'Institut Français d'Athènes, Athens. Useful, factual.

Morgan, Gareth (ed. Kalokairinos), *Cretan Poetry: Sources and Inspiration*, Iraklion, 1960 (offprint from *Kritika Chronica*, Vol. XIV).

Notopoulos, James A., 'Homer and Cretan Homeric Poetry', *American Journal of Philology*, Vol. LXXIII, 3.

Pashley, Robert, *Travels in Crete*, 2 vols., Cambridge, 1837. Endlessly rewarding.

Smith, Michael Llewellyn, *The Great Island, A Study of Crete*, Longmans, London, 1965. Best contemporary book on modern and historic Crete and particularly good on Cretan song.

Spratt, Captain T. A. B., *Travels and Researches in Crete*, 2 vols., London, 1865. More straitlaced than Pashley but full of interest.

Tournefort, J. P. de (transl. John Ozell), *A Voyage in the Levant*, London, 1718. Another curious and compelling book.

(In Greek only: outstanding and beautifully illustrated essay on 'Byzantine Art in the province of Iraklion' by Emmanuel Borboudakis in the official volume *Iraklion and its province*. Also available as offprint.)

WORLD WAR II

BATTLE

Buckley, Christopher, *Greece and Crete*, H.M.S.O., London, 1952.

Clark, Alan, *The Fall of Crete*, Blond, London, 1962, Nel Mentor, 1969.

Davin, D. M., 'Crete' (in *Official History of New Zealand in the Second World War*), Wellington, New Zealand, 1953.

Heydte, Baron von der (transl. W. Stanley Moss), *Daedalus Returned, Crete 1941*, Hutchinson, London, 1958.

Stewart, I. McD. G., *The Struggle for Crete*, Oxford, 1966. The most authoritative account.

Waugh, Evelyn, *Officers and Gentlemen*, Chapman and Hall, London, 1955.
Evelyn Waugh Diaries, Weidenfeld and Nicolson, London, 1976.

RESISTANCE

Fielding, Xan, *Hide and Seek*, Secker and Warburg, London, 1954.
Moss, W. Stanley, *Ill Met by Moonlight*, Harrap, London, 1948.
Psychoundakis, George, *The Cretan Runner*, John Murray, London, 1955. Introduction by Patrick Leigh Fermor.
Rendel, A. M., *Appointment in Crete*, Wingate, London, 1953.
Woodhouse, C. M., *Apple of Discord*, Hutchinson, London, 1948.

GENERAL READING

Fielding, Xan, *The Stronghold*, Secker and Warburg, London, 1953. A return to post-war Crete by a wartime agent.
Kazantzakis, Nikos, *Freedom and Death*, Bruno Cassirer, Oxford, 1956; Faber Paperbacks, London, 1966. A fine novel of Cretan revolution against the Turks.
— *Zorba*, Bruno Cassirer, Oxford, 1959; Faber Paperbacks, 1961. Energetic novel on Cretan themes.
Marshall, F. H. and Mavrogordato, J. (transl.), *Three Cretan Plays*, Oxford, 1929. Contains *The Sacrifice of Abraham*, *Erophile* and *Gyparis*.
Miller, Henry, *The Colossus of Maroussi*, Heinemann, London, 1960 (first published in 1941). Miller's romp round Greece includes Crete.
Prevelakis, P., *Chronique d'une Cité*, Gallimard, Paris, 1960. A tale of Rethimnon.

GUIDES

Bowman, John, *A Traveller's Guide to Crete*, Jonathan Cape, London, new and revised edition 1974.
Spanakis, Sterghios, *Crete, A Guide*, 2 vols., Sfakianakis, Iraklion. Especially useful on Crete in historic times.

Index